THE LINK: WELCOME TO HUMANITY

WILLIAM ZANOTTI

BACK HILL PRESS

/

Zanotti, William. The Link: Welcome to Humanity
eBook ISBN: 978-1-7372429-1-8
Print ISBN: 978-1-7372429-0-1
Library of Congress Number: 2021921822

Cover by RLSather - SelPubBookCovers.com

CONTENTS

Prologue   1

PART I
EARTHFOLK

1. Classroom In A Cloud   5
2. Fieldwork   15
3. Observations At Las Cruces   23
4. Progress   33
5. Paulina And Mariluz   39
6. Poonam Murthy   43
7. Martino And Fitz   47
8. Trauma Center   55
9. Waves   60
10. The Team   69
11. Doctor Who?   78

PART II
VENUSFOLK

12. Mess Exit   87
13. Bright Sands At Dawn   102
14. A Soldier   111
15. Real Home   135

PART III
EARTHFOLK

16. Memory Or Dream   157
17. Theoremifics   175
18. Little More Than Savages   188

PART IV
VENUSFOLK

19. A Crusty Turd   197
20. Chase In Space   208
21. Reflection   225

PART V
FOLK

22. A Reasonable Assumption	229
23. Following The Rules	236
24. Not Much To See	242
25. Human Understanding	256
26. Guastamo Cavanus	262
27. Just Beginning	273
28. The Academy	275
29. Connections	284
30. The Message	293
About the Author	305
Acknowledgments	307
Also by William Zanotti	309

PROLOGUE

Reggie could hear muffled laughter coming from inside the heavy canvas tent. He ran around the pavilion's exterior like a squirrel scurrying from tree to tree. He was desperate to get a peek inside or at least hear what was happening. Music and voices filtered out, but they were subdued. The low thump of drums and the muted wail of horns vibrated in the air. The energy was unmistakable. He stopped and pressed his ear against the canvas, tracing its rough texture with his fingertips. The pounding in his chest matched the thumps that pushed against the sides of the tent. When the reverberations receded, his sense of urgency rose. He feared he'd never get in.

Frustration shook him like the ground beneath a rocket at liftoff. All the other kids got to enjoy the circus together. Reggie wanted to share in the laughter. What was the point of laughter if it wasn't shared? If only someone else had been left out, too. But there was no one. How had everyone gotten in but him? Did anyone even know he was outside? Did anyone care? The tension in his limbs slackened with each question. Eventually, his shoulders dropped. A billowing cloud of sadness formed inside him, and hot tears began to descend. They stung his cheeks.

This was how Earthfolk lived.

That day's observation was one of the earliest and most painful memories from Reggie's early education on Earthfolk. He and his classmates had been projected into a small town in North America to observe the humans of Earth attending a circus. Everyone was *inside* the circus tent. Not Reggie. The object of the exercise had been to teach the children about the fickleness of Earthfolk emotion. It was an effective lesson for Reggie. So many orbits later, the loneliness of that demonstration still gave him a twinge.

The need for belonging ran deep in Earthfolk, as did fear. Their desire to belong could be useful in acclimating them to *the link*. But irrational fear, anger, and despair led to poor decisions and violence, which could compromise *the link* itself.

He'd learned a sad lesson, but one that ignited a life-long passion to elevate Folk.

PART I

EARTHFOLK

1

CLASSROOM IN A CLOUD

REGGIE COULD COMMUNICATE with any person anywhere in the cosmos. There were habitable worlds everywhere. He could blink and visit any of them. Yet he drifted alone, an imponderable speck of nothing in the vastness of space. He chose to float in silent suspension in his tiny nebular hollow, his classroom in a cloud. He could have remained in the field, collecting data, making observations, getting closer to the completion of his greatest work. Instead, he'd chosen to share some of what he'd learned. He knew now that he'd chosen poorly. He'd waited too long to act. His life was about to slide away from him faster than the universe raced to meet the unknown.

Countless stars surrounded him as he slowly swiveled his head, scanning the .2 lightyear area of the nebula. They appeared immovable, yet their light sped toward him, always tantalizingly shining before him, like his dream for Earthfolk.

Reggie tried to rest his mind, stretching out within the celestial sphere that served as his teaching platform. He gazed out at the distant blues and reds in the space surrounding him. He didn't often allow himself to relax and contemplate his life. His research and his students received the bulk of his energy. Moments of introspection were so few as to have become precious to him.

He stretched a bit further and thought about the ideal characteristics of a mate he might someday have petitioned for. She would be thoroughly familiar with Earthfolk. Her eyes would be colorful and bright, her sphere of influence vast. Reggie smiled at the thought of an exclusive partner. Their eyes would meet, and each would know they had been seeking the other. They would share themselves, their minds commingling as they travelled *the link* and explored exotic star systems. Their bonding would be vigorous. She would be understanding, kind, and true. He could almost see her.

These were beautiful thoughts. But did someone like this really exist? Or was she just an unreality, like an Earthfolk dream? He sighed, thinking of how Earthfolk falsely conceived of dreams as unreality. Of course, none of it mattered. Not after the notice he'd just received.

A swirl interrupted his thoughts. Another unexpected visit? The first had brought troubling news. What now? A curving laser light approached. It split into two lights, a pair of eyes. Reggie gathered himself to receive a greeting.

He knew who it was before she was even focused. While maybe not worse, this second visit wouldn't help. His mother had a knack for seeking him out when he was most engaged in self-exploration, rare as those moments were.

"*Reggie*," she said, emphasizing the peculiar name. It was weird coming from his mother. Throughout his life, she seldom addressed him with an appellation other than Son.

"Hello, Mother. I was just thinking of you," Reggie responded.

"You're a terrible liar, dear. I thought I'd come to you. If we had to wait for you to visit, your father and I would never see you. You look tired. Are you getting enough rest? Is something troubling you? I hope your students aren't vexing you too much."

"Good to see you, too, Mother." Reggie lowered his head.

"Oh, don't be cross. You know I miss you. Let me have a look at you," she said. Her chin tilted upward as she appraised him. "Ah, still handsome. Your father said to tell you to come and see him when your teaching commitment is over. He has something he wants to discuss with you. I suspect he just wants you to go exploring with him. He won't admit how much he enjoys the idle time you spend together."

Reggie, too, enjoyed spending time with his father. The exploring they did was nothing more than projections to exotic locations, always chosen by his father, where they typically studied flora and fauna while sweeping auroras or some other dazzling display bloomed across the skies. His father always managed to pick the best spots for educational enrichment. The worlds tended to be uninhabited or sparsely inhabited by Folk, so there was little chance of contact.

Reggie wondered why his mother never went with them. He thought to ask her, but that would extend the conversation. He needed time to think, to get his affairs in order. His mother looked the same as ever in her billowy lavender blouse and matching smooth pants. She'd appeared in the same outfit for as long as he could remember. It was the style on Mega back before she partnered with Father. It was all an image in space, of course, but the familiarity of it was not displeasing.

There was no way he could tell her about the turn his life had just taken. Still, he found himself glad she'd come. It was nice to see a friendly face in the emptiness of the nebula, after the Universal Study Collective representative's visit.

"Mother, I can't really chat right now. I have to give the final lesson of the term today, and I need to prepare. I'll come see you and Father as soon as I'm free," he said, unsure if freedom would be part of his future.

"You're always so busy. You need a partner to settle you down. Have you given any thought to petitioning for one?" she said.

"Not interested. Too much going on right now," Reggie said.

"Sometimes I think the only partner you're ever going to have is at the other end of your examining glasses," she said, still appraising him.

"I really need to get my thoughts together for class, Mother."

She stared at him for a long moment, looked around, then reluctantly said goodbye. Mercifully, she faded out. It was uncanny how she always knew what was on his mind.

Reggie lingered in the classroom, pondering his mother's words. He thought about what actually *was* at the other end of his examining glass—a potential Earthfolk test subject, and a pretty one.

TWENTY PAIRS OF eyes began to recede through the diffuse gas cloud that surrounded the classroom. They left, slowly at first, then faster, fanning out into the darkness of space like so many colorful shooting stars. One by one, the lights faded from his sight.

Reggie sighed deeply. He would miss his students. He knew them by their eyes. He knew when they were engaged, when they were confused, when they couldn't care less. The eyes always told the story. He hoped they would use his lessons as a foundation for forming their own opinions on Folk. Some might even keep the Earthfolk names he'd required them to research and select for themselves, to be used while in class. It was the tradition of Folk researchers to use academic monikers related to their field of interest. He was Aurigae—Reggie. He announced it proudly at the start of every term. They could choose whoever, whatever name they wanted. They didn't have to agree with his methods, but they should at least know the facts about isolated planets and their unenlightened inhabitants, of which Earth and Venus were Reggie's specialties.

He held out his hands and turned them over, examining them. He closed them into fists and mused. Here he was, observing the movement of his hands, watching the wisps of soothing blue and pink in suspension all around his little bubble in space, while his body rested light-years away on Mega. He was a configuration of light, soundlessly floating in his nebular classroom. Alone again.

The tiny nebula, known to the unenlightened Folk of Earth as NGC 6543, hadn't changed much in the four Mega orbits he'd been teaching from it. He thought maybe the misty, pale blue gas surrounding his immediate area was a little lighter, the deep pink gas a touch less dense, as they stretched into the distance in all directions. But his hollow in the middle of the nebula—his classroom—was almost exactly the same as it had been in the beginning. His image was suspended at the exact same locus at the center of the sphere. The position of the gas cloud was virtually unchanged, despite its movement through space and four orbits' worth of electromagnetic waves passing through it. But the location put him close to Earth, and he enjoyed being close to those particular unenlightened humans.

The memory of being sent to Earth as a student, and the feeling of being excluded asserted itself again. It was an empty feeling, similar to the emptiness of space. Lessons of the type he'd been given were no longer permitted. Projections to Earth had been restricted to commissioned researchers orbits ago. The risk of exposing *the link* to Earthfolk, such as they were, was too great, and the benefits of firsthand emotional experience were deemed dubious at best. Emotion clouded things. As far as the Academy was concerned, that's all any elementary student needed to know.

Reggie had kept his latest research from his students at the Universal Study Collective. The data he collected was from projections to, indeed reconstitutions on, Earth. Even though they were graduate level classes, his students didn't need to know about his visits to Earth. It had been difficult. In his heart, he wanted everyone to know that he and his team were on the precipice of revolutionizing the study of Folk to include direct contact and interaction. But he needed to protect his commission. Close to the end of the term, he'd nearly revealed the scope of his work. He'd been teaching a lesson on Venusfolk when he slipped. "The skin is thick and gray with a slightly metallic sheen. They are invariably thin, emaciated in comparison to Earthfolk. Their eyes are small and black like obsidian, about one third the size of those of Earthfolk," he'd said. The class had been mesmerized by his description of the dim Folk of Venus, so unlike all other humans in appearance.

"The thick skin is like a protective polymer, sleek and smooth. Their bodies have no hair, and they wear no coverings. The males and females present quite similarly. The most striking thing about them physically is not, as you might imagine, their metallic, glistening skin and small eyes; it is their lack of teeth, which gives their faces a sloping, burnished quality. In Earthfolk terms, you can picture a balloon in process of deflating. At full maturity, both the males and females reach a height of no more than one meter six. You're all familiar with alternative Earthfolk measurement metrics? Does everyone know what one meter six is in Earthfolk *imperial* measurement?"

The question had been met with silence and shifting eyes. Twenty pairs of eyes, twenty individuals, diligently avoiding his gaze, many using the question as a prompt to look out of the classroom and through the thin wisps of gas in the distance, their attention suddenly drawn to some far-off star or other.

"Well, we seem to have forgotten our lesson on Earthfolk measurement systems. Venusfolk reach a maximum height of five feet." He'd deliberately used the obscure Earth term. "That's right—*feet*," he'd repeated, as the students' eyes showed a hint of mirth. "Keep in mind that only a very small subset of Earthfolk currently use this measurement scheme."

Reggie's image glowed slightly brighter. He always seemed to circle back to Earthfolk, even while giving a lecture on Venusfolk.

"You should also note that Venusfolk do not generally measure themselves. The size of their own bodies is not something they think about. This is probably because they are all so much alike," he'd said.

It was then that he'd begun to lose himself. It had pleased him that his students appreciated the subject. Mentioning Earthfolk had stirred him and called to mind his fieldwork. He hadn't attempted to suppress the rising excitement he felt. Emotion ultimately clouded things. He knew that. Yet he'd accepted, even reveled in, the muted mirth he'd triggered in his students. The twinkling in their eyes had encouraged him.

"Fascinating Folk, Venusfolk," he'd said. "They are human, in the sense that they have the same root anatomical features as us and as Earthfolk. Venusfolk evolution, however, reflects environmental considerations not present for Earthfolk or ourselves. Venusfolk live entirely underground, receiving their ultraviolet light through a system of relays and filters. They, like all Folk, lack the intellectual complexity of greater humanity. Neither Venusfolk nor Earthfolk are aware of *the link,* and neither are likely to connect on their own. Venusfolk's existence is comfortable, peaceful, even Utopian, and so they do not search. Earthfolk search but because of their violent nature, the Academy has forbidden revelation of *the link* to them. Sad, don't you think? Earthfolk need a lot of help. That's why, very shortly, my team and I will be conducting a series of . . . uh . . . things."

Reggie had caught himself. He'd nearly revealed his plan to give a small group of Earthfolk a glimpse of *the link*.

He kept on talking as if nothing had happened. "We have studied Earth far more extensively and for far longer than we have Venus. The advanced techniques we developed as we studied many generations of Earthfolk have allowed us to make tremendously rapid progress in our understanding of Venusfolk. We attribute this swift advancement to our great strides in theoremifics. We learned that emotion is as tightly bound to the thought patterns of Venusfolk, as it is for Earthfolk. Also, my research team and I recently confirmed that Earthfolk consider dreams to be insignificant—an unreality."

He stammered through the rest of the lesson on Venusfolk, hoping the students hadn't noticed his slip.

Perhaps he should have shared with them his pioneering research, his elegant theories, and the data from his fieldwork. It was his duty to objectively and dispassionately provide them with all the information he knew. He hadn't done that. But his work was too advanced and would likely bring unwanted scrutiny from the Academy. Ironically, as it turned out, it didn't matter what his students knew or didn't know.

Despite his secrecy, the Academy must have surmised that Reggie was going beyond his commission to observe only. He was to collect data on Earthfolk *without contact*. The appearance of a messenger from the Universal Study Collective on behalf of the Academy, his unexpected visitor, had signaled the end for him.

The messenger's appearance had found him alone in his nebular hollow. The terse message was that he had exactly seven rotations to present himself at Academy Reconfiguration Station

13 off Mega. He was to appear in the flesh. There'd been no discussion—just the message, and then the emissary was gone. He didn't even merit receiving word directly from a USC administrator or Academy official. Having to present himself in the flesh, fully reconstituted, was bad. Having to appear at ARS-13 was worse. If all they wanted was to discuss his findings and preparations, or to warn him off, he wouldn't need to appear there in corporeal form. There was no thought to flee. The Academy had his wave signatures. They'd find him immediately.

The summons itself had elicited no emotion in Reggie. He accepted the order with the same equanimity as the messenger who'd issued it. He thought he should have felt something. He didn't. Feelings were the boost that he'd hoped would make his experiment work. Otherwise, he would need to infuse his electromagnetic wave transmissions to Earthfolk with artificially produced emotion. He had no idea if the replication of an emotion was the same as the real thing? Maybe. Super-positioned quantum particles were identical. He needed to know if emotion worked the same way.

His thoughts vacillated between what he needed to do to make his formulas work and the imminent accounting before the Academy.

The Academy talked of the dangers of OTH—Other Than Human—presence attaching to *the link*. As far as Reggie was concerned, this was institutional myth on a grand scale. *The link* was a naturally occurring process that allowed people to harness existing energy, nothing more, nothing less. He didn't understand how an eminently rational administration could bend itself to the paranoia of the abstract. The existence of OTH had never been proven. Advanced humanity, comfortable being the highest form of life in the universe, was uncomfortable with unknowns. The concept of OTH teetered on the edge of mysticism. Yet the notion of a force beyond humanity's reach, indeed beyond its comprehension, continued. Reggie considered it nonsense. It hinted of fear.

He closed his eyes inside his bubble. He was a tiny dot of nothingness in a universe that existed more in people's minds than in the flesh. A disconnected future of permanent corporeal life would be no life at all.

He was sure his work would cause no damage to *the link.*

Appearing in the flesh meant subsuming himself into his body on Mega and taking a shuttle to ARS-13. He could do it in a single rotation. That would leave him six rotations to take the greatest leap ever made in Folk connectivity.

2

FIELDWORK

PRISM-LINED EXAMINING glasses were positioned in a semicircle before Reggie. Each had its own tether connecting it through the vast, deep-red, nebular cloud known to Earthfolk as NGC 7293 with some distant point in space of his choosing.

Reggie hovered directly in front of the largest of his twelve examining glasses. A hospital, surrounded by vehicles, in an arid location on Earth was on display. The words NEW MEXICO were printed on several of the vehicles. Reggie glanced at measurements and calculations slowly scrolling on the adjacent screen under the heading *Earthfolk in situ*.

The time for passive silence in the lab was over. He waited patiently for Zoe. He wanted to see her once before he acted. She and Sig might not understand why he chose this path. He wouldn't tell them until after he was successful. He told himself this was to protect them from the consequences. But really, he wanted to avoid their trying to persuade him to wait. Zoe might understand. She was always agreeable to his suggestions and they seemed to share the same zeal for Folk betterment. Sig would be a tougher sell. Although a committed Folk researcher, he was steeped in Academy dogma.

Zoe's signaled clearly, no surprises. Two green dots from a long way off took their time materializing, a respectful approach. She was always considerate of Reggie's solitude. Even though the lab was for the whole team. Finally, a swirl of light and her full image appeared.

"Hello," she said, followed by a ready smile that usually elicited the same in Reggie. Not this time.

"Hello," Reggie said shifting his focus from the screens

"Whoa, you've got all the examining glasses trained on one location. What's going on?" she said, her green eyes widening. She wore Earthfolk clothes, that made her rather look like a musical artist or rock performer as it were, he thought. Earthfolk names and clothes were de rigueur in the Folk Studies Department. They allowed for a bit of self-expression in an otherwise clinical environment.

"Just some observations. I asked you to come so I could get a look at your most recent data," Reggie said.

Zoe moved closer to the big display and the scrolling data. "You're not planning a Glimmerwac style transmission?" she said.

Reggie said nothing. How was it the females in his life saw through him so easily?

Direct transmission to live creatures on Folk planets was prohibited in order to prevent disaster. He knew he wouldn't be the first scientist to test rogue transmissions. Any Doctor of Folk Research worthy of the title knew the story of the first unauthorized experiment on Earth, and it didn't even involve humans. Reggie hadn't done anything yet and he was about to be sanctioned as if he had.

The first transgressor of Academy protocol was banished from *the link* thirty orbits ago. Dr. Marc Glimmerwac, brilliant scholar, Assistant-Chief of the Folk Studies Department at the Universal Study Collective, pursued a theory revolving around the similarities in socialization between the humans and the chimpanzees of Earth. It had great potential. But his work with psychoactive wave stimulants was ill conceived and poorly executed. The Academy's response was swift and severe. Glimmerwac's mind was reconditioned to prevent connection to *the link*. He was, thereafter, permanently corporeal.

Reggie bristled at the popular characterization of Glimmerwac's enhanced electromagnetic waves as a madman's concoction. Reggie liked to think of his own work as complex, esoteric sequencing. *Concoction* made Folk wave research sound imprecise, cavalier, even frivolous. And maybe it was. But Glimmerwac didn't have the benefit of theoremifics, developed twenty-five orbits after his failed trial. Theoremifics was good science. Find a way to infuse emotion into the wave sequencing transmitted to emotional beings, and success couldn't be far behind. Logical.

Dr. Marc Glimmerwac, disgraced scientist, was an eccentric, but he wasn't crazy. If he was crazy then so was Reggie, for contemplating a similarly radical experiment, even as the Academy bore down on him.

Glimmerwac had focused on an area deep within the African continent on Earth. The old scientist set off with a devoted team of students. They transmitted to exactly one adult male chimpanzee. Just one. The test subject and a band of adult male chimpanzees, whipped into a frenzy, became extremely aggressive and brutally killed all the male chimpanzees from a neighboring community. Over the course of one orbit, they savagely ripped, bit, stomped, and pounded to death chimpanzees with whom they had previously coexisted peacefully. An entire community was wiped out within a single orbit because of one test subject. Though mitigated by a slightly higher intellect, the same potential for brutality was in Earth-folk. Reggie's plan could have the same devastating effect, only this time on human souls. He'd been working his mind to the point of extreme fatigue. Things were complicated, as they always were. He didn't have 100 percent confidence in himself and his weary mind. Something could go terribly wrong. But there was no way of knowing whether his theory was correct without testing it. He believed in Folk in general and Earthfolk in particular. He believed their emotions could work in their favor, violent tendencies notwithstanding. Reggie had spent too much of his life studying them, to let it all end on ARS-13 without attempting at least one test.

He believed an innate desire for peace and belonging was buried somewhere in Folk. He was driven, like Glimmerwac; but he knew the subject matter better. He wasn't going to make the same mistakes. He was going to interact carefully with human subjects, for whom emotional and executive functioning capacity was great. Properly guided, the Earthfolk response to new energy could be controlled. Feelings of connection and belonging would help with exposure to *the link*. A precise dose of theoremifics was the key to helping Earthfolk adjust.

Reggie had traced Glimmerwac's steps. He'd reconstructed the wave formulas. He'd recalculated the socio-kinetic algorithms used on the African continent. He was confident that Glimmerwac had missed something. Many believed he had chosen a malfunctioning or maladjusted chimpanzee. Not Reggie. He believed the flaw was selecting *any* chimpanzee. He wasn't interested in chimpanzees. Glimmerwac hadn't been either. They were supposed to be a means to an end. Glimmerwac was trying to gain an understanding of Earthfolk, not of chimpanzees. The similarity between humans and primates had enthralled Glimmerwac. But the real issue was the compatibility of Earthfolk with *the link*, with expanded awareness, not with their similarity to primates. Given the capability to connect instantaneously with others, could Earthfolk survive? Could *the link* survive the Earthfolk proclivity to harm each other in prodigious numbers?

There was no time for independent cross-verification calculations of his formulas. There was no need for the development of intermediary transmission devices, as the Academy would surely recommend, if it ever seriously considered his work. *The link* was natural. His techniques should be natural. No technology, just mental wave manipulation. The right waves could do it. He could make it work with the right subject—multiple subjects, so they could support each other. The innate Earthfolk need to belong would be met.

How could he wait? Lives were being wasted in petty violence on Earth. Reggie wanted to save people. Bring people together. Earthfolk to Earthfolk. Earthfolk to him. Earthfolk to the universe. It would work. It would work. The more he said it, the more he believed it. He would not let fear be his undoing. He just needed a little bit more data.

"No, no. Just wanted to compare what I've got with what you and Sig have come up with so far," he said, avoiding eye contact.

Reggie's experiment was at the vanguard of science itself. Everything was unpredictable, and outcomes could never be guaranteed. He accepted the risk, but didn't expect them to do the same. Sig and Zoe had been doing some preliminaries on his behalf. He just hadn't told them the full extent of his ambition.

And he was certain that a female human, not a male chimp, was the ideal test subject. Throughout his studies, Reggie had found less violent behavior in females than in males; the margin for error was more favorable.

The Academy harbored misgivings about the license they'd

begrudgingly given him. If it hadn't been for Sig's standing in
the scientific community and his assurances that *the link* would
not be exposed, Reggie felt sure that his work in dream theory
would not have been enough for them to have granted authorization to do the observations and long-term study his approval
provided.

In order to satisfy the orthodoxy of the Academy, even
limited non-contact observation of Earthfolk required detailed
reports and advance notice. The consequences of Glimmerwac's
failed work had lasted for many orbits and continue to inform
Academy policy. The Academy Review Board had obviously
been watching him more closely than he'd expected. The
burden of reporting was intense, and clearly the Academy was
nervous and wanted to reign him in. He had to move quickly.

It had become clear to Reggie that transmitting waves to a
singular test subject would not address the full social aspect of
expanded sight. The chimps, like Earthfolk, were social creatures. Multiple subjects should have been tested simultaneously.
How could a sole test subject be expected to smoothly process
life-altering mind expansion without the network of interactive
relationships they had relied upon their whole life? And why
test chimpanzees?

Reggie's observations of Earthfolk had shown that females
were more docile than males, making them a focal point of his
research. He'd concluded that it was best to test a group of
Earthfolk that included females.

Earthfolk demonstrated curiosity and effective use of technology. Their minds were receptive to the possibilities of
science. Chimpanzees were simply inferior. Reggie *had* to test
his electromagnetic waves on Earthfolk. He would not use stan-
dard trial methods. He would interact directly and use theoremifics to soften any violent impulses upon exposure to *the link*.
He would cap any long-term negative fallout by utilizing his

dream theory to give the Earthfolk a feeling of unreality. At least that was the plan. If all went well, the Earthfolk subjects would think the trial was a dream, and hence, less disruptive to their lives.

Glimmerwac was a lover of humanity. He had at least tried to offer hope to Earthfolk. Reggie thought him to be a gentle soul who wanted to bring peace to Folk, and Reggie quite admired him for this. Glimmerwac never would've hurt a living being on purpose. He was misunderstood, like Reggie.

"Oh, okay, well I was about to head out for some close in observations, no direct mind-to-mind work of course," she said, raising an eyebrow. "Why don't you come with me?"

"Can't. I'm off for my own fieldwork," he said.

"All right, well, you want to meet back here in an Earth rotation?" she said.

"Sounds good," he said, closing off the examining glasses.

He disliked being dishonest with Zoe. She was his oldest friend.

He couldn't tell Sig either. He wouldn't understand. He was almost twice Reggie's age. He came from a long line of researchers and high intellectuals, all of whom wrestled with issues concerning Folk in one capacity or another. He was well respected and had been on staff at USC for many orbits before Reggie's arrival. Technically, Sig was Reggie's advisor, but currently he was more of a colleague. Sig had lobbied to get Reggie into the Contemporary Folk Studies Department, and eventually gave up all his other students and his own research of The Beyond to focus exclusively on working with Reggie.

By virtue of Reggie's extensive field experience observing Earthfolk, and his promising research on dream theory, Reggie was given much autonomy, and was allowed to bring his long-time colleague, Zoe, on board. The two, along with Sig, formed a unique but effective team. Reggie's team.

Reggie appreciated that Sig actively participated in research. He could have used his position to try and control them, but he didn't. "Tell me what I can do," he had declared at their very first project meeting. They saw this as a humble commitment to what they could accomplish together. One of Sig's biggest contributions was the historical perspective he brought, having advised researchers who had gone on to have leadership roles at the Academy. He was a strong advocate of thoroughness and comprehensive preparation, something that he said would keep them all out of trouble. It also didn't hurt that he had many connections at the Academy and could facilitate approvals that might otherwise elude them.

Sig had shown great enthusiasm about getting Reggie to join him and having him as part of a team. The other academicians were apprehensive about Reggie's ability to be productive in a team environment. Reggie's best work had been done alone, outside the parameters of his primary study cohort. The same was true of his time at USC before joining Sig. His mathematics and Folk study were solitary pursuits. Reggie was notorious at USC for not responding to the swirl of a proposed connection. Sig had suggested that this was due to an underdeveloped connection to *the link*. When most children were solidifying attachment to their peers through group projects, Reggie pored over old texts on Folk, with singular fascination, always taking notes. Zoe was the only one who seemed to appreciate his singlemindedness.

3

OBSERVATIONS AT LAS CRUCES

TOTAL POPULATION, CRIME rates, metadata from psychological studies, comparative data from other planets, anything she thought relevant from the entire anthology of Academy-published data on Earthfolk, Zoe had gathered and studied, at Reggie's request. His instruction to the team was to concentrate on identifying subjects who had shown an interest in life beyond Earth and thus open-mindedness. He'd suggested using people from an astronomy class in Las Cruces, New Mexico. Zoe supported him. She would follow Academy protocol but only so far as it involved precluding exposure to *the link*. She would need to make her own contact in order to evaluate potential subjects.

~

ZOE FOUND IT odd that Mr. Fuzzytail, whom she'd named immediately upon spotting him, had zero interest in the people in and around the playground. He wasn't the least bit afraid. At one point, he got to within feet of some of the children. He was the only squirrel who actually went inside the wood planks marking the perimeter of the playground equipment area. He was adept at picking out the nuts hidden in the wide pond of faded wood chips that served as a soft-landing surface for tumbling children. It seemed all he cared about were the nuts. It was as if his shiny black eyes didn't even see the people.

Munching in earnest as he stood on his hind legs, Mr. Fuzzytail ratcheted his head left and right, observing the environs while Zoe observed him. He spied a couple of other squirrels—distant relations, no doubt. There was a dog lying near a bench on the opposite side of the playground, looking at him. The dog seemed harmless enough, though. He hadn't moved once since Mr. Fuzzytail snatched his first nut from the playground's wood chips. The dog's lack of serious interest was perhaps the product of advanced age, which showed in the form of a gray soul patch on his otherwise-black, furry chin. He was on a leash strapped to the bench, but Mr. Fuzzytail should probably keep an eye on him anyway.

Zoe, on the other hand, was keenly interested in the people. She didn't often do close-up observation of Earthfolk—too risky. She couldn't help smiling. There was a carefree feeling in the air. Those at the playground who weren't actively smiling wore looks of contentment, satisfaction, and ease. It would have been difficult for anyone to remain stoic while watching the children play.

There was the older Earthfolk male with white hair pushing a small child on a swing. It was hard to tell which of them was having more fun. Each time the swing squeaked to its apex, the little girl yelled "Alleeeeey . . ." then paused and waited for the swing to squonk speedily back toward the ground to yell, "Oooop!" to the old man's delight. There were the two adult females standing together and nodding at each other as one slowly rocked a large-wheeled carriage back and forth. An occasional laugh passed between them.

It was difficult to imagine these people making war with each other at a cost of millions of lives. She hoped what she saw here was who they really were: fun-loving, gentle people, not the humans known for war and violence.

Zoe watched those who watched the children. They were mostly adult females, though there were a few males and a couple of pairs. She had come to see one of the pairs.

She zeroed in on the couple seated on a wood bench, their shoulders and thighs touching. The woman smiled and followed the movements of a little girl. Zoe tracked the girl, who was vainly trying to keep up with a boy running a circuit: up the ladder, down the slide, one full circle on the spinning wheel, then a dizzy run back to the ladder. The little girl stopped and began walking. Then she sat. She spotted Mr. Fuzzytail and examined him. Mr. Fuzzytail, for his part, stopped chewing for all of two seconds to consider the little blond creature who appeared to be interested in him. Ordinarily, he wouldn't have wasted his time on her, but he noticed that she seemed to be curious about the nuts. He saw her pick one up. Was she going to toss it his way? It looked like he would be amenable to this.

Zoe turned her attention back to the couple. The name spelled out in red script on an oval patch of the man's pressed work shirt was MIKE. On the opposite breast was MIKE'S TIRE AND AUTO. He wore matching dark blue work pants. His face was relaxed. Under his eyes was a small web of wrinkles where fatigue refused to be suppressed. His veiny hands were clean—fingernails notwithstanding—and smelled of scented soap. He sat expressionless, his eyes occasionally shifting from the little girl to a little boy.

Beside Mike sat a woman smiling as she watched. Behind the children were a slide, some monkey bars, and a couple of swings that had seen better days. But the condition of the equipment didn't seem to bother anyone, least of all the two children the couple watched.

It was the way of greater humanity that children taught each other as much as their elders.

Zoe observed the children as she approached the bench where the couple sat. The little blond girl had tangled hair and the remnants of a red substance on her face. The boy, slightly taller and of a sturdier build, had a broad grin on his faced distinguished by a missing front tooth.

Standing just to the side of the couple, Zoe noticed the woman's smile begin to fade just a touch.

"Izzy. What's up?" Mike said.

"Nothing. Just thinking. It's a beautiful day, isn't it?" the woman responded.

"Yeah. Wish I didn't have to go to work." He nodded in the direction of their son. "He's having a blast."

Zoe walked over to the bench and sat down. "Good morning," she said.

"Morning," Mike and Izzy said in unison.

Zoe nodded at the little girl and the squirrel. "She seems to have made a friend."

"That's our daughter, Elle," said Izzy. "She loves animals."

"Excuse me," Mike said, setting down a notebook, getting up and walking over to the boys.

"She's cute," said Zoe.

Izzy nodded in agreement and looked at Zoe, taking in her short brown hair slightly layered on one side, green eyes, and the variety of glistening rings on her fingers. Zoe smiled as the woman seemed to assess her. Zoe chosen to clothe herself in tight jeans and close-fitting leather jacket.

"Any of yours?" Izzy asked, throwing a nod at the scene before them.

"No, not yet. Someday."

"I love your rings," said Izzy.

"Thanks."

Zoe looked toward the boys and Mike, who was now increasing the velocity of the spinning wheel with both hands so the boys on it dare not jump off. Elle, spotting her dad in the play area, jumped up and trotted over to him. She tried to add to the speed of the wheel, mimicking her father.

"That's my husband, Mike," said Izzy. "The smaller of the two boys is our son, Mike Jr."

"I'm Zoe."

Izzy held out her hand. "Isabella."

They looked at each other.

"Have we met?" asked Izzy.

"Maybe," Zoe said. "Did you take a class on astronomy at the Albuquerque Public Library on Central Ave, not long ago?"

"Yes. Were you there?"

"Yes, I was uh . . . an observer," Zoe said.

"That's amazing, I have to tell my husband."

"I think he's a little busy at the moment," Zoe said, pointing at Mike Jr., whose knowledge of centrifugal force had just dramatically increased when he attempted to dismount the spinning wheel. Mike Sr. also got a lesson on the subject when he attempted to grab Mike Jr. as he flew from the wheel. They both fell to the ground—one with skinned knees, too dizzy to cry, and the other dusting himself off and trying to suppress words he didn't want to end up in his son's vocabulary.

Zoe could tell that Isabella took no small amount of pleasure from the wipeout. She laughed and put her hand over her mouth to hide her amusement.

"Oh, dear," Izzy said, rising and approaching the scene of the accident. Zoe watched as Isabella pulled Mike Jr. to his feet, only to have him slink down and dangle from her hand like a dead weight. She let him slump to the ground to recover his equilibrium and approached her husband. He was on one knee. Isabella said something to him, and they both laughed. She reached out her hand to help him up. He took it, but instead of pulling himself up, he pulled Isabella close to him, and the two kissed.

The kiss seemed almost magical to Zoe. There was joy, a powerful emotional-physical connection, and energy, all in an instant. She could see it, feel it. A picture of Reggie in his corporeal Earth form came to mind. Dark, curly brown hair. Serious light brown eyes that were always searching—that sometimes searched her, she thought. She saw his thin curved lips and wondered if they could do more than lecture on Folk. Did they have feeling? If she kissed them, would they connect him to her the way Mike and Isabella were connected? Could Reggie feel the emotion? Could he handle it?

She'd known Reggie for most of her life. They'd gone to school together, played together, traveled together, worked together. There was no one she knew better than him, and yet she felt he hardly knew her at all. For all his searching eyes, she was nothing to him but a fellow student, a travel companion, a colleague. She was certain that if Reggie petitioned for a partner, he would be matched with someone totally unlike herself. Yet she knew with equal certainty that they were happy when they were together and that if they were partnered, they would grow together. Their knowledge would combine smoothly. Their fusion would be vigorous and intense. If she were to seek a partner, she would put Reggie's name on the petition.

Zoe looked at the marble notebook on the now-vacated bench. She picked it up and read from the top of the first page:

Cicadas and birds and squirrels and frogs, cows, horses, flies, and people. All give voice to the day. Clicks and chirps and bellows and croaks, grunts, whines, buzzes, and yells herald the march out of night's nervous keep. The scent of grass and leaves and trees and a stream, the cool mountain air. It all fills the senses. But there is a special time in the thick of the forest, at the height of day's beauty, when sound fades. The animals rest. The burble of the stream becomes a distant memory, and the wind alone speaks to the soul. Stillness embraces all. The compassion of silence, which calms all disquiet, is offered as a gift. It is quietly received and understood to be the joy of simply being alive. A man lets fall his defenses, and a gentle heart knows peace. The voice of God is met with gratitude and praise and a single life-affirming tear.

~

ZOE'S FOOTSTEPS LANDED, soft and welcome, thousands of light years from Earth. She walked the meandering path of the Long Trail on Greenworld, listening to birds call and answer each other before coming to rest in a clearing full of freshly fallen green leaves. The Long Trail wound its way across the entire planet, sometimes alongside rivers, sometimes through valleys or over mountains, always lush and teeming with life.

She stood still for a time, letting the warmth of the day soak into her body. She tiptoed a few steps farther, to the middle of the clearing, and slowly sat down on her heels. She stayed there a long time, quieting her mind. After a while, she lay on her back. Lying among the many shades of green, she contemplated the canopy high above. Long branches from towering trees bent into arcs and intertwined. The branches supported one another like a large group of friends huddled together, resting their outstretched arms on each other's shoulders. Each slow pass of the wind rippled across shimmering leaves, rocking the twinkling sunlight back and forth.

Eventually, her eyelids grew heavy and closed. She could still see the glistening green sway of the treetops in her mind as sleep descended. Her slow pirouette into slumber brought airy dreams that drifted on the scent of leaves and fresh earth, sweeping her into the rhythm of the forest.

When she opened her eyes, the sparkle of the sun had gone, and the treetops were a darker green. USC came to mind in the cool air of dusk. She thought of Sig and when she'd first joined the Earthfolk research team. Sig had told her that she'd come to his attention not through achievements in research, or even through Reggie's recommendation, but through her accomplishments in reform at USC. She had the ability to integrate the most powerful elements of emotional philosophy, her specialty, with pragmatic application, he'd told her. She had succeeded in getting USC to reorganize an entire division, something that hadn't been done in half a millennium. She was proud of this. She'd achieved it by challenging the traditional machinations of the Academy itself. Her logic and natural ability to connect people with the ideas they wished to express and explore were compared by critics and observers to the way ancient computers might have used algorithms, had those computers possessed a measure of emotional intelligence. Sig saw her as the ballast that would keep Reggie's precocious intellect and unbridled enthusiasm centered as they grappled with the complexity of Folk.

Zoe looked around. The cradle of the warm, leafy field had become like a looking glass in the laboratory, cold and scientific. She turned her head to one side and looked closely at the leaves around her. She reached over and grabbed a handful. In the dim of twilight, they'd lost their individual hues. They were all the same shade of dull green. The beauty and vitality of Greenworld had gone with the sunset. It was enough to make one cry, she thought. She didn't. She felt nothing. Everything around her had become dull. Was light alone the arbiter of her mental state?

She was capable of emotion. She knew she was. She felt things all the time. Well, that wasn't true. She felt things when she was with Reggie. Well, that wasn't entirely true, either. She felt *one* thing when she was with Reggie, and it was pain. A tiny twinge in her abdomen gave rise to pressure in her chest that was like a fine mist tickling her lungs so that she had to think about her breathing. Sometimes, the mist grew into a lush cloud of ache whose only release was to weep a cold rain inside her.

She'd awakened with a chill. And the world was gray. She rolled onto her side. The smell of nuts and grass and earth was stronger now in the cool of night. She breathed deeply and pulled herself up. Even though her body had rested, her mind was weary. Being present in physical form had this effect. She stretched and raised her eyes to the treetops, so lovely before, so lifeless now. She wondered how they would restore themselves to glistening beauty. The answer, she knew, was that they wouldn't need to. The trees were the same by night and by day regardless of light. It was she who changed, her perspective. She knew this intellectually. Still, she wished for day.

Zoe headed back to her quarters, keeping her eyes mostly on her feet. The path became wide, and she could see well enough without the canopy overhead. She glanced at the sky. There was no moon, only emerging stars. To either side of her, knee-high bushes with tightly packed trees behind them lined the earthen path. The bushes and trees held no interest for her. The multitude of birdsongs had given way to solitary chirps, lost and lonely in the dark.

At last, during a long, uphill climb, she spotted the outline of a structure. Her accommodations on Greenworld consisted of a chalet made entirely of glass, overlooking Greenworld's largest river. There were few people inhabiting the surrounding woodlands. The glass chalets were spaced far enough apart as to feel completely isolated. Trees rose up through the floor of each chalet, forming the walls of rooms. Carve-outs in the trees provided tables, shelves, and a bed. The chalets had no artificial climate control; none was needed. At night, moonlight reflected off the scattered chalets and would appear from a distance as sparkles on the mountainside.

Zoe climbed the tree in front of her chalet and entered at the center of the structure. The sounds of the forest became muted. It was almost full dark now. She sat on a stump and listened to the quieting night, alone.

4

PROGRESS

R EGGIE APPEARED AT the laboratory, ruminating about the framework he'd set up on Earth. Zoe was the only one there. She was quietly examining Earth text on a virtual screen before her.

"Hello, Reg," she greeted him with a quick glance.

"Hello," he said.

"How's the search for a target going?" Zoe asked, turning back to her text.

"I think it's going well. Have I ever mentioned that Earthfolk fascinate me?"

"Just every day, all day," Zoe said.

"Mmm. It's just that I want so much to help them, but they're so incredibly complex. They need so much help. It's fascinating," Reggie said.

"Don't apologize. It's why I love you." Zoe quickly straightened up. "Um. I mean it's why *we* love you. You know what I mean. There's a reason Sig and I stick around. Your passion is inspiring. Earthfolk are remarkable with their emotions, their love and their sadness. I think Sig is more Venus oriented. But the way you talk about Earthfolk has really drawn us in. What you're doing is important. I couldn't imagine working with anyone but you," Zoe said.

Reggie moved over beside Zoe and looked at her screen.

"Thanks for saying that, Zoe. I wouldn't know where to begin without you. I mean, without you *all*," he clarified.

Both looked at the screen. Neither said anything for a few seconds. Zoe turned and looked at Reggie. He looked at her. He couldn't match her composure. He had to look away. He felt a flash of anxiety. He felt the need to look anywhere but at Zoe. Was he not in control of himself? He wanted to be somewhere else, but he also didn't want to stop looking at her. How odd.

Recognizing that there was danger of this becoming extremely awkward, he asked her how her research was going, if she had any new data. She turned from the screen toward the examining glass.

"I'm examining a complete family unit. The male seems docile in the context of the family. He demonstrates far less aggression than when he is with only males, or worse, when he is with other males in the presence of a female. The female exhibits tender feelings and seeks ways to demonstrate them, expressing herself to each of the family members. The children are brimming with energy. I need to study them further. I have a written text here in the glass. It is an expression of love from the female child to the female adult. It's called a birthday card."

"I'm familiar with birthday cards. They're acknowledgements of aging."

Zoe turned and looked at Reggie's profile. "Yes, but they're much more than that. In this one, the child expresses an abundance of love for the adult female. I suspect that it is an accurate reflection of the child's feelings. But that's not the intriguing part. I've transcribed an audio recording. It's the female child saying, 'I love you, Mommy. You're the best, Mommy.'"

Reggie continued looking at the examining glass. "It's an expression of love."

"Yes, Reggie. But you can't detect the depth and purity of emotion without hearing the voice," she said.

"What are you getting at?" He was puzzled.

"You know that the spoken word of Earth has nuanced meaning, yes?" Zoe said, looking off into the distance.

"Yes," Reggie agreed.

"Well, I believe that with the right electromagnetic treatment, we can sort out the spoken words that have purity and depth of meaning from those that are superficial. I've been working on an algorithm," she said.

"I'm listening," Reggie said.

"Not exactly. But you need to listen—*really* listen. Here in space, we have no sound, only simulation. It's not the same. Let's try a quick experiment. Follow me," she said, and she streaked off.

Reggie thought she was a bit erratic, like a child. He quickly followed.

REGGIE CAME IN right behind Zoe. He didn't recognize their location. The first thing he became aware of was that they were standing on a glass floor high above trees. As he looked around, he saw that they'd reconstituted themselves inside a glass enclosure in a treetop. There was a large trunk running up the center of the room.

Zoe gestured to a stump. "Sit," she said with a smile. "Welcome to Greenworld." Zoe took a deep breath, stood, and dissembled her form momentarily. She swirled, then reconstituted herself.

"OK. Look at me, Reggie," she said, her smile gone, but her

face no less lovely.

Reggie regarded her, poised above him. She was a handsome woman in full form. He looked into her familiar eyes. They sparkled and then became subdued. She said nothing, just looked at him, canting her head slightly. Then she spoke.

"Reggie. I love you."

His name sounded different this time. It seemed to capture him. It was as if *Reggie* were more than a label or moniker, the way she spoke it. He, all of him, was Reggie. It wasn't just a word. As she said *I love you*, he watched her eyes go from subdued to sparkling to subdued again. A charge ran through him—a feeling from the past, maybe. It felt good. Then it was gone, and he was left looking at the familiar face of his friend.

He was confused. "I don't understand," he said.

"It's just an experiment. Something I've been tinkering with. In contrast, if you were to say the same words to me, there would be a variation—less intensity, I think, and less depth. Try it," she said, moving closer and holding his stare.

He was unsure of what to do or why his thoughts seemed to narrow into a myopic focus on the words *I love you*. A different feeling ran through him. Then it was gone. Was it fear? Reggie managed to mumble, "How did you formulate this?"

"I've compiled many recordings, starting with the first anomalous auditory laughter and expressions received from Earth and leading up to communications within the family unit I've been studying as part of your project. There is something in the voice that gives meaning. When Earthfolk speak with each other, even they cannot always detect the true meaning. I've been working on an electromagnetic filter for Earthfolk auditory communication," she said.

Reggie, still uncertain about the nature of his excitement, stated evenly, "Wonderful. I need to see your data, your measurements, sources, techniques. I want all that you have."

He wanted to tell Zoe about the impending ruin of his career, about his intentions for his Earthfolk experiment, about the feelings he'd just had. But emotion was constricting his judgement, and he believed emotion was at the root of his problems. Best to move on.

"Sure, Reggie. I'll put it all together to show you and Sig at the same time. It's a lot," Zoe said with a wan smile.

"Let's move fast. Zoe, this is real progress," he said, knowing there wasn't enough time to explore her findings.

ZOE NODDED, AS Reggie spoke of progress. Was it really? Here they were in a peaceful nook, thousands of light years from the Academy and its protocols, talking of feelings. Talking of emotion. Emotion she felt, as sure as the light that constituted Reggie's and her images. But did he feel it? He was never really present. What did he mean by progress? She wondered if he would ever understand emotion the way she did.

REGGIE WAS GRATEFUL for Zoe's effort and the lesson on emotion. He didn't understand it, but maybe what little he did comprehend would help. He really did need to move fast. His deadline loomed large. He said his goodbye and was off. He'd already lost time preparing. The Academy could intervene at any point and insist he go to Mega sooner. They could be watching him right now, for all he knew. He wondered if it was fear he was feeling. He had to appear at ARS-13. That meant he would likely be sent to Mega or some far-off planet to live out his days in corporeal form with his neural pathways reconfigured to prevent connection to *the link*. No more travel or transmissions of any kind. That was how the Academy dealt with those who went beyond their commissioned studies. He would spend a few rotations on Mega being reconditioned for acclimation to full-time physical existence, and then it would be farewell to the rest of the universe. This was the consequence of just planning a transgression.

His image reappeared in his classroom. As he floated soundlessly, he considered where he'd gone wrong, how the Academy had found him out. It must have been his last report. He had revealed too much, hinted too plainly at the risks he was prepared to take with Earthfolk. His tinkering with emotional waves and dream theory was too progressive for the Academy, too dangerous for *the link*. And perhaps they were right.

It would be back to the flesh. His image would be limited to the light reflected from his corporeal form, seen only by those who were physically close to his body.

He needed to go to the desert. He needed to go to New Mexico, where things were as far along as he could manage. As for the risk to *the link*, he didn't for an instant believe that the exposure of an infinitesimal number of Folk to its channels and waves would cause the mayhem the Academy predicted. *The link* was a natural phenomenon. It had always been and always would be. He understood that the Academy had a responsibility to regulate its use. But his plan involved a mere handful of Folk, and only for a very short time—just long enough to determine if they could actually see and make sense of it. He had no concern about the stasis of their bodies, as the exposure would be brief. His research strongly suggested they would survive and thrive. All he wanted to do was prove it so that others greater than himself could take up the cause.

Folk had not been introduced to *the link* in eons. Meanwhile, they wallowed in cycles of war and violence. Reggie told himself he was being altruistic. He knew in his core that he was right, that he could save people.

Fear was not going to stop him.

5

PAULINA AND MARILUZ

P AULINA AND MARILUZ received a look from the young barista behind the counter, who'd had to ask the customer in front of her to repeat his order. The girl looked away, then shot another glance over the customer's shoulder to the corner where the two were seated. She didn't seem annoyed so much as curious to know what they were all worked up about so early in the morning. The answer was life at school and life in outer space. Mariluz would contend that sometimes they seemed to be one and the same, especially on parent-teacher day.

"I didn't know what to say to his mother. What if using the smelly mothballs as planets in the galaxy diorama was her idea?" Mariluz said with a smile.

The ladies burst out laughing, Paulina covering her mouth and giggling, a stark contrast to Mariluz' guffaws.

"Speaking of the Milky Way, have you seen the new vice principal?" asked Mariluz. "He's right up your alley, Paulina. White hair, pale skin, blue eyes."

Paulina raised her eyebrows. "I haven't seen him, but I heard there was going to be a new administrator. I think his name is Jack something. Silva. Jack Silva."

"Silva fox, more like it!" Mariluz shouted.

Paulina smiled. "Well, I hope he doesn't have sticky fingers like the last one."

Mariluz kept at it. "Paulina, you need to meet this guy." She looked over to the table next to theirs. A heavyset woman with a toddler seated across from her looked back. Mariluz lowered her voice and added, "*En serio, es un caballero de aspecto muy distinguido. Está divorciado.*"

"I thought we were here to talk about our trip to the observatory, not men," said Paulina. She, unlike Mariluz, had an ex-husband. She figured she'd had enough experience with men, more than Mariluz. She knew enough to know that silver foxes were not in her future.

The ladies continued chatting. After a bit more unsuccessful prodding by Mariluz, they got down to the business of planning their visit to the Very Large Array. They agreed that they would announce their trip on Dr. K's Cosmos Connection forum, just to see if anyone else was interested in making the trek with them. It would be more fun that way and maybe give Mariluz a chance to check out AlienWheelman, if he came. The two clashed famously on the forum. Sparks flew when she and 'Wheelie' collided over what would happen if a hypothetical car traveling through space at the speed of light turned on its headlights. Would light shine out in front of the car, or would nothing happen? The make and model of the car was their first obstacle. It was stupid, but it was great fun. She assumed Wheelie wasn't serious—at least she hoped he wasn't serious—in thinking the lights would project out.

REGGIE WRIGGLED IN his chair. The lightweight aluminum of the chair pressed awkwardly into his lower back. He pinched the fabric on his shoulders and wondered why they called what he was wearing a leisure suit. It hung on him, making him uncomfortably warm. Not his conception of leisure. Nonetheless, he didn't take his eyes off the plate glass window. He could clearly see the two females inside. It was doubtful they could see him, even if they looked out; he was tucked under the shade of a wide green umbrella. How long could the two talk? He wondered what they were discussing. They both seemed to be talking at once, and they laughed a lot. That was probably the point of the exercise. Silly, really, when compared with the breadth of connections they could be making.

THE LADIES' MEETING wound down, as did the volume of their chatter. Mariluz announced that she was getting a coffee refill for the road.

"Need anything?" Mariluz asked, heading toward the counter. Paulina shook her head.

"May I have a refill, please?" Mariluz asked the young barista.

"Sure thing," replied the girl. She took Mariluz's travel mug with a smile and held her eye for a moment. "Pardon me, but I heard y'all talking about space. Didn't you used to teach science at the middle school?"

Mariluz searched the girl's face to see if she could remember having her as a student. Nothing registered. "I taught Spanish and science both for two years. You weren't one of my students?" she asked.

"No. I'm Sarah. My brother Sam had you. I think he was in your Spanish class. I love science, space," the bubbly barista said.

"Ah," Mariluz said.

"Did you know Voyager 2 just left the solar system?" Sarah said, wide-eyed.

"Yes, I know. It's very exciting. I always tell my students to keep track of the Voyagers. They might someday make contact with aliens," Mariluz said with a wink.

The girl nodded enthusiastically.

Mariluz got her coffee and returned to the table. Paulina was already standing, ready to go.

"Shall we?" Mariluz announced, leading the way to the door. She looked toward the front counter and waved. "*Hasta luego,* Sarah."

"*Buenos tardes,*" shouted the girl, mangled Spanish stumbling off her tongue.

REGGIE STOOD. FINALLY. He walked toward the parked cars in front of the coffee shop, keeping his eyes on the females— laughing, again. If there had to be emotion, happiness was probably a good one to share, he considered.

THE LADIES STEPPED out into the light of the rising sun. The hot air was welcomed by both after twenty minutes in the air-conditioned coffee shop. The sky was a magnificent blue, but dark clouds were visible in the distance. The two ladies huddled briefly in the parking lot for a quick parting hug. Mariluz, ever ebullient, was the first to reach her arms out. No sooner did she embrace Paulina than a massive bright light swept over them.

6

POONAM MURTHY

M RS. POONAM MURTHY, late of Davangere, Karnataka, India, late of Iselin, New Jersey, late of Richardson, Texas, most recently transplanted to Las Cruces, NM, couldn't be accused of not supporting her husband, Venkata.

While Venkata strove to secure a permanent position at New Mexico State University by teaching three classes a week, tutoring five days a week, doing consulting work in the evenings, and writing code in between, Poonam smiled at guests and poured ready-made batter into a waffle-making machine.

Breakfast at King's Quarter Inn off of Interstate 10 was the motel's busiest time. Poonam had graduated with distinction from Osmania University in Hyderabad, India, held a master's degree in chemistry, and was certified to teach in New Jersey, Texas, and New Mexico. Unfortunately, most of the teaching she did these days was on how to make a proper bed. Her most impressive chemical research now was on how much water could be mixed with orange juice and still have it taste like orange juice.

She and her husband were part owners of the Inn, along

with Venkata's cousin-brother and an uncle in New Jersey. Venkata handled the finances for the motel on weekends and was busy at the university during the week. Poonam hadn't thought it was a good idea to go into business with Uncle Chakraborty-Ji and his son. She had politely mentioned this to her husband several dozen times. Chakraborty-Ji owned two hotels and a restaurant with a liquor license in New Jersey, as well as a convenience store in Texas. He would stay in New Jersey, making liberal use of his liquor license, and Ravi, his son, would be in Texas running the convenience store. Who would run the motel while Venkata worked at the university? She knew the answer to this question, and she humbly repeated it again and again. She discretely mentioned that it might be hard for her to find a job in Las Cruces if he took a position at the university, especially if she had to spend all her time running a motel. Venkata's answer was that it would give them breathing room financially until he could secure a permanent teaching job. It was a fallback. Poonam expressed to her husband that the only falling back would be in her career. And yet she agreed.

After the morning setup, Poonam could usually be found seated behind the Inn, tapping on her laptop and sipping orange water. Today, she was sitting out there giving dubious thumbs-ups to friends on social media and catching up on what news she could get from Karnataka. She'd already sent two e-mails to Chakraborty-Ji's wife, trying to figure out if Chakraborty-Ji was going to help out with the upcoming taxes and inspection. The e-mails were sure to go unanswered.

She checked some online reviews of the motel. It was always gratifying when guests gave compliments on the friendliness of the staff. Fortunately, this was a recurring theme across platforms.

After a few minutes of checking reviews, satisfied that no mention of bedbugs was circulating, she logged into Dr. K's

Cosmos Connection forum. A thread on mathematics caught her eye. She knew a few people who posted on the site. She'd met them while substitute teaching. They were either substitute teachers themselves or parents. The owner of the site was a local neurologist who'd originally posted an essay called "Cosmos from Chaos: The Birth of a Brain," which drew parallels between the universe and the human brain. But most people on the site just wanted to talk about space or aliens. A couple were scientifically oriented, though, like the ones going on about calculating parsecs between galaxies using ridiculously large numbers. Poonam wondered about the stars and infinity but rarely took to a calculator over it.

She heard footsteps and glanced up from her screen. A handsome man in a powder blue polyester jacket and matching trousers had just rounded the corner. She smiled at him and looked back at her screen.

She reached for the plastic cup of thin juice when *zip,* the laptop screen glitched and went blank. She stared at the blank screen for a few moments, then lifted the laptop, examined it back and front, and shook it hard—an advanced recovery technique Venkata had taught her. Nothing. She muttered a few phrases in Hindi, interspersed with her husband's name and a less-than-flattering assessment of his computer science acumen. She usually blamed him for technical malfunctions, regardless of the device. Actually, she blamed him for any malfunctions, period.

REGGIE TUGGED AT his collar as he walked along the side of the structure. The warm morning air had followed him around each corner. Earthfolk generally considered sunrise to be pleasing. They had a point. It was nice to see layers of sunlight across a wide sky. He thought it likely that Mrs. Poonam Murthy was enjoying the sunrise. He hoped she'd enjoy the light in *the link* just as much. It was probably a good thing for her to be happy when he transmitted.

IN AN INSTANT, with her eyes still focused on the blank screen, Poonam lost her sense of distance and depth. Everything became a blur of colors. There was movement. There wasn't anything to give her context, but she knew there was movement.

Someone spoke. She was being watched. The voice told her to be calm. She didn't trust it. She couldn't figure out what the hell was going on. She was near panic. Had she passed out? Had she been kidnapped? She couldn't feel her body. There were colors. First there was white, as if she were blind. Then there was green—acute, deep, bright—only the color green. And she was *in* the color green. There were no shapes, no objects. The voice told her to be at peace.

She had no time to contemplate the green before it turned to red, and then she was coming back to herself. There was a sensation. Pain. Slow. Was it behind her eyes? She had no body, but damn it if the pain wasn't behind her eyes.

A new sensation. She was rising and falling on large waves. She feared that if her motion stopped, she would be consumed by the waves. She felt pressure and queasiness. What the hell was happening? Nothing made sense. It was Venkata's fault. Orange juice should not be mixed with water. A mind can explode. No more thoughts. Now she was running and talking but not thinking. She could feel her body again. Running. She stopped, and a deep sleep immediately took her.

7

MARTINO AND FITZ

F ITZ ALREADY HAD a tiny bead of sweat just above his right eyebrow. In the distance, to the east of Route 213, a crack of bleary red squinted over the horizon. The sun was just beginning to rise, cranky as hell. It often woke that way out in the desert.

"*Agua fría, jefe?*" asked Tino, not for the first time.

"Yeah, *agua fría,*" Fitz answered, also not for the first time, as the two hoisted a cooler with a large duffel bag stacked on top into the back of a New Mexico Department of Transportation pickup truck parked in a fenced-in carport. The two men had just parked their own trucks under twin piñon trees close to the road.

Martino "Tino" Martinez knew he annoyed Fitz every time he asked, but ever since the time the cooler had been loaded with warm water and no ice, he seemed to feel it was his duty to question the water's status before heading out for a day in the sun.

It was an unwritten rule that part of Fitz's job as the boss was to make sure they had what they needed. He was a smart guy, an engineer. Unfortunately, he sometimes forgot the little things that made a difference in the day's heat.

Today's mission was straightforward, some ditch surveys and a couple readings from the active infrared sensors over a large sector of isolated roads in Doña Ana County. The concern was flash flooding and the roads' capacity to drain water. Failing proper drainage, they needed to know the impact of closing certain roads during monsoons. He was the only engineer in the office who did his own grunt work. But he liked being out of the office, even if the sun continued to bleach his silver-gray hair.

Tino latched the tailgate while Fitz took up his command post in the passenger seat. Fitz had his laptop out and was pulling up GPS coordinates by the time Tino started the truck.

"Jackman Hollow first, boss?" Tino asked.

"Yeah. You remember how to get there?" Fitz said.

"Sí."

The air conditioning was blowing warm, and the radio was still loud from the day before as they crunched their way onto the highway, heading south. No headlights or movement for miles around. Tino swung the sun visor across to the driver's side window in expectation of the jab that would come as the sun rose higher. He lowered the volume on the radio and changed the station to the news. It was the same drill every morning.

"Probably no rain today, *sí*?" Tino said.

"You never know during monsoon season. You can change the station back after the weather report," Fitz said. They got official reports back at the office, but no would call them this early unless it was an emergency.

Twelve miles along, they pulled off the road just before a bridge. Fitz grabbed the two-way radio from his belt, clicked it on, and called out, "Edwin. *Buenos días.*"

"Good morning, sir," came a quick reply.

"We're here. Let's get going."

"Yes, sir," the walkie crackled back.

Fitz clipped the walkie to his belt and looked toward the side of the flat bridge where it met the top of a gulley.

A SHORT DISTANCE away at the mouth of a culvert leading to the gulley Reggie watched as Edwin Figueroa sat in his car under the bridge. Edwin was wearing a bright-colored vest, but it was fairly dark, and Reggie could just see the top half of the man as he spoke into a device. The man got out and started up the embankment. Finally. The other two must have arrived. It was the same every morning. Reggie clambered out of the culvert, brushing cobwebs from his jacket. He walked fast toward the bridge. By the time he got to the embankment, the man was out of sight. He would have to hurry. Reggie reached the top of the hill, slightly out of breath. Edwin was already close to the truck.

EDWIN WORE HIS lime-green, reflective vest loose over a DOT T-shirt. The vest rose up slightly in the warm morning breeze as he strode toward the truck. He carried a backpack with a white hard hat fastened to it in one hand and a small cooler in the other.

"Morning," Fitz called out from the passenger side window of the truck.

"Water cold?" Edwin asked, hopping in the back seat.

Fitz ignored the question. "I hope you remembered not to bring lunch. We're going to Anita's again. And this'll be the last time. The water's been cold for the past two weeks."

Tino rolled the pickup back onto the road as Edwin buckled up.

Edwin laughed, "Just messing with you, Fitz. I didn't bring lunch today. Only thing I brought was some cold water," he said, holding up his small cooler.

Fitz turned around and gave Edwin an unamused smirk, though his twinkling blue eyes conveyed the opposite.

"What? Just in case," Edwin said, chuckling along with Tino.

"Not funny. By the way . . ."

Fitz didn't get to finish his sentence. The radio went silent, the dashboard and headlights flickered, and the engine coughed and cut off. The truck swerved sharply toward the shoulder.

"What the hell?" Fitz managed to get out before light blasted through the window, turning everything to bright white.

TINO INSTINCTIVELY HIT the brake and cut the wheel, thinking they'd been hit by a truck or a train. He thought he was dead, and that he was lucky to have died a pain-free, instantaneous death. The light was there to take him to heaven. He was grateful it hadn't hurt. He had a vision of broken bones, mashed internal organs, blood. All of these things could have happened, but they hadn't. A tremendous relief. He had an aversion to pain in all its forms.

So, now what? His mind was at ease, as it usually was. There was all this light. Actually, now that he thought about it, that's all there was. Bright white light. He tried listening, but there was no sound. Would an angel be coming for him? There was movement. He was glad his wife had insisted the whole family go to confession before mass last Saturday night at Saint Theresa's. He was good to go. He thought to make the sign of the cross but couldn't.

Wow, he thought, realizing he had no body but was moving anyway.

It felt like he was at the beach with his kids back in Corpus

Christi and had gotten submerged in a strong wave. Then everything went blue.

OK.

After a period, everything went red.

Not OK.

Red was the color of the devil, of hell. Dang. He thought about Saint Theresa's. He'd confessed all the things he could think of. He hadn't committed any of the heavy hitters: murder, adultery, stealing, putting a wad of gum in the collection basket instead of the money his mother had given him for the offering when he was a kid. Wait, that last one was a real possibility. It came back to him. He was eight when he did that. But he'd never confessed it. Did that mean he wasn't forgiven? Dang!

He was still moving. He couldn't tell direction. He didn't think it was down, but he didn't know for sure. If he was moving downward, he was definitely going to hell. He felt a tingling that would have been behind his eyes, if he had eyes. He had a slightly ill feeling. Oh boy, here he comes—El Diablo.

I should've swallowed the dang gum. He felt dizzy. Everything faded to black.

AS SOON AS the truck cut off and swerved, Fitz braced himself, for an impact that didn't come. Bright white flooded the pickup, then subsided, but everything was still white. Fitz waited. He was scared. He'd never blacked out or hallucinated before. It was a good thing he hadn't been driving. He could have killed them all. Was he having a reaction to some ultra-high-frequency transmission from the nearby military base? God knows what jamming tech they might be testing over there. Maybe it was deliberate, or maybe something had gone haywire. He knew how close they were to government land, and flight-testing areas. He was convinced he'd been hit with something.

The white changed to blue changed to red. There was motion, somehow, very faint. Then a tingling sensation. He tried to say, "What the hell?" but wasn't sure anything came out. He became disoriented—not surprising, as he had no frame of reference. Someone said, "All is right and well." Then, black.

The next thing he knew, he was whole again and seeing the inside of the truck. The truck was dead and resting at an odd angle just off the road. He leaned his head back against the headrest and glanced over at Tino. "All is right and well?" he mimicked.

"Huh?" Tino said, massaging his right temple.

"You said, 'All is right and well.'"

"No. That's what you said," Tino shot back.

"No. I said, 'What the hell?' and then you said, 'All is right and well.'"

Tino frowned and shook his head.

Fitz sat up and turned his upper body toward the back seat. Edwin looked more or less OK, no obvious injuries. "You say it?" he asked.

Edwin slowly shook his head. He didn't seem ready to talk.

"But you heard someone say, 'All is right and well,' right?"

Edwin nodded.

Fitz turned back to Tino. "What the hell happened?"

"*No sé.* I thought maybe I was dead," Tino said. It occurred to him that he needed to verify he was, in fact, not dead. He looked out the driver's side window. It was day, and they were stopped at a forty-five-degree angle, facing away from the highway. He craned his neck and looked through the windshield, over the hood of the truck. They were on the edge of a drainage ditch. Another few feet, and they would have gone right in. This was all reassuring to Tino. They were in the truck. They weren't moving, and their position was consistent with him pulling off the road when they got hit. It was a miracle they hadn't died. But what had hit them?

He gently pulled the parking brake on and put the gear in park. He popped the door open, peeked out onto the ground, and got out. Nothing. No other vehicles. The road was quiet. He walked around behind the truck. Nothing out of the ordinary. He looked up. The sun wasn't very high in the sky. He pulled his sunglasses from his shirt pocket and continued looking up. He whispered out loud, "*En el nombre del Padre, del Hijo, y del Espíritu Santo,*" as he quickly crossed himself. He went on to say a silent prayer of thanks and concluded by asking forgiveness for putting his gum in the collection basket when he was eight. He promised to donate the money he was supposed to give, plus interest, to Saint Theresa's, and forego gum forever.

FITZ WATCHED TINO walk around the truck and bless himself. He looked over at the ignition. The key was in it, and it was in the on position. He reached over and took the key out. He put it back in and turned the switch. The truck started right up, the exhaust displacing a small dust cloud. Tino jumped, cried out, and stumbled backward onto the ground behind the truck. After a few seconds, he sat up. Realizing what happened, he muttered his disapproval, "*Pinche güey!*"—followed immediately by, "*Perdóname, Dios, mío,*" as he glanced up at the sky.

Tino got back in the driver's seat. Just as he pulled his seat belt firmly across his lap, a massive white light blinded him. Then everything went black.

REGGIE HAD NEARLY blown this one. The men had almost driven off. He had to transmit in two stages to be sure he got all three. He'd been a little slow catching up to the truck; his body had lumbered under the strain of trying to run up the hill at the bridge. But running was good practice. He'd likely spend the rest of his life in corporeal form on Mega. He hoped it would all be worth it. Transmitting to an entire group, for the purpose of emotional support, when he was really most interested in the females, or rather, one particular female, was a lot more work than he'd expected.

8

TRAUMA CENTER

LITTLE PAWS SCRATCHED at the bedroom door as a garbage truck rumbled outside. Lisa looked at her dresser mirror. She canted her head and stared at the mirror's beveled edge. If she tilted her head just right, the sunlight and angled glass trim produced a prism effect, making the edge reflect all the colors of the visible spectrum—Red, Orange, Yellow, Green, Blue, Indigo, and Violet—in perfect order. It was a ROY G. BIV autograph on the side of her mirror. As she squinted and tilted her head, taking in the colors, the scratching at the door grew more determined.

"Patience, kitty cat. Mama's sleeping," she groaned.

But she wasn't sleeping. She pulled the covers up to her chin, closed her eyes, and tried to recall the dream she'd been having. Something about seeing colors and waves. There had been a man's voice. Was it her father? She often dreamed of him. Her father was gentle in her dreams, as he had been in life before he died. The voice in her dream had been gentle as well, and she'd trusted it, but it had been distant. Was it Flash? Besides her father, Flash was the only man who made repeat appearances in her dreams, and she trusted him. She hadn't dreamed about him for close to a year, yet she still remembered that last dream clearly. It was a good dream. Flash was driving. They were in his beat-up little convertible with the top down, heading up the coast back in California. Wild streaks of blond hair whipped her face, but she didn't care. She was flying. They were in love.

She lay very quietly, concentrating on the voice from her bizarre dream. It wasn't Flash. There was no reason she'd start dreaming about him again now. What had the voice said? The only thing she remembered for certain was that it was a very strange dream, stranger than her usual strange dreams.

As she lay there, a low *phwumph* sound broke the silence of her room.

She paused, listening.

Phwumph.

She raised her head slightly.

Phwumph.

"Go away!" Lisa yelled. Dale was hurling herself headfirst at the bedroom door. Were all cats this batshit crazy, or was Dale a special kind of wingnut? Then a low *buzz, buzz, buzz . . .*

Her cell phone was vibrating. She flung off the covers, bounced out of bed, and fumbled for her work cell. She glanced at the top of the screen. *July 12, 2019—6:31 a.m.* Six thirty? What the hell?

She recognized the number. It was the hospital. She swiped her finger across the bottom of the screen.

"Hello, this is Dr. Kulowski," she said, clearing her throat.

"Good morning, Dr. K. It's Clara."

"Morning, Clara. This can't be good," Lisa murmured.

Phwumph!

Lisa stamped her foot in the direction of the door, which was immediately answered by the sound of paws scrambling down the hall.

"Good morning. It's not good. We've got three simultaneous trauma cases, unresponsive but stable."

"Wow. OK," Lisa said, her attention firmly fixed to the voice on the phone.

"Yeah. Apparently, they all lost consciousness at the same time, no accident, no sign of head injuries."

"Tox?" Lisa asked.

"We're waiting on analysis. I don't think it's drugs. Maybe some kind of gas? I don't know. Cops said they all work for the county—some kind of road crew or something. They found them in a pickup out near White Sands."

"CT?" Lisa asked.

"Being done as we speak. But what are the odds of three people having strokes at the same time? I mean . . . I don't know what it is. The attending neuro is here, but honestly, I think he's waiting for you."

"OK, Clara. Have someone upload the scans to the shared drive as soon as they're ready. I'll check them from my office, then head down to you," Lisa said.

"Thank you. See you in a bit," Clara said, and the line went dead.

Lisa lay back down on the bed and rubbed her eyes. Her lower eyelids were wet. In fact, her cheeks and chin were damp, too. What the hell? She was crying in her sleep now? An old familiar feeling came over her, something akin to déjà vu. The feeling didn't come often, but when it did, it was unsettling. She felt like a little girl again. She wanted someone to hold her, carry her. She wanted to let everything go and quietly watch the world from atop someone's shoulders, without all the cares, without all the considerations and implications, diagnoses, outcomes, precautions. Then the feeling passed.

She thought for a few moments longer and concluded that she didn't have time for this crap. No time for a shower, either.

She needed to get to the hospital. Three county workers collapsing near a missile test site was odd. She ran through the most likely scenarios. Probably drugs. Maybe they were electrocuted. No—gas. Carbon monoxide?

Phwumph.

It was going to be a long day.

SIRENS FADED IN and out across the city, winding their way toward the trauma center. Shiny, slippery roads slowed the emergency vehicles at every turn. Traffic lights flashed red. Bad timing for a monsoon, even a small one. Idling ambulances were piling up outside the Mount Vista Regional Trauma Center on the outskirts of Las Cruces, NM.

"MVR Main, this is LCFD. We are en route with an Asian female, approximately thirty years old. Subject experienced syncope and possible head injury. Subject is unconscious, vitals stable. Please advise . . ."

Dr. Lisa Kulowski looked up from the CT scan on her laptop and spoke in a calm voice. "Clara, contact Air Evac. We can't take any more. That'll make six cases. Contact El Paso Level I Trauma and let them know that if any more come in, we'll be sending them their way." After three seconds of Clara remaining still, Lisa raised her voice. "Move it!"

Lisa despised tyrannical doctors, but there was a difference between being a tyrant and getting people to act fast. Clara needed a jolt. Lisa understood the older woman's hesitation. There was something going on here that neither one of them had seen before. Unease was in the air. The EMTs and cops had an unusual grimness in their expressions as they compared notes on their way in and out of the hospital. Most of these patients would likely lose their lives or have their lives permanently altered, and the first responders knew it. No one, including Lisa, had a handle on the situation. Her immediate diagnosis was edema of synaptic connectivity tissue, possibly ischemic, possible peripheral neuropathy, but she wasn't sure of anything. Basically, she had six people who'd all collapsed. Three were brought in together. The other three were individual cases from different parts of the city.

She'd been near the top of her class at the University of Southern California and had years of surgical and research experience with brain trauma, yet she could not figure out what was going on. There was no hemorrhaging, no sign of external trauma, and only slight swelling. There was minimal neural activity, just a single high-frequency electrical signal in the gamma range. Bloodwork was negative. Maybe it was something environmental. Was it contagious? That's what made Lisa uneasy. Did she need to initiate isolation and containment protocols? She figured she'd better have someone contact the Centers for Disease Control. Something was off. Damn.

ALL THE EXAMINING glasses displayed vivid scenes from Earth.

Those who had received the transmission were in distress. Serious distress. It wasn't supposed to be like this. Reggie's mind was swirling. What had he missed? How had his formula failed so terribly? Was there something wrong in his calculations? This shouldn't have happened. Something was off. Damn.

9

WAVES

L ISA NO LONGER had control of her muscles and limbs. She wasn't sure if she even had muscles and limbs. She was moving. She was going in different directions, simultaneously spreading out, underwater maybe? *I shouldn't be able to do that*, she thought. She should have felt her stomach dropping or the force of acceleration or something. It didn't feel like a dream or like she was imagining it. But it had to be a dream. She wondered if time had stopped. Words were inadequate to describe what she saw. Who would she tell, anyway? It had to be seen to be believed.

The water surrounded her. It was frozen but not cold. It moved with her. But how? How did she know it was water at all? Because of the vast, wide waves. But the waves weren't moving. They were frozen. They should have been moving past her. They should have swelled and crested.

The water was a pattern of lines, helices, double, triple, quadruple. A tunnel. It moved with her. She didn't pass through it. She was in it. The waves were many and of varying heights and frequencies. The pattern embraced her, allowing her to remain steady as she moved with it. Impossible. She knew she was moving because she could see orbs on the waves, and the orbs passed her. They were strange. Maybe they were moving and she the one remaining still? No. *I am moving,* she told herself.

Lisa.

Lisa.

"Lisa."

Lisa scrunched one eye closed and slightly opened the other.

"Lisa, dear. You all right? I think you were dreaming." Clara carefully slid a steaming Styrofoam cup across the cafeteria table toward Lisa's elbow.

Clara's puffy face and the ambient noise of the hospital cafeteria put an end to the movement of the patterns. Noise filled her senses. A couple of people were talking loudly over the hum of an orbiting floor-buffing machine in the hallway; a can dropped in a soda machine somewhere. There had been no noise in the pattern, not a solitary sound during her frozen flight.

"Lisa. You there? You were mumbling about moving and the water being frozen. Thought you might like some hot tea."

"Thanks, Clara."

"You should go home and get some sleep, dear. It's three a.m. Don't you have office hours tomorrow?"

"Yeah. No, wait, I canceled them. I need to be here. What about you?"

"Don't worry about me, I'm off for the weekend. It's been some couple of days, huh? Makes me think it might be time for me to retire. Or maybe catch a nine-to-fiver in some doctor's office. Maybe yours?" Clara raised an eyebrow.

"Don't say that, Clara. If you leave, there'll be nobody to tell the doctors what needs get done around here . . . and how to do it."

They both smiled. Clara bounced up from the table, belying

her fifty-nine years. She gave Lisa a tender pat on the shoulder, told her to get some rest, and headed down the hallway toward the sound of the buffing machine.

Lisa was relieved Clara wasn't holding a grudge over her sharp words in the ER. Barking at Clara to move her ass was unheard of. It was usually Clara doing the barking, and on some days, the growling and biting, too. Lisa had no doubt the emergency room's senior nurse could reduce her to tears if she wanted. All it would take was a withering look and an implication that she'd lost the woman's respect. Tonight, thankfully, Clara was still a friend. Holding the cup between her hands, she appreciated the warmth of the tea and the warmth of a hardened ER nurse whom she admired.

The dream, though—it had been so incredibly lifelike, but at the same time implausibly bizarre. She was starting to regret not having contacted a professional. Maybe the weird dreams were somehow related to the diagnostic sleep study she'd had the day before the crisis hit. Could be a side effect. Weird dreams might just be the cost of sleep. With all the trauma patients coming in, she had barely had time for a cup of tea, let alone sleep. Maybe she should mention the dreams to the consultant. He might have some insights. She never dreamed so vividly. She hardly ever napped, even after a long surgery.

Anyway, it might be worth reaching out to him. He seemed to know his stuff, and he wasn't hard on the eyes. But what was she thinking? She was a neurologist, for goodness' sake. Physician, heal thyself, and all that. Two days into a crisis was not a good time to think about herself. Still, she knew she needed more sleep, or she wouldn't be worth much. She decided feeling guilty would only slow her down. When she'd decided to get serious about her poor sleep, she had no way of knowing six serious cases would materialize the next day.

She didn't have time to follow up with the sleep specialist

now. She needed to stay focused on her patients. The pathology of their affliction escaped her. The epidemiologist from the CDC hadn't shed much light on things. There were no obvious commonalities in the patients. The group consisted of males and females, ranging in age from eighteen to forty-two. They lived in different areas of the city and on the outskirts. There were three episode sites—two groups of coworkers and a lone female. All six were in good health. In fact, good health might've been the only thing they shared.

Then it occurred to her. If it was an airborne pathogen, she had been exposed to it. What if that was the reason she was dreaming in such a strange way? Was her brain getting a little slushy? Would she start wompin' around and collapse? That was her mother's expression—*wompin' around*—applied to children who ran around, excitedly waving their arms and yammering.

She needed to rule out her own exposure being the cause of the symptoms she was experiencing. She *did* need to speak with the doctor from the sleep center to confirm that the dreams she'd experienced were in the vicinity of normal.

LISA LOOKED AT the handsome doctor with his serious light brown eyes and curly dark hair. "At first, it was like static on a TV when a station goes off the air in the wee hours of the morning, you know?" she said.

He just nodded.

She continued, "And it was all around me. There was no buzz to go along with it. Just the static. That's all I saw. But it wasn't exactly like TV static. This static had color. Lots of color. All the colors, I think. Colors I can't even describe. There's nothing to compare them with. I couldn't say this one was like red or that one was like blue, because they weren't. I don't know what their names are. Red and blue and green and all the regular ones were there, but there were more, too. I thought I might have gone blind. I was just sitting alone in the cafeteria, too tired to eat. It was a long day, you know?"

"Mm," the handsome doctor agreed.

Lisa considered his expression. He definitely looked sympathetic. He was hanging on her every word and didn't take his eyes off her. But he didn't smile. Serious type. He wasn't taking notes. She thought maybe he should be writing this stuff down, but she shrugged it off and continued, "The only things available in the cafeteria after eight p.m. are candy bars, chips, and soda from the machines. They'd only make me feel gross, so I just sat there looking at pictures of Dale, my calico, on my phone. I remember thinking she was going to be pissed at me for not feeding her on time. I was hoping she hadn't trashed the house in protest. She demands punctuality, you know?"

The sleep doctor nodded. Not so much as a hint of a smile. He was still in sympathy mode, though. Something told Lisa that he was good at what he did. She just kind of felt it. He was clearly all business, which was fine with her. Of course, he might've been one of those people who thought it was better to remain silent and be considered a fool than to open one's mouth and remove all doubt.

She'd been worried about her sleeping and dreaming. After she'd worked through dinner, with no progress in diagnosing the trauma patients, she'd wound up in the cafeteria.

"As I was looking at my phone, the picture kind of wrinkled and turned to static. Then the static spread to everything around me until that was all I could see—not the phone, not the cafeteria, just static. I felt my head turn just a bit, kind of like a dog when he hears a strange sound, you know?"

Still no reaction. Must not have been a dog or cat person.

"Then the static had color. It was weird. It happened so fast; I didn't know what to think. I wondered if I'd gone blind. I knew that couldn't be, though, because things wouldn't be as distinct if I were blind. I didn't know what to do. I felt like I was awake. Tired, yes, but fully awake. It was quiet. When I was looking at the picture of Dale, the one from when she was a kitten, peeking out of my cocoa mug, I could hear two janitors talking in the hallway, rolling a buffing machine around. Once the static started, I heard nothing. The static expanded— like, it lengthened—and then I was moving. All the colors of the static became part of a pattern of ribbons, then waves, and then I saw eyes! That's it, I saw eyes!" she said, remembering them clearly now.

Lisa looked out the office window. She could see wide, flat land and mountains jutting up in the distance. There was something appealing about the plainness of the desert. Its simplicity was soothing. The sun had just made its way up over the mountains. The view was stunning from the first floor of the old brick building where the sleep center was tucked away. She hadn't noticed the view upon arriving; too much on her mind. The old brick building had the appearance of being abandoned, as there were no cars in the parking lot. But she'd found Dr. Reggie Homer's office just inside on the first floor of the two-story building.

She looked around the room. The walls were bare, a matte light mocha color, like the flat earth outside. She looked back over the sparse desktop at her host. She felt obligated to fill the growing silence. "I saw eyes everywhere. Just eyes. They were different colors. One pair was looking at me. I saw that I was in water, frozen. I didn't feel cold, but I figured I was in water because there were waves. And I was amazed by the colors of the waves, like when I was a kid watching the finale of a fireworks show, completely transported. The waves were like multicolored ribbons on a vast topographical map."

At this point, Lisa stopped talking, figuring it was well past time for some feedback. She let the silence hang.

REGGIE LOOKED AT Lisa in silence for a few moments. She was still smiling faintly, perhaps at the memory of the colors. Reggie inspected her face. He knew something hadn't gone quite right. She shouldn't have been able to see anyone other than her group. Still, she didn't seem to have any ill effects. That was most important. He searched her soft brown eyes and wondered that the "frozen water" hadn't melted in the warmth of her gaze. It radiated from her. Excitement, curiosity, and the glow of abundant life. He understood that there was some anxiety. Still, he'd given her a glimpse of *the link* with no major damage. And he'd done it according to plan, using his dream theory paired with theoremifics. She thought it was a dream and hadn't really happened. This was the result he was hoping for.

"Am I losing my mind, Dr. Homer?" Lisa said.

"No. Just the opposite. I think you're finding it . . . though it's odd that you saw so many pairs of eyes. The eyes you saw, did they have faces?" Reggie asked.

"No. No faces. No bodies. They were all different. Only one pair was looking at me."

"How did they make you feel?" he said.

"They scared me, actually. But as long as I was moving, or they were moving, I thought I'd be fine. I was sort of mesmerized by the colors of their eyes," Lisa said, looking off to the side.

Reggie noted that if there was fear, she was likely not suited to connecting for a longer period. Mesmerized was OK. Fear was not. He couldn't allow Earthfolk fear, or the potential for violence it brought with it, into *the link*.

"I'd like to introduce you to my team. They are very much

going to want to speak with you about what you saw and felt. Can you come back tomorrow?" Reggie asked.

"I shouldn't have come here today. Dr. Homer, there are six people in my hospital with unexplained brain trauma, waiting for me to properly diagnose them. I really appreciate your seeing me on such short notice and so early in the morning. But you're welcome to bring your team by my office at the hospital. I could probably get away for a few minutes. I need to know if something happened to me at your center," Lisa said.

LISA DIDN'T REALLY expect that a team of doctors would make a special trip just for her, but she was in the middle of a crisis. Maybe it was just a professional courtesy. Dr. Homer seemed eager and sincere.

"Sounds like a plan. Speaking of plans, if you're hungry, maybe you'd like to get breakfast with me? There's a diner near the bus station, excellent French toast," Reggie said.

Lisa was surprised by how quickly he'd agreed to come to her office with his entire team, and she was doubly surprised by his breakfast invitation.

"Dr. Homer, are you asking me on a *date*?" she said.

REGGIE HAD A flash of panic. He hadn't realized he was holding his breath, but he exhaled and laughed nervously. He wondered if he'd crossed a line. "Would that be inappropriate?" he said, wondering where he was going with this.

"To hell with inappropriate. I haven't eaten in . . . since yesterday. I really do need to eat. But I don't have much time. I'll drive, you navigate," she said.

Reggie was surprised by the readiness of her response.

There was something about Lisa that he liked. She felt familiar to him.

Lisa's enthusiasm for breakfast tickled Reggie. The thought of being alone in a small conveyance with this Earthfolk woman of her own free will made his heart pound. Then he realized she might just be in it for the French toast, and his heart rate came down. He wasn't even sure the diner had French toast. It was the only typical Earthfolk breakfast food he could call to mind. Had he offered to buy? He should have. That would be custom. He would. She wanted to call it a date? Curious. The thump in his chest increased again.

He got up from his desk and opened the door for her. She got up, and he followed her to the elevators. In the elevator, she reached across to press the lobby button; he noticed her scent. Anesthetic gas perhaps, he thought. Appropriate. He was feeling light as air. No—anesthetic gas would not have a detectable scent. More likely, it was hospital disinfectant. Either way, it was perfume to him.

10

THE TEAM

S IG AND ZOE filed into the room. Four chairs stood in front of Lisa's desk. They were interlocked at the legs and faced the large glass-topped desk. Zoe figured that when this doctor spoke with patients, she spoke with the people in their lives as well, all together. Points for that. Looking around, Zoe spied a couch and several wood-framed certificates hanging on the baby blue walls. There was one from the University of Central Arkansas. There was a big one from the University of Southern California with the name LISA URSULA CATHERINE KULOWSKI written out in fancy type. Zoe smiled. She and her colleagues were also from USC, albeit a slightly different institution. Zoe had a good feeling about the coincidence and about Lisa Ursula Kulowski in general. There was a framed magazine article titled "Mass Spectrometry in Neuroscience with Dr. Lisa Ursula Kulowski." It hung next to a framed comic book cover with an inscription signed in marker on the lower right. Next to that was a framed picture that looked like bands of light in space. It was captioned "Pale Blue Dot."

Zoe shifted her attention to Dr. Kulowski. The pretty doctor set down an oversized mug of tea, the only thing on her desk besides a laptop and phone. On the mug, it said HOORAY FOR DR. K surrounded by lots of clapping hands. "Dr. K" smiled and walked around the desk. She offered her hand to Sig first. That was no surprise. Sig had gravitas in his tweed three-piece suit and bow tie. Older than the rest and completely bald, he was the natural guess for leader of the group. No one would peg Zoe for a boss. As Lisa made her way down the line, Reggie, who was seated in one of the four linked chairs, got up, stood off to the side, and watched the greetings. Zoe noticed his keen interest in the interactions.

Zoe smiled and reached out her hand. "Zoe."

"A pleasure to meet you. What gorgeous rings you're wearing," said Lisa, her eyes tracking the iridescence of a delicate, bevel-edged, glass-like piece.

More points for noticing Zoe's *gorgeous* rings. She had good taste. *The session is going well,* Zoe thought.

"Thanks. I've got a thing for unusual rings, especially bright shiny ones," Zoe said.

"Nothing wrong with that. A girl needs her shiny things. Please, everyone, have a seat," Lisa said, waving her arm.

"That's OK, Lisa, I prefer to stand," said Reggie.

Zoe casually turned her head to make eye contact with Sig, who was already looking at her. Sig mouthed the word *Lisa,* raising an eyebrow as a question mark. Zoe made a mental note under the category of "needs further discussion." Reggie being on such familiar terms with the subject of a study was unusual. Zoe felt a pit in her stomach and turned back to Lisa with a different sort of interest.

Lisa sat down again and began, "All right. First off, I've never done a complete sleep study. I didn't realize there was a psychoanalytical aspect extensive enough to require four doctors. I did do some sleep research when I worked in pediatrics at Mount Sinai in New York, where I gained a lot of respect for sleep experts. We had a patient who'd had a seizure, and one of the effects was insomnia. I was consulted on what was happening with certain signals in the brain, but I came at it from a purely physical response analysis. Stimulation in the cortex here equals a nerve response there—that sort of thing. Psychology and 'dream interpretation,' for lack of a better term, are foreign territory to me. I appreciate anyone who can demonstrate cause and effect in this area. My question for you all is how, or if, you guys messed with my head."

Sig wasted no time. "Of course. Your uneasiness is perfectly understandable, especially given your unique expertise in neurology. You've seen us at work, seen our equipment, and you know we don't use any psychoactive drugs. We have printouts of all the data collected from your evaluation. It's really just readings from our monitors." Sig glanced uneasily at Reggie, then resumed. "As a brain surgeon, I'm sure you appreciate the significance of stimulation to specific areas of the brain. But your first visit to the clinic was, as we agreed, just to get a baseline. It's true that we use electrical stimulation as part of our therapy, but that comes much later and with explicit written consent. We're still some way off from actually giving you an electrical charge. You were simply spoken to by Dr. Homer while we monitored electrical activity through electroencephalography and so forth. The electrodes attached to your body were merely monitors, ones I'm sure you're very familiar with from your line of work. The stimulation you received was a whisper in your ear, nothing more. And yet you report significant change in your dream activity. Your experience thus far has been different from what we have seen in other cases."

The readings and everything else were merely pro forma work to support the ruse surrounding Reggie's transmission.

. . .

LISA CONSIDERED REGGIE's words. She furrowed her brow. This business of whispering in her ear was news to her. She thought she'd just fallen asleep for a little bit at the sleep center. "Whatever the stimulation was, it had an effect on me," she said.

"That's why we're here," Sig said in his clipped German accent. "We very much want to document what you experienced while you were sleeping." That was certainly true.

"I'll tell you something else," Lisa went on. "I think I know now what it's like for someone who has taken LSD. I had the most realistic yet far-out fantasy dream ever. It felt real. I know everybody says that about their dreams, but this one was different. Like everybody else, I forget most of my dreams almost immediately. This one feels more like a memory. I can remember details clearly."

"As I said," Sig responded, "we administered no drugs, not even a sedative. You fell asleep in the normal way."

"Here's the problem," Lisa said, removing a pen from the chest pocket of her blouse and twirling it around each of her fingers. "The dream I'm concerned about was not the one I had while at the clinic. It happened here, in the cafeteria. I'm not accusing you of giving me drugs, but you did something to me." She was animated now. She hoped they could convince her that something they'd done had caused her dream, something that could rule out exposure to a pathogen from the trauma patients.

She stopped twirling the pen and pointed it at Sig, "Let me see the printouts."

Sig made a show of rustling through his leather attaché case.

Zoe came to his rescue, "Dr. Kulowski, we understand that you're very busy. Would you mind telling us the specifics of your dream?"

Lisa spent the next twenty minutes recounting almost verbatim what she'd told Reggie at his office. They asked her a lot of very specific questions, most dealing with how she felt at certain points in the dream. The last question they asked was whether or not she had talked to anyone in her dream.

"I was too excited. I don't think I could have spoken if I'd wanted to. I'm not sure how long the dream lasted."

Sig thanked her for sharing her experience in such great detail and for taking time away from her day in the midst of a crisis. Zoe did the same. They rose.

"Wait, that's it? Don't you have some explanation or advice for me?" She looked from one of them to the other, then finally said, "Reggie, you've been quiet. What do you have to say?"

Lisa caught Zoe shooting a glance at Sig.

"Give us a couple of days to compare notes," Reggie deflected.

"Look, I came to you guys because I needed help sleeping. I thought you'd at least talk to me about stress reduction. Maybe recommend I make my bedroom darker or something. A certain type of pillow, perhaps?" Lisa said.

Reggie spoke in a soft voice. "Lisa, you had no trouble falling asleep in the clinic or, apparently, in the hospital cafeteria. From what I've seen, you manage stress very well. Give us a couple of days, and we'll work up a comprehensive report."

The rest of the team started for the door.

"Wait. What about the printouts?" Lisa said.

Sig stammered, "I accidentally brought the wrong file. I'll send them along with our full report."

SIG AND ZOE said their goodbyes and fled. Reggie stayed behind. He was sensing some distress and no small amount of annoyance building up in Lisa. Her lips were pursed. Yes, he believed that was annoyance or anger. Distrust, maybe. Definitely suspicion. All of the above, most likely. He was getting better at reading her. He wanted to study her more, but he knew the team would have much to say.

"Lisa, my team really is the very best in the field. They'll have a thorough analysis for you, including the readings. Don't worry. I think it was just a vivid dream. I hope you don't increase your stress level by worrying about a dream-filled nap," Reggie said.

She got up, walked around the glass desk, and stood in front of Reggie. She looked him full in the eyes. She was close, just inside handshake distance. He could smell her again. He breathed in. She was wearing actual perfume now. It was even more intoxicating than the vague disinfectant smell from earlier. Was it lilac? Was that what it was called? Jasmine? Wonderful.

"What did you say?" she asked.

He paused, trying to master his senses, which were quickly filling up. The creamy smoothness of her face, the smell of her perfume, the sound of her voice, the silky blond hair, the nearness of her.

He managed to get out, "I said I'm concerned about you worrying over nothing."

"That's not what I mean. Sig said you spoke to me while I slept. What did you say? And what did you mean this morning when you said it was odd that I saw eyes in my dream?"

Reggie averted his gaze for an instant, then said, "All dreams are *odd*, of course. As far as what I said to you during the study, I can't remember exactly. You'll get a full transcript along with the report. My team is very thorough, Lisa. We record readings from all our instruments, and the audio recordings are automatically transcribed."

"Do you record video?" she asked.

"No," Reggie said.

"That gives me an idea," she said.

"What gives you an idea?" Reggie said.

"You use sophisticated equipment, right? Top of the line?"

"Yes," answered Reggie warily.

"Do you happen to have a SPECT camera?" she asked.

"I'm sorry, what now?" he countered, clearing his throat. Reggie's heart rate was going up. He could feel it pounding in his chest, a very unpleasant sensation. He backed up ever so slightly and crossed his arms, trying to remain composed.

"You know, Single Photon Emission Computed Tomography. You did your residency in neurology, I presume? The reason I ask is that it's something we haven't tried with the trauma patients I told you about. Our machine is being repaired. If you have one, we could use the help," she explained.

"Of course. Yes, right. No. I mean. We would help if we could, but we don't use the SPECT," he said, feeling oddly timid.

Lisa looked at him for a few moments. Then she glanced over his shoulder at the clock. "I have to get to the ICU," she said, opening the door for him.

"Of course. We'll get you the full report from your study. Try not worry. Everything is just fine."

LISA SAT ALONE in her office for a minute, dissatisfied with Reggie's perfunctory answer about what he'd whispered in her ear. He was a bit quirky. She wondered what he'd said to her.

A voice interrupted her thoughts, "Doctor, you have a call from the Centers for Disease Control."

Lisa glanced up to see her receptionist in the doorway. She nodded and told her to transfer the call.

"Hello, this is Dr. Kulowski." She put the phone on speaker.

The investigator, whose CDC Emergency Management polo shirt didn't seem to fit quite right when he'd stood in front of her two days earlier explaining how little they had to work with, now reiterated how little they had to go on. Lisa scrolled through the patients' test results on her laptop. Somewhere between CT scans, she got a poke in the ear.

". . . investigation, and there may be a connection to a sleep center. At least two of the patients went to one. The sleep center seems to have closed up shop, and there's no record of it ever having been incorporated or otherwise licensed. Detectives have interviewed the landlord. He adamantly denies renting the place to anyone."

She grabbed the phone. "Where was it located?"

"Off I-25, north of town."

"How many went there?"

"As I said, at least two, maybe more. We're not sure."

"Do you know if they received any medication or other form of treatment or intervention?"

"Family members said they were prepared to receive electrical stimulation. We have no way of knowing if they actually did. Of the two confirmed patients, one went for help with sleeping, and the other went out of interest in developing lucid dreaming abilities. Detectives are working on establishing other commonalities, and they're actively looking for the people who ran the clinic. The FBI has been contacted and has offered assistance."

"So, we're still unsure if there is a risk of contagion?"

"It's looking more and more like an isolated event based on some type of electrical stimulation introduced at the bogus sleep center. But that doesn't explain all the patients. We just don't know if the others had similar interactions. If any of the patients regain consciousness, please call me immediately. We must interview them. In the meantime, we recommend that you maintain quarantine."

"Thank you. Please keep me posted."

"Sure thing."

Lisa ended the call. She looked out her window, then picked

up the phone and punched in a couple of numbers. "Maria, do you still have the number for Dr. Homer? Please call him and let me know when you get him. I need to speak with him right away. It's urgent."

Lisa didn't reveal to the investigator what she knew about the sleep center. Maybe it was her previous experience with the bureaucracy of the CDC, but she didn't trust the investigator to be discreet about her personal involvement. She'd be quarantined and unable to help anyone, including herself.

Her conversation with the investigator had, however, assuaged some of her fear. She no longer worried that it was something contagious, which was good news for everyone. Then again, there seemed to be a group of nutjobs messing with people's brains, including her own. Would she experience some latent effect and black out? She needed to know what Sig's data looked like or if it even existed. Hell, she needed her own brain scan.

11

DOCTOR WHO?

A S SOON AS Reggie arrived back at her office, Lisa met him just inside the door.

"You're a medical doctor, right? Where did you study medicine?" Lisa asked.

He looked past her to see if anyone else was in the office. "USC," he said, pronouncing each letter slowly.

"So you're a fellow Trojan?" she asked, forcing a tight smile.

"Mm." Reggie swallowed, the dryness in his mouth making the effort pronounced.

There was an edge to her sharp focus. She had the same look as when she'd asked him about the SPECT. He had no idea what she was talking about.

"That was what you said when I first came to your center. Funny thing is, I checked California's database of licensed physicians, and there is no Dr. Reggie Homer listed. I also checked the nationwide database. Guess what? No Dr. Homer of USC. You're a terrible liar, Reggie."

Reggie thought for a second. He knew when she'd summoned him back to her office so quickly that she was suspicious. He needed to get out in front of it. "Lisa, I'm not who you think I am. I'm not a physician. But I *am* a doctor, a researcher. I'm sort of a field anthropologist. The sleep studies I've done are research on Earthfolk's . . . I mean on *people's* capacity to perceive and assimilate to wireless communication." He was trying hard to keep things simple so that Lisa could understand. He didn't like lying to her. "Can we go into your office?" He took a small step toward her.

She backed away from him, then quickly retreated into the office, putting her desk between them. She didn't seem afraid of him, even now, but he could tell his admission was disconcerting. She probably thought him some kind of scammer and dangerous to the public health. Prudence demanded that she put some distance between them. Prudence demanded a call to the authorities. She casually reached inside her blazer pocket and slid out her cell phone. She glanced at the cell phone, then looked up at him, taking in his features.

"Leave the door open," she ordered.

"Don't be afraid," he pleaded. "I'm your friend, and I can explain everything."

Lisa was too smart to accept any attempt to characterize his sleep center subterfuge as innocuous, collegial, or in any way necessary for what he purported to be doing. Any more lies would not hold up to the scrutiny that was sure to follow. More lies would lead to more distrust, fear, and attention.

He decided to tell her everything. "Lisa, I think you should sit down."

She eyed him suspiciously.

"Please. There are some things you need to know, and they may come as a bit of a shock to you."

"You mean more of a shock than finding out you're a complete fraud and impostor and responsible for putting six people into a coma?"

"In a word, yes."

She eyed him, suspicion evident in a slight smirk. Reggie felt somewhat trapped.

"Please," he said, shaking his head and sitting down in front of her desk.

Lisa remained standing, only taking her eyes off Reggie for an instant, calculating the distance to the open door, he thought. She clearly thought he was some sort of criminal, but given that, he believed she didn't fear him, not really. She was uncomfortable, yes, but not afraid.

"Please, just listen. I care a great deal for you, Lisa."

Lisa raised an eyebrow.

"I'm not a doctor the way you think of doctors. I am not on staff . . . anywhere. I am not from around here. In point of fact, I am not from Earth."

"Hold on one second," she interrupted, holding up an index finger. She sat down, grabbed her desk phone, and punched in a few numbers. She waited, then commanded, "Maria, get in touch with Dr. Yoon and ask him to come up to my office right away. Tell him it's important. And call the front desk and tell them I may need to have someone escorted out. Quickly, please. Thank you."

"Who is Dr. Yoon?" asked Reggie.

"He's the psychologist on call," Lisa replied. "I think it best he hears this as well."

"Fair enough, but will you hear me out in the meantime?"

"Sure," she said, placing her cell phone on the desk. She slid open the middle drawer of the desk and took out a yellow legal pad. She grabbed a pen, then opened another drawer and looked up at Reggie. "Do you mind if I record this?" She started fumbling with her cell phone again.

"Lisa, please, that won't be necessary. It's important that I tell you what's going on. Just listen."

She paused. His urgency was having an effect on her. He

sensed she might just hear him out. The next few moments were key. He needed to convince her not to call any authorities and escalate things. He remained calm.

"Do you believe in life beyond your planet?" he asked.

"*My* planet?"

"Earth."

"What does that have to do with any of this?" she asked, impatiently sliding the drawer closed.

"It has everything to do with it," he said.

"Fine. Sure, I guess so."

"Is that a yes?"

"Yes."

"Do you *really* believe there is life beyond your planet?"

"I said yes."

"No. I mean, do you truly, truly believe it?"

"I cannot say with one hundred percent certainty that there is life on other planets. There is no proof of it, but I guess there must be. The universe is too big for there not to be," Lisa said, matching his tone.

"I am not asking if you *know* there is life beyond your planet, just whether or not you truly believe there is."

"I believe there is life out there," she declared. "I believe God created man. Why not lots of them in other parts of universe? Nothing in the bible precludes it. Certainly, science tells us it's likely."

"OK. If you truly believe that, then logic dictates it is possible alien life may come into contact with life on Earth. Yes?"

"I guess."

"No, no guessing. You just said you believe there is life out there. If there is life out there, then it is possible contact may be made. Somehow, someday."

"Yes," she conceded.

"Today is that day. For you."

Reggie didn't blink. He wanted her to know he was serious.

"So, you're some alien from outer space? Is that what you're saying? You landed here in your flying saucer, and you're poking around in people's brains while they sleep?"

"What you just said is not terribly far from the truth."

"Maria!" Lisa called to the outer office. There was no response. She picked up the desk phone again.

"Lisa, wait," he said in as soft a tone as he could manage. "I know this is difficult to believe. Please be patient. Think rationally, not emotionally. Do you recall how you found out about the sleep center?"

She thought for a minute, then confessed that she could not remember.

"Do you remember going there, driving there, parking, what the building looks like?"

Of course, she couldn't.

"You can't remember because it was all arranged by me."

She seemed confused.

"You need solid proof?"

"Absolutely," she said without hesitation.

"What if I were to disappear right in front of you? Right now. Just disappear."

"You're full of crap."

"Will you believe me?"

"No."

"You won't believe your own eyes? Why not?"

"Because you're full of crap."

Reggie became fuzzy before her eyes. Everything in the room was in clear focus except for him. Then he was all particles, like a magnified dot matrix image. The dots shimmered and faded. Finally, there was only a pair of multicolored eyes, then nothing but an empty seat in front of her.

. . .

"HOLY CRAP!" SHE stood. "Holy crap. Holy crap. Holy crap."

Lisa walked around her desk. She walked back and forth, did two laps around the desk and chairs. He had to be a magician. Her heart was pounding. Had he just escaped? There was no way. She went back to her chair and sat heavily. *No one is going to believe this. I don't believe this.* He was just gone. In a flash. Like Flash from the comics. Just like losing her real-life Flash. Just gone. She realized she was holding her pen in a death grip, like a knife. Who was this man? Confusion enveloped her.

Reggie materialized again in reverse order. Lisa sat stunned, bringing the pen in close to her chest. At just the moment Reggie became fully present, Maria stepped into the office.

"Is everything OK, Dr. K? I heard someone shouting."

You just missed the magic show, Lisa thought. She stared at Reggie and gently placed the pen back on the desk. "Everything is fine, Maria. Call Dr. Yoon and let him know I don't need him."

"That's good," Maria said, "because I couldn't get hold of him. What about security? They asked if it was an emergency."

"No. Call them back and tell them the issue was resolved. Sorry. And thank you."

Maria looked from Dr. K to Dr. Homer, obviously wondering what was going on. Then she twirled and disappeared back into the outer room as quickly as she'd come in.

"Lisa, are you OK?" Reggie said.

She sat speechless.

"I am a researcher from something called the Universal Study Collective, USC—a gathering of minds focused on the accumulation and dissemination of knowledge and peace. The Collective is similar to what you would call a university, but it is universal in scope. I suppose you could say I hold a doctorate in physics. I am called Aurigae. When it comes to study and research, my colleagues and students refer to me as Dr. Reginald Homer. I come from far away, but I have ancestors who were local. They came from a place roughly two thousand light-years from Earth."

"I'm sorry, you're Doctor *who*?" asked Lisa, snapping herself out of a daze.

"Dr. Homer. How about we go to the diner again, second breakfast? Early lunch?" Reggie suggested, hoping for the same enthusiasm from earlier.

PART II

VENUSFOLK

12

MESS EXIT

S TEWART GORDON STOOD for almost a full minute, studying a neat row of aluminum chafing dishes. He reluctantly slid an entrée onto his plate.

"This crud looks like it's been sitting here since Abe shot the goat," he proclaimed.

From the other side of the counter, shielded by a short glass partition, an inscrutable old soldier in a white apron raised his eyebrows and pointed a ladle at Stewart. "You like-a da juice?"

"Juice? No, I'm gonna have milk."

In line behind Stewart, Specialist William Orestes, known to most of the base as Billy O. or just plain B.O., offered his translation, "Uh, I think he's asking if you want gravy on your chicken loaf."

Stewart turned to Billy. "Gravy? Looks more like boiled cottage cheese. Well, at least I won't be able to see the meat. I'll take some," he said, looking back at the swarthy cook.

"I think—" Billy started to reply. Before he could get anything out, there was a stir at the entrance to the mess hall.

"Atten-*tion*!" someone called out. Unusual during chow time.

"That doesn't sound good," whispered Stewart without turning around.

The captain, approaching from the entryway put an end to all movement and sound in the hall. "You, Gordon," he demanded in a deep voice. "Are you disturbing the serenity of my chow hall?"

Stewart turned and stood at his best approximation of attention. He tried to sound confident. "Sir, no, sir."

"What's your issue?" demanded the captain, closing in on Stewart.

"Sir, I don't have any issues, sir," Stewart replied.

"Did you just hit me with a *sir* sandwich?"

"With respect, sir, when we first met in your office, you told me I'm not a soldier, but that I should try to blend in, sir."

"And are you blending in right now?"

"Sir, yes, sir . . . I mean, yes, sir," Stewart stammered. He was nervous in the face of the captain's close-range stare. He could see the pores in the captain's dark skin. This was the first time any officer had come into the chow hall. The whole room seemed to be watching Stewart. "I didn't mean to give you a sandwich, sir . . . a sir sandwich, sir."

"Mm hm. You," Captain Archibald said, fixing his gaze on Billy. "You're the escort?"

"Yes, sir," Billy replied, standing at crisp attention.

"When Mr. Gordon is checked back into the research facility, report to my office."

"Yes, sir."

Billy served as Stewart's military escort. He was the first soldier Stewart had met when he'd arrived at Air Force Compound 50. Billy was army, like Captain Bertrand Archibald —B-Ball. The Army had a detachment operating on the base. They were the ones responsible for Stewart. They ran their own operation, even though they were technically part of the joint task force responsible for setting up the very first United States Space Force Cyber and Signals Counterespionage Command, or USSFCSCC for short. Stewart considered Billy more of a friend than a chaperone. Billy's having to report to B-Ball's office did not sound good. Stewart wondered if the only reason B-Ball had come to the chow hall was to check on him.

∼

STEWART KNOCKED ON Billy's door.

"Come in,"

"Everything all right, Billy?" asked Stewart as he stepped into the cool air of the tent.

Billy was sitting on his cot, wearing shorts and putting on a pair of sneakers.

"You screwed me over, Stew, holding up the line and talking smack about the chow. B-Ball ordered me to run the perimeter."

"I'm sorry, Billy, really. But I can't take it anymore. I haven't had a good meal in months. Months! Look at me. I've turned into a grunt, working twelve-hour days, eating gruel. No girls. Not a one. The only entertainment is the five-dollar movie theater in town. No decent restaurants. No one told me when I was wined and dined for this project that I'd be sweating my gonads off in the desert, eating loaves of mystery meat. I have a master's degree in physics, for heaven's sake. I was told air force chow was the best in the military. I distinctly remember being told task force personnel ate like kings."

Billy shook his head, "Air force chow *is* good, and they do eat like kings, but you're attached to the army, and we run our own facility—the entire supply chain."

"I'm sorry for getting you into trouble," repeated Stewart. "What do you have to do?"

"Three laps around the perimeter. It's about ten kilometers.

At least he's letting me do it at sunset. You should join me. You look like you're good for at least one lap," Billy said. "It'll show B-Ball you're taking things seriously."

"Just because I have a crew cut doesn't mean I'm in shape. They made me get it so I'd look like everyone else around here. It's true, I haven't got an ounce of fat on me, but I haven't got an ounce of muscle, either. I'm skin and bones. If I thought I could do one lap around, I'd join you in a heartbeat. Unfortunately, if I ran, you'd end up having to give me CPR. Listen, there's something I want to talk to you about."

"Can't talk now. Gotta head out," said Billy.

Billy got up from his neatly made cot, smoothed out the bedding with his palms, and headed for the door. Stewart stared at him as he walked past. "Wait," Stewart said. Billy didn't even turn around.

∾

STEWART WATCHED BILLY try to wipe his eyes with the shoulder of his sweat-soaked T-shirt as he lumbered to the end of his final lap.

"Well, that was fun," Billy said, hunching over beside the bench where Stewart sat.

Stewart handed Billy a bottle of water.

"Thanks."

"Billy, listen. You gotta help me get out of here. My buddy Chase from the Cultural Center in town, says he's got a unique research opportunity for me."

"What the hell are you talking about? You can leave anytime you want. You're a civilian." Billy drained the water bottle and crushed it into a ball.

"No. I need your help with something. I don't want to quit. I just need to take a short trip without anyone finding out. I just need to get off base and onto the reservation. Chase can help me from there."

"Why? B-Ball will be on your ass. Operational security and all that."

"Listen," said Stewart.

"OK," said Billy, trying to control the sweat on his forehead with his forearm, then stretching to touch his toes.

"Don't laugh. My friend says he knows someone who makes regular runs off the reservation to . . . are you listening?"

"I'm listening," Billy said, standing up and tossing the crushed bottle into his gym bag.

"This is some heavy stuff, Billy. I meant to tell you about this before now. Promise you'll hear me out and take what I tell you seriously."

"Sure."

"Seriously. Keep an open mind. And don't freak out," Stewart demanded.

"Sure," said Billy. He stopped moving around and looked squarely at Stewart. There was a small bead of sweat on the tip of his nose.

Stewart knew what he was about to say was crazy, but he had to tell Billy. He was willing to rely on Billy's discretion. He was a friend. "Chase says he can arrange to get me to another planet." Stewart said it quickly, before he lost his nerve or had time to rethink the whole thing. He immediately regretted saying it. He knew it was crazy. To hear it said out loud made it even more ridiculous.

"I'm sorry. What?" Billy's eyes widened. He didn't blink.

"Another planet."

"*Another planet?* You mean like Roswell or Portland or something? Miami?" Billy folded his arms and searched Stewart's eyes, probably trying to figure if he was joking. Neither one smiled.

"No, no, like . . . Venus or something. I just need you to get me a few things."

Billy stood stock still for a few moments. Then said, "Cool. Cool. So, what is it you need? Besides counseling, that is. Venus, huh? That's off the reservation all right—*way* off the reservation." He let his arms drop and looked away.

"Get me a utility truck or a minivan. Bring it out to Serenity East tonight, behind the zip line, near that old confidence course, past the first security fence. You'll have to drive all the way around. There's construction out there. I can get out, no problem. I'll make sure the car gets back. I know someone at the infirmary who can tell B-Ball I left with an air force doctor if he asks. But he won't. He barely knows I exist. Make sure the truck is there by twenty-two thirty. It's a Friday night, so no one will miss me for the next couple of days. Chase can get me back by Monday morning."

"Are you out of your mother-loving mind. I could be arrested for stealing government property."

"I'll have the truck back by Monday. People use vehicles from the motor pool for all kinds of personal stuff. Look, it'll be on me. I'm the one using it. And it's technically atmospheric research, just not our atmosphere."

"No way. I'm supposed to be keeping an eye on you. What do I do if someone finds out you're gone? How will it look if I say I haven't seen you, when watching you is part of my job?"

"Tell them I took the shuttle to town; I was heading to the movies, and that was the last time you saw me."

"They'll check the shuttle log," Billy said. He looked at Stewart as if looking at an overturned truck that had dumped watermelons all over the highway—half amused, half distressed.

"Doesn't matter. It won't be on you, Billy."

"It's a bad idea, dude. Just take the authorized shuttle into town, then go do whatever you want. I only need to watch you while you're on base."

"Can't. I have to head out tonight. It's already arranged. C'mon Billy. I need a little bit of freedom. You trust me, don't you?" Stewart pleaded. He could see that Billy thought he was nuts. They'd been friends since the beginning of Stewart's detail, but one could only ask so much of a friend. Stewart knew and appreciated the sensitive work being done on the base. Billy would be taking a risk. For Stewart, it didn't matter; he was a civilian. As long as he didn't divulge any classified information, he figured he'd have no problem, no matter where he went. It wasn't like he was going to meet with a foreign power or anything. Were aliens considered foreign powers? The whole thing really was ridiculous, even to Stewart. But he was committed to seeing the wild scheme through to conclusion.

"I'm going to take a shower, man," said Billy.

"I know it sounds like I'm loony tunes. I'm not. I just need a break for the weekend. Get my mind off of my ex-girlfriend. Probably the whole thing is some kind of hoax or scam, but I just want to check it out anyway. It'll be fun. Did I mention the spaceship in the desert?"

"You did not."

"There is a spaceship parked out in the desert. That's all I know. I've got to see it."

"Where are you getting all this information?" Billy asked.

"From Chase. You met him. From the museum at the Cultural Center?"

"The guy in the suit?"

"Yeah, that's him."

"So you're both nuts, then."

Stewart had an idea. He didn't think Chase would mind him bringing an extra person along for the ride. In fact, if the whole thing was a load of crap, which it surely was, it would be good to have Billy there. He could handle himself physically. "What if you and I took a drive out to the reservation together? No one would really care if we used a truck. We could come up with some legit reason."

Billy didn't answer right away. He looked like he was thinking about it. No doubt about it—he was curious. But he also had no reason to do this for Stewart.

"No can do," he finally answered.

"Well, what if we were to take a drive out to the confidence course to work out, get in shape? That's up your alley. If you were to jog back and leave me to drive the truck, that could be the last time you saw me, if anyone were to ask. But no one's going to ask. I'll take pictures of the ship."

Stewart could tell Billy was thinking hard about it. This plan gave him an out.

"No one's going to believe you wanted to go work out late at night, or any other time, for that matter," Billy said, finally cracking a smile.

"Tell them I felt bad for getting you into hot water with B-Ball and wanted to do my own physical training. Just think what it will mean if it's real, Billy," Stewart pleaded. "Even if it's not, I'm sure there's *something* interesting out there."

"Fine. I'll get the wheels, but leave me out of whatever fantasy trip you're on. You want to split, that's fine. You're a free man, whatever. I have to get back."

"You'll bring the truck? I have some things I need to do. I'll meet you at the confidence course tonight?"

"If I can."

"Twenty-two thirty?"

"Right."

~

MIDNIGHT. A DARK green silhouette slowly clunked and crunched its way along the gravel road. Headlights off, the truck was barely discernable from the gray landscape under the waning moon. It creaked to a halt next to a rusted metal sign, twisted by years of heavy vehicles doing exactly what the sign said: YOU WILL REACH THE FINISH. JUST DON'T STOP.

The driver's door swung open, and a pair of dark boots stepped out into the dim quiet. Billy swiveled his head in a 180-degree scan. In the darkness, his hair looked gray rather than blond.

Serenity East was no longer used as a confidence course. Its days of confidence had left it behind like so many two-and-a-half-ton trucks in a fading caravan. The blood and sweat of determined young men and women had long since been absorbed into the earth and returned to the sky as vapors rising from the hard-baked New Mexico ground. The place was grim now, especially at night. It was as if the colorless shapes knew there would be no more blood and sweat to nourish them. Some of the shapes slowly rocked, brooding in the warm wind. Other shapes stood deathly still, resolved to move no more.

"Stew. Stew. You there? Stew, come on, man," Billy called out, sounding nervous.

"Shhh. I'm here." Stewart's voice came from one of the motionless shapes, a wooden box fastened to petrified posts standing some fifteen feet high.

Billy's eyes followed the length of a rickety old ladder to see Stewart's pale face leaning over the side of the box. "This ain't cool, man," he shouted up to Stewart. "B-Ball's gonna be pissed. I don't need this grief. It's friggin' creepy out here, dude."

"Shhh. To heck with him. Come with me, Billy," Stewart said from atop his perch. He shimmied clumsily down the ladder. When he hit the ground, out of breath, he had a big grin on his face.

Stewart looked at his friend. The poor guy seemed genuinely nervous. More so than the borrowing a vehicle should have allowed for. He clearly thought Stewart had no understanding of the gravity of the situation. But Stewart knew. He just didn't care. He was grinning like a twelve-year-old.

Billy cut right to the heart of things, "You want me to go with you to another planet? You're aware of the drug problem on the reservation, right? I'm thinking your Indian buddy from the Cultural Center might have spiked the ol' peace pipe on you. Maybe you had a couple of tokes too many?" Billy mimed taking a smoke, his eyes going wide.

"I'm serious. Come with me. Chase says he's been there. He's *been* there, my man! It's unbelievable, I know. The person he knows has taken him there. They leave from the bottom of a deep arroyo somewhere out in the desert. The trip takes about an hour and a half one way. Well, really only about half an hour, but there's like a half hour of preparation and a half hour of recovery time or something," Stewart said.

"Oh, I'm sure it's a trip. Do me a favor—swing by Mars on your way back and pick me up some snacks. Is this the part where I ask you what it's supposed to be like up on Venus?"

Stewart could tell Billy was masking his interest with disbelief. "People live there. They're human. Mostly female, Chase says. He also says that humans have lived on Venus for thousands of years, maybe longer than people have lived on Earth. They speak some wacky language like Italian and Chinese combined, only it sounds like they're underwater when they talk, because their vocal cords are denser than ours. When they speak, you can see their breath. It's like a yellow mist. Something to do with the food they eat. Chase has been learning the language. But it's not necessary, because his connection has a device that translates their language into all of Earth's languages and vice versa."

"Oh. Well, that's a relief," Billy said. The sarcasm was thick. "This is crazy. You're willing to risk your life and your career? You don't have any training for space travel. Even if everything you say is true—which I'm here to tell you it's absolutely not—don't you think you should report it?"

"Not until I've checked it out. If it turns out to be a hoax, no harm done. I won't be the head case who sees alien spaceships in the desert. I have to take this opportunity to explore, to get away. Besides, mostly chicks, Billy. Who knows? Now that I'm free maybe I'll hookup with an alien," Stewart said with a smile.

"Dude. Are you friggin' insane?" Billy said.

"Nope, just desperate. Look, if you don't want to come, it's OK. Just don't tell anybody. I'll make sure the truck is back by Monday," Stewart said.

"Seriously, dude. Are you insane?"

~

IT WAS THE middle of the night, but still hot—a dry heat.

Stewart trekked up the east side of Organ Mountain, leaving the truck about one hundred yards from the trailhead. He had arranged to meet Chase in a cave they'd found a few months back while hiking in the national park. The Organ Mountain range was like a ten-thousand-foot-high rock castle pockmarked with brush. It rose out of flat ground that stretched around it as far as the eye could see. The cave was off a twelve-mile trail on the side of a rocky rise and overlooked the national park's official campground. Stewart had first spotted the cave while following an eagle's path through his binoculars. He and Chase had chanced a climb up the steep cliff to check it out. It wasn't far, as the eagle flies, from the campground to the cave, but it was strenuous.

Now, in the high heat of summer, it was the off-season. The

campground would be empty. They'd chosen the cave as their meeting spot because Stewart wasn't interested in getting reacquainted with the gigantic flies that had tortured him on his last visit to the campground. Dealing with flies in this heat would not be tolerable. Besides, he didn't want to risk being spotted by anyone connected to the base. He was tired and thirsty. He wished he'd thrown more water in his pack.

It would be dawn in an hour or so. He needed to get up that cliff. Hopefully, Chase would already be there so they could start toward the reservation.

Chase wasn't there when Stewart, perspiring liberally, got to the cave. It was small, maybe the size of a panel van, and black inside. Before entering, he cracked a glow stick. Something was sure to be living in there. He hoped whatever it was would be small and would scurry away in the light. He proceeded cautiously. First, he took a couple of quick peeks. Then, mustering his courage, he crouched down and inched his way in. To his relief, there were no other occupants. Just cool, earthy-smelling air. There were footprints on the ground inside, probably from the last time he and Chase had explored the cave. The ground and the walls were smooth. He hunched his way over to the far wall and shined the glow stick close to it. Midway up the wall, he spotted the petroglyph they'd discovered last time. It was a carving of a long-haired woman with absurdly large breasts, wearing a polka-dotted dress. Next to the carving were the words, MRS. RUBIN, CLASS TRIP '04. Stewart chuckled, just like the first time he'd seen it. He wondered what archaeologists would make of it in a few hundred years.

STEWART SAT WITH his back against the cave wall and waited. Might as well eat. He reached into his pack and pulled out an MRE. The gray-green pouch was labeled JERK CHICKEN in block letters. He tore it open and went right for the cookie. While he munched on it, he heard a whistle. An actual whistle, like a referee's whistle. Uh-oh. He heard it again: two short bursts. Crap. A few seconds passed. Then he heard the whistle once more; this time, it was to the rhythm of "shave and a haircut . . . two bits." He stowed the MRE and glow stick in his bag. There was total darkness in the cave again. Then the shave and a haircut rhythm repeated, followed by a faint, "Hey, Stew!" that sounded a lot like Chase. He crawled to the opening of the cave.

"Chase?" Stewart called back.

"Yes. It is me," said Chase—one of his characteristically complete sentences.

"Are you kidding me, man? People can probably hear that whistle a mile from here. Come on up."

"Why would I come up? We have to go back to my truck and get moving. Also, your glow stick is noticeable from farther away than my whistle. You are a physics guy. You know light travels farther and faster than sound."

"Don't you want to say hello to Mrs. Rubin?" Stewart made his way toward Chase's voice.

Spotting a white T-shirt, Stewart saw Chase sitting on a rock, looking east at a hint of dawn. Stewart could tell by his expression that he didn't approve of the joke about Mrs. Rubin.

"I do not find the handiwork of vandals amusing," Chase said. "Also, tell me again why we are all the way up here, only to go back down again to the truck?"

"I can't stand the flies at the campground, and it's safer here," Stewart said.

"Stew, there is no one around at this time of year."

"We're here," Stewart said.

"Fair point. Are you ready for this, my friend?" Chase said, smiling.

"Let's do it, while it's still dark," Stewart said.

They trooped back down the mountain. According to Chase, the mysterious arroyo was on the edge of the reservation in a stretch of desert some fifty miles from the highest peak.

Stewart trusted Chase. They'd met not long after Stewart arrived from California. It was at the library in Las Cruces. Chase was in a tweed three-piece suit. Stewart came to learn that Chase's affinity for tweed was well documented at the cultural center, where Chase volunteered. Stewart recalled seeing a hand-drawn picture of Chase in his suit tacked to the office bulletin board at the center. The artist was the six-year-old daughter of one of his coworkers.

It seemed to Stewart that the staff at the center was puzzled about why Chase wore a three-piece tweed suit to conduct tours of the Native American exhibits. The other guides all wore polo shirts with the Center's logo. It was curious, to be sure, but it could be written off as a quirk. What the staff couldn't countenance was that Chase wore suits out into the searing New Mexico summer—to lunch, to outdoor events, to all center functions. There were theories, of course. During one of his visits to the center, a young employee had told Stewart that some of the staff thought Chase had a small hole in his marble bag, or maybe a touch of obsessive-compulsive disorder. Stewart figured that he just valued the history and sanctity of the artifacts and was committed to bringing an appropriate respectability to the Center. Chase apparently also wore his suits at the high school where he taught history.

One of the older security guards at the center had once asked Chase, in front of Stewart, how old he was. Chase answered matter-of-factly that he was twenty-seven. The guard pressed him, "Aren't you a little young to be wearing an old getup like that?" Chase told Stewart later that he'd wanted to answer, "Are *you* not a little old to be wearing a shiny square badge and a pair of polyester slacks with racing stripes down the legs?" Instead, he politely informed the old-timer that they both had their uniforms, and in any case, the suit was brand new. Then he asked if the guard had ever owned a tweed suit. Without waiting for an answer, he winked and nodded, as if the two shared a secret regarding the magical properties of tweed. Then he smiled and went on his way. The perplexed guard looked after him.

Stewart wondered what the crowd at the Cultural Center would make of Chase's penchant for wearing blue jeans, a Texas Rangers baseball cap, and a white T-shirt when they went hiking. Chase was definitely a mystery. Stewart wondered about the arroyo his friend had described. He hoped it was real.

The last time the two had been hiking, not far from where they were now, they'd camped overnight. Chase had gotten up in the deep of night. Stewart had heard his crunching footsteps behind the tents. Camping etiquette dictated that if he was going to relieve himself, he should do it away from the tents, but Chase hadn't returned till just before dawn. When Stewart had asked him about his late-night stroll, Chase had said he wanted to feel the quiet of the darkness and see the approaching light. Man of mystery, indeed.

13

BRIGHT SANDS AT DAWN

"DO WE REALLY have to do this without headlights?" Stewart said.

Chase glanced over at Stewart. "The public is not exactly welcome where we are going," he said.

"How unwelcome are we talking?" Stewart said.

"Close to shoot-on-sight unwelcome," Chase replied.

"Oh. Keep the headlights off, then. And turn down the dash lights. Why are we going so slow?" Stewart said, sitting up straighter and swiveling his head.

"We cannot risk creating too big a dust cloud, even in this low light. Someone might spot it from a distance. As it is, we will be lucky if we can avoid the motion sensors. Fortunately, I have it on good authority that near dawn, the entire sensor system reboots, which takes about an hour. Also, dawn is when the most false-positives light up the sensors, thanks to our good friends, the roadrunners. It is good that there are roadrunners here," Chase said, taking his eyes off the dim desert in front of them and looking over at Stewart, who stared back at him. Chase's voice deepened. "Tradition has it that roadrunners keep evil spirits away."

"Yeah, but we're not going to need them to do that, right? Because there won't be any evil spirits to worry about? You said these people are benevolent, didn't you?" Stewart said.

"Sure. Sure. I do have one confession, though," Chase said, smiling.

"Oh, God. Here we go," Stewart said, looking up at the ceiling of the vehicle.

"I have not exactly been to the planet myself," Chase said.

"What? You said in no uncertain terms that you'd been there! That the people were mostly females, very gentle and welcoming and helpful and all that. Are you friggin' kidding me?" Stewart said.

"No," replied Chase, his smile waning only slightly.

Stewart took a deep breath, "You've seen the ship, though, right? The spaceship?"

"No," Chase said.

"Oh, lord. B.O. was right. You're tripping on peyote or weed or horse manure or whatever it is that you stuff in that friggin' pipe of yours. Stop the truck—turn around before it's fully light. We're gonna get arrested." Stewart was beginning to get a clearer picture of where they were. "Oh, man! We're on the missile testing range, aren't we? How did we get past the fence? You know there are places out here that are radioactive, right? Oh, lord, I knew it couldn't be real. Good thing B.O. didn't come with me," Stewart said, shaking his head and rubbing the tops of his thighs.

"Quit hyperventilating," Chase said in a calm but firm voice.

"Do you know what I'm risking? How did I let you talk me into this? I should have stayed at USC, taken that associate professorship, and lived a quiet normal life. I never should have let myself be recruited for a *special* military research project. I wouldn't have had to put up with B-Ball, the bad food, or the heat. And I wouldn't be a moving target on a missile range right now. I told you I believe in life on other planets, and you took advantage of that."

"Who is B-Ball? You didn't tell me you were on a 'special' project," Chase said, letting go of the steering wheel and making air quotes. "You told me you were doing mechanical testing in the motor pool."

Stewart continued shaking his head. "I told you I was working with motors. It's all classified. I can't talk about it. You wanna know who B-Ball is?" Stewart turned and looked out the passenger side window. "I'll tell you who B-Ball is. He's the guy who's gonna make sure I do my prison time in a cell with someone named Demon Killer who is six foot five, has serious anger management issues, and was abused in high school by a science teacher . . . who happened to be named Stewart."

"We are not going to get arrested. We are close to the reservation; we can tell anyone we might see that we are tracking road-runners to tag them and research them for a history of Pueblo traditions I'm working on. It is not that big a stretch," Chase said.

"Yeah, that'll work for you. You're a local. Hell, you look like a friggin' young Geronimo. I'm a physicist from LA on contract with the U.S. Army. Why would I be chasing roadrunners in a highly classified and extremely dangerous area? I'm supposed to know better," Stewart said.

"I will tell them I recruited you to study the dynamics of the roadrunner in flight," Chase said.

"Those things can fly?"

"Sure. How else would they keep away the evil spirits?" Chase said, his smile returning fully.

"Not funny. I've got a very high security clearance. The highest, I think. And still, if I go someplace other than the three usual spots on my day off, I have to write a three-page essay in advance about where I'm going and why. How would I explain running around the desert with Geronimo, chasing roadrunners for science?" Stewart said, making a rapid scissor motion with his fingers meant to mimic roadrunners on the move.

"I really am working on a book. Listen, we are not going to get caught. I told you, I have a good source on base—my friend Bert. We grew up together."

"The air force takes a dim view of their people sharing operational security info unnecessarily. Especially with civilians," Stewart said.

"He is not in the air force. He is in the army, like you."

Stewart pondered this. There wasn't a large contingent of army personnel on base, and those who were assigned there were all specialists. The population of the base was made up mostly of air force personnel and a host of alphabet soup secret agency types. He knew most of the army contingent by name and general function. He didn't know any Bert. Maybe it was an alias. Anyone giving out sensitive information was likely to use an alias. Hell, this whole thing could be some espionage play to get classified information out of him and Chase.

Damn, it all made sense. There wasn't really an extraterrestrial presence out here. There was an extra*territorial* presence, maybe Chinese or Russian. *What an idiot!* he thought. He had wanted to believe so badly that he'd let himself be duped. Chase had probably been tricked, too. Unless he was in on it? Shit. Could he trust Chase? What did Stewart really know about him? He'd known him for less than a year. Sure, they were friends. They'd camped and hiked together, and they shared a passion for astronomy and history. Was it a coincidence that they'd met at an astronomy lecture at the Las Cruces Public Library? Or had Chase been planted there? Maybe he wasn't even really Native American. Stewart turned and looked closely at Chase's profile. He could be Filipino? Nah, he was a dead ringer for a young Geronimo.

"Tell me about this contact of yours. Bert?" Stewart said.

"Not much to tell. Great guy. We grew up together. Played a lot of basketball. We're still friends," Chase replied.

"Wait, you played basketball? What are you, all of one meter seven?" Stewart said, looking Chase over from head to toe in the dim dashboard light.

"One meter seven?" Chase echoed.

"About five foot six," Stewart clarified.

"You wound me. I was actually pretty good—varsity point guard for four years," Chase said with a nod.

"Continue," Stewart said, as calmly as he could manage.

"Well, Birdy and I went to the same high school. He was a few years older than me. No one knew how old I really was in high school. I used my older brother's birth certificate and transcripts after he moved to Ruidoso with my father. I walked tall. I was articulate and well dressed. No one asked any questions. Elementary school was rough for me. It was all boys, and the teachers were not particularly good. I wanted to learn, and the high school was coed. So, I just enrolled myself. I lived with my uncle. He was clueless.

"I knew Bert from town and from playing basketball at the rec center. He was good friends with my older brother. He looked out for me. Birdy was a senior, but we served many a detention period together. I got sent to detention for getting beat up. Birdy got detention for demonstrating the proper way to beat someone up on those who beat *me* up. After high school, Birdy joined the army. We kept in touch, and he visited whenever he was back home. He eventually got stationed at Fort Bliss, close enough for us to get together now and then. We still do. He is a good man," Chase concluded.

"How come you've never mentioned him before?" Stewart asked.

"I am sure I have. When you and I first met, I told you I had a good friend who was on base," Chase said.

"I assumed he was an air force guy."

"No, he is army through and through. Loves it. Been all over the world, has all sorts of medals. I think he is a captain or something—"

"What?" Stewart interrupted.

"I am not certain of his rank now. What are you ranked?"

"I'm not a soldier. Hold on a second—Bert as in *Bertrand*?"

"Yes," Chase replied.

"As in Bertrand *Archibald*?" Stewart spat out.

"Yes. You know him?" Chase said casually.

"Yeah, I know him! He's the guy who'll be throwing me in jail with Demon Killer. Why do you call him Birdy?"

"He used to talk a lot about wanting to fly, plus it sounds like Bert—*Berty*. I guess that's why."

Stewart held his tongue for a minute. Then couldn't contain himself. "This is just too weird."

"Weird? No. But we are getting close," Chase said, making a slow turn and rolling the truck to a stop. "We'll walk from here."

Chase got out, walked around to the back of the truck, and opened the tailgate. He climbed up, grabbed a backpack, and slung it over his shoulder. He also grabbed Stewart's pack, then jumped down off the tailgate. Stewart was still in the truck.

"Stew," Chase said, "you coming?"

Chase walked around to the passenger side window. He looked at Stewart, who stared back at him through the glass. After a few seconds, Stewart rolled down the window, scowled, and looked Chase in the eye.

"You're not Filipino, are you?" Stewart said.

"What?"

"Never mind," said Stewart, rolling up the window and popping open the door. "Are we gonna just leave the truck here?"

"Yes, but give me a hand with the tarp. It is in the back," Chase said, gesturing with his thumb.

They unrolled a brown tarp and covered the entire truck, staking it to the hard-packed earth with small metal tent stakes. Then they set out, walking away from the rising sun. As he walked, Chase fixed his eyes on a small GPS in his hand. After a few minutes, the terrain started to rise. The grade steepened abruptly, and Chase slowed. They were on the edge of a wide arroyo, looking down some thirty feet into darkness. The sun was still too low to penetrate the depth of the arroyo.

Chase crouched low. Stewart followed suit, not knowing exactly why they were crouching. "OK. This is where it gets weird," Chase whispered.

"How weird?"

"A lot weirder than me wearing a three-piece suit to work in one-hundred-degree weather."

"Why *do* you do that?" Stewart asked.

Chase winked. "Keeps people guessing every day."

"Yeah, guessing what institution you escaped from," Stewart said.

"Shhhh. Put these on," Chase reached into his pack and pulled out two pairs of dark sunglasses.

"What's this?" Stewart asked.

"They're 3D glasses."

"Why?" Stewart asked.

Chase put his glasses on. "Keeps your brain from going blind."

"But it's dark down there," Stewart pointed out.

"It won't be shortly."

Chase reached back into his pack and pulled out a small bongo drum. He started beating out a rhythm. Stewart eyed him and didn't say a word. Here was Geronimo, crouching in the desert wearing *Blues Brothers* shades and a white T-shirt with

'Rock 'n' Roll' printed on it., beating out an incantation. Stewart wondered if he was summoning the spirit of some long-dead warrior to guide them or some such business.

After a few minutes, the rhythm became familiar. He started humming it to himself. Yep, he got it—"Yankee Doodle Dandy," without a doubt. Could this be the most elaborate practical joke ever? Did Chase really wear a full suit every day in this heat? The dude was nuts. What the hell were they doing here?

Then the heavens opened up . . . from the bottom of the arroyo.

"Let's go," said Chase, stuffing the drum in his pack and bounding down the embankment. Stewart followed him into the light.

LIGHT DID NOT come up from the arroyo. It went down, as if the bottom had fallen out. Sand and brush on the sides of the embankment lightened to a bright white. Light was not being reflected off the sides of the arroyo—it was being drawn down.

Stewart caught up with Chase near the bottom. The two paused, then took a slow step into a shimmering pond of light together. All it took was the one step. They were both sucked forward into a wash of white light so bright they could no longer see each other. Just as quickly as they fell, all movement ceased. They were suspended deep in an ocean of light.

A calm voice speaking English with a German accent said, "Good day, Chase. Welcome. Mr. Gordon, nice to have you joining us. Forgive me for any unpleasant sensation you may have felt on your descent. Please don't be alarmed. It will take only a moment for us to reach the magnetic South Pole. From there, we will launch, provided you have been fully configured.

We will be casting off into the obliquity of the ecliptic. Please try
to relax your minds."

SIG WATCHED THE two awestruck Earthfolk. They seemed
like little kids. He hoped this would work. It was good that they
showed no signs of being blinded by the light. It just might
work. He wondered what they would make of Venus, of Venusfolk. He thought of his scientist friend on Venus. He pictured
her, smiled, and off they went.

14

A SOLDIER

I F A CELLO were being played along with a whistling wind blowing a tune into a giant foghorn, the resulting sound would be a weak approximation of the music coming from behind the walls. The melody was faint. Stewart couldn't concentrate on the rich, blustery, vaguely classical strains. He sat before a bare table; a person sat across from him. Stewart could see himself reflected in the glass wall behind the person. The expression on his face reminded him not so much of a man engrossed in conversation as it did his childhood dog, Beppo. Whenever Stewart's mother opened a can of dog food, Beppo sat staring at the can with an exquisite singularity of focus. His head tilted in sync with every millimeter of the can's movement. While Stewart's head didn't tilt like Beppo's, the profound mixture of intensity and patience was the same.

"You are a soldier?" she asked.

Stewart didn't blink. "No."

"I understand you are in the army," she said.

"Not exactly," Stewart said, with hardly a clue of how to convey his contractual role with the military.

"You kill people," she said, more a statement than a question.

"No," Stewart said, shifting in his seat. The smooth, tubular chair was cool to the touch. It was one continuous curve with just enough surface area for him to rest his backside.

"But you are with the army?" she insisted, after thinking about his answer for a while.

"I help defend people," Stewart said, feeling obligated to justify himself. The real reason he was working on the special project with the military was curiosity and the fact that he could get experience working on extra-atmospheric systems.

"From what?" she said.

"Bad guys," Stewart said.

There was a long pause, then, "Who are the bad guys?"

"People who want to kill us," Stewart said. That hadn't come out right.

Now Madam the Physical Scientist shifted. "People?"

"Yes."

Again there was a long pause. "Who is *us*?" she asked.

"My country," he said.

Another pause, and then she said, "I see. How many people have you killed?" The question was matter-of-fact, as if it were merely academic, a data point needed to complete some sort of rubric.

"I haven't killed anyone," Stewart said.

"But you will?" Madam asked.

Stewart thought he detected a genuine curiosity in his hostess.

"I hope not," he said.

An uncomfortable silence set in. Stewart was mesmerized not by the surroundings, which he hoped to get the opportunity to examine, but by the *person* before him. One of her curiosities was the way she always paused for a great length of time before speaking.

"Do other soldiers kill people?" she said finally.

"Yes."

"To defend your country?"

He thought she meant to be helpful in answering for him.

"Yes," he said, hoping she really did understand that he was not some sort of mercenary.

"How do *you* defend your country?" she asked, sitting still in her own smooth metal chair.

"By demonstrating that our weapons and technology are overwhelmingly superior, so that our enemies will be afraid to attack us. That's our main defense."

"I see. Other countries, *people*, should fear you."

Stewart felt his cheeks flushing. He squirmed in his seat. He asked Madam the Physical Scientist a question of his own. "How do *you* protect yourselves here on Venus?"

"From whom?" she said after not that long a pause.

"From your enemies," he said.

"What enemies? We are one, why would we try to harm ourselves?"

Stewart was surprised. "So you have no enemies?"

"Correct," she said.

"What about crime? Do you have crime?" he asked. He was both fascinated and disbelieving.

"Of course. We have laws. They are sometimes broken. We are a civilized society. That is why we have arbiters. To determine resolution."

"Why are there no men here?" This was the question he had most wanted to ask from the moment Madam the Physical Scientist had led him through the dim corridors of this place. Exactly where the heck he was, he didn't know. It was clearly underground, a network of corridors and chambers.

"Of course there are men. How else would we procreate?" she answered.

Stewart paused to think. The hum of the wall music wafted softly around them. "Where are they?" he asked.

"They are at work. Where else would they be? If they are not at work, then they are in their cells."

"The men?" he asked, surprised by the term *cells*. He wondered if she was using it to define a group or to indicate incarceration.

"Yes," she said.

"All the men?"

"Yes."

"In their *cells*?" Communication was awkward. It worked, but it was awkward. He spoke into a pendant that hung around his neck, and the person before him did the same. For the most part, he resisted the temptation to lower his head as if talking into a microphone. It was easy enough. His eyes were fixed on Madam the Physical Scientist. She was like nothing he'd ever seen before, the stuff of science fiction. A creature who was supposed to be human. And she kind of was human, he thought. He was grateful for the device, in any case. He'd heard the "Venusfolk," as Sig had called them, speaking to each other in the room where he and Chase had first arrived. It seemed impossible that anyone could understand the peculiar gurgling patois of clipped words that came out of their tiny mouths.

"If they're not at work, they are in their cells," she answered.

Stewart couldn't tell if she was smiling through the barely perceptible yellow mist that came out of her mouth every time she spoke. "Where's my friend, Chase?" he asked.

"He is speaking with Madam the Spiritual Scientist," she said.

Madam the Physical Scientist answered this last question with a deferential flourish of her hand and a nod of her head.

"May I speak with him?" Stewart asked in as even a tone as he could manage.

"Of course. Have you concern for him?" Madam asked, moving slightly in her chair.

"No, no. Uh, I would just like to speak with him," Stewart said.

"Of course," she said, after a long pause.

"DUDE, WE NEED to get the hell out of here! Where's your man Sig?" Stewart's eyes were wide, and he talked fast.

"Calm down. We just got here. This is absolutely amazing. I do not know where to begin. Do you know what this all means? It is all *real*. When I told you about Venus, I was not sure I believed it myself. After meeting Sig, I was convinced of the possibility that it could be real. But to see it all with my own eyes is amazing. I do not have the words to describe what I am feeling," Chase said in his usual even, complete sentences with nary a contraction.

"Well, I can describe how I'm feeling. These chicks are crazy, and I don't want to end up on Madam the Manfood Scientist's R & D table. Have you been told yet where all the men are?" Stewart said.

"I have not."

"I can tell you. They're in jail. Unless they're on work furlough. Where's Sig?" Stewart said.

Chase took a few seconds to process this information. He looked around at the glass walls and ceiling of the room. It smelled vaguely of chlorine and was humid, but not uncomfortably so. The chairs and table in the center of the room were glass. In fact, almost everything in the room was glass. Some objects were familiar. Others, he had no idea what they were used for. The table, the chairs, and the other objects were different colors and consistencies. Some were multicolored, like the table he and Stewart sat at. It had a rainbow swirl pattern on the top with solid light blue legs. There was stone visible behind the clear glass of the ceiling and walls. Granite ductwork emerged from the center of the walls and ran across the ceiling. It was almost as if they'd taken a kids' dining area from a fast-food restaurant, turned it to glass, and fused it to the inside of a cave.

He turned back to Stewart. "So, what are you saying? Our hostesses are a sinister race of man-eaters? Do not be rash. We cannot judge how society works here. We certainly cannot leave. Not yet. Do you realize that we are probably the only people on Earth beside Sig who know that life on Venus exists?"

"Why is that, Chase? Why us? How well do you know Sig? Where is he from? What's his last name?" Stewart asked.

"I met Sig at the library about the same time I met you. He was doing research there in the evenings, like I was. I could tell he was excited about what he was doing. He practically ran from shelf to shelf. He pounded away on his laptop and was always smiling to himself. I finally asked him one night what it was that had him so lit up. At first, he just said, 'Astronomy' and went about his business. But we started to talk after that, and he eventually told me that he was focused on UFOs and electromagnetism and Venus. We became friends, and he got me hooked. Some of what he showed me was mind-boggling. I am not a hard science guy, so I did not understand most of it. You probably would have."

"I'll tell you what I understand," said Stewart. "The temperature on the surface of Venus is supposed to be about eight hundred degrees Fahrenheit. There's no water, and the oxygen is in concentrations we shouldn't be able to breathe. I'm willing concede that maybe there is water below the surface, insulated by certain kinds of rock, and maybe that water contains phytoplankton that produces oxygen. What I don't understand is how the hell we got here."

Seeing that Stewart's scientific curiosity was piqued, Chase encouraged him. "How do you suppose there are people living here? And why can we see their breath when they speak? It is not cold enough. And why don't we see *our* breath?"

"We must be underground, which might account for the moisture in the air. It has been a mystery why Venus evolved differently from Earth when it comes to water. It's generally believed that the water was lost due to the intense heat and greenhouse effects. But it is possible that water is somehow shielded from the heat belowground.

"Venus does not generate its own magnetic field. Sig said that we were going to launch from magnetic source to magnetic source, the 'obliquity of the ecliptic' and all that business. That should not have been possible. None of this should be possible. There should not be people living here, black-eyed humans or otherwise. As far as their breath, an internal temperature much, much higher than our own might be a factor. They could be hot-blooded—like, seriously hot-blooded.

"You know, we never entered a spacecraft of any sort to get here. Are we sure we're not still just somewhere in the desert? All we saw of the trip was lots of lights and misty clouds and weird grid patterns and a tunnel. We could be in a virtual reality bunker, for all we know."

Chase chuckled. "You do not believe that. If you did, you would not be afraid of the man-eating women of Venus."

"Maybe we're all tweaked up on hallucinogens. Have you noticed they don't have teeth? What do you think they eat?"

"I do not know. Maybe *stew*." Chase paused for effect. Nothing but a deadpan look from Stewart. "OK, bad joke. Let us set about asking them, then, and not run scared because their existence is strange to us. This is a monumental opportunity. To say it is a once-in-a-lifetime thing does not come close to the magnitude of this."

"I want to see what the dudes look like. I want to talk to one," said Stewart.

Chase looked down at his chest and considered the shiny silver pendant that hung from his neck. It resembled a cross. He tried appealing to Stewart's curiosity again. "These devices are amazing. Sig told me that without them, the Venusfolk voices are garbled, and the language sounds like French and Chinese combined."

Stewart looked at his own device. "I hope they can't control us with these, like some kind of dog collar zapper."

Chase shook his head, and after much cajoling, he managed to convince Stewart that they owed it to science and to Earth not to panic. They needed to see where this visit would go and what they could learn, no matter what. Stewart was curious, but he was scared. They agreed that they would risk offending their hostesses by asking to speak with a man, but if it caused any issues, they would quickly back off. They also agreed to request that they remain together and that Sig join them.

They knocked on the glass door. It was a thick plate of dark blue glass. Neither one of them could figure out how to open it. Eventually, it opened by sliding up into the ceiling. There didn't appear to be any buttons or levers to activate it. It closed behind them. They tried waving their hands and walking back toward it to open it again.

While they were making gestures and groping the wall near the door, it lifted open, and Madam the Physical Scientist walked in. Her gray sheen and shiny black eyes were startling, so much so that it was hardly noticeable to them that she wore no clothes. There was no hair anywhere on her body. Her chest was firm and somewhat muscular, almost like a man's. Her face was long, with high cheeks and a small mouth. Her voice was feminine and sounded very Earthlike through the translator. She was incredibly thin, but there was little discernable bone structure. She was like a slender ghost. Stewart found her oddly appealing.

Behind her stood Sig with a big smile on his face. Stewart was as curious about Sig as he was about Madam the Physical Scientist and life on Venus. Perhaps Sig was from Venus. No, that couldn't be—if he were a man from Venus, he'd be in a cell or at work. Also, he was probably too tall, and his flesh was not shiny gray. Stewart thought, with some sarcasm, that Sig was probably smiling because everyone here was as bald as him.

Stepping into the room, Sig spoke up. "I'm afraid I must apologize to you gentlemen. I fear my initial introductions were wholly inadequate. Leaving you alone to interact was clumsy of me. Allow me to properly present to you Madam the Physical Scientist. Madam is chief of all physical science advancement for Venus. That is why I recommended she first meet with you, Stewart, since you are a man of science." Sig lifted his chin and stared deep into Stewart's eyes. "I hope you had an opportunity to explain to Madam the Physical Scientist that you are principally a man of science and *not* a soldier, as she seems to have surmised."

Sig looked from Stewart to Madam the Physical Scientist and back. "I would not have been so indelicate as to bring a soldier to the peaceful people of Venus. I hope there has been no misunderstanding between you and her grace, Madam the Physical Scientist. You understand, Stewart, that having a soldier here would cause certain apprehensions on the part of our hosts. I think a meeting with Madam-the-Social Scientist may have been a better start."

Stewart didn't need any more hints.

"I didn't quite get a chance to tell Madam that I was merely an advisor to the U.S. Army, and I must emphasize *was*. I left the army." He wasn't exactly lying. He had, in fact, left. He just didn't mention that it was only for the weekend. Besides, what he had told Madam was true. He was no killer. He believed that by improving the U.S. government's technological capabilities, lives would be saved. "I believe wholeheartedly in peace," he said in a solemn tone. He attempted an awkward half curtsy, half bow that amused Chase.

"Excellent," Sig said. "Madam the Physical Scientist is the one who made it possible for us to come here. I in no way wish to offend her. I wish only to thank her for the exchange she has cordially and graciously facilitated. I had hoped you would trade technical information."

Madam the Physical Scientist stepped close to Sig and placed her thin hand on his arm.

"Sig, Thank you for your kind words. I am not offended. And it is you who was most responsible for arranging this meeting. Even if this young man were a soldier, I can see in his eyes that he is a man of peace. I accept that one can be a soldier in his world and still want peace. Shall I introduce you to the other Scientists? We have many questions. Please . . ." Madam the Physical Scientist gestured for them to follow her.

THEY PASSED SEVERAL people as they followed Madam down a long dark hallway with lighted railing. They were led to another room with the same walls of stone behind the glass. This room was much bigger, though. It had a large round table of translucent purple with darker purple chairs arranged all around it. The room seemed to be lit by the glass structures themselves. The big table provided most of the light, giving the room a purple hue. There were people milling about. Their movements were smooth, almost sensual in the soft purple light. They all wore translation neck-laces and spoke closely with one another, the mist of their yellow breath turning a diaphanous magenta in the light of the table. They spoke in low tones, so it was hard to distinguish their words.

Some people began taking seats, and others stood with their backs against the wall, forming a large circle. Chase and Stewart followed Madam to chairs on the far side of the table. Sig paused in the entryway, completing the ring of people standing. No one wore clothing except Chase, Stewart, and Sig, who were also the only men.

What followed was an odd sort of game show–style questioning. Each person who wished to speak pressed the table in front of them, which glowed white and gave off a low buzz. The people around the perimeter asked no questions. They made up the studio audience. Chase and Stew fell into the rhythm, duly pressing the table each time before they spoke. There were long pauses between questions, which felt odd at first but then made perfect sense. It gave everyone time to think before asking a question or answering one.

Stewart didn't know how long they were in the conference hall. His brain couldn't keep up with all the information. He was excited, and the more he learned, the more ebullient he became. At the same time, he was somewhat charmed by the Venusfolk's mild voices and thoughtful dialogue. Their lips didn't really move when they spoke. They just kind of breathed out their words. Each speaker asked for permission to address them before speaking, and then followed up with an inquiry as to their well-being, fatigue, or comfort.

THE CIVILITY AND genuine kindness were endearing, Chase thought. As he looked around the room, he was drawn to their eyes. They were slightly different shapes and sizes, but all were the shiniest black, like glass.

Chase was relaxed from the start but grew even more so as the discussion progressed. He let Stewart do most of the talking. He was fascinated by the faces. His study of them was interrupted only by glances at the variety of glass objects in the room. There were two purple glass cylinders, one to the side of each door. They looked like giant test tubes with flat, solid tops. Chase figured they were podiums of some sort. They were short, but that was no surprise. All the people in the room were short. Sig towered over the others standing beside him.

Madam the Physical Scientist announced to the other Madams seated at the table that they would take a break to rest their minds. She informed the audience that the next discussion would be of a sensitive nature. They would not be permitted to observe but would be informed of the outcome afterward.

Chase and Stewart were shown back to the room with the blue glass door. This time when they entered, the door did not come down. Two pieces of furniture had been added to the room in their absence. They looked like reclining lawn chairs made of clear glass and were arranged against the walls across from each other.

They sat down at the table in the center of the room and looked at each other. Neither knew where to begin. Stewart smiled. Then Chase smiled. Stewart started laughing. Then Chase started laughing. And just like that, they were both belly laughing, with Stewart slowly sliding out of his chair onto the glass floor. He held his sides and laughed so hard he had to gasp for air. Chase had a low volume/high pressure laugh that turned his cheeks red and necessitated wiping his eyes, which were watering freely.

When they had exhausted themselves laughing, Chase

composed himself enough to speak. "That was like no other meeting I have ever attended."

"I don't know what to say. Hell, I don't know what to think," said Stewart.

"It is real. Life on other planets. Life on Venus. We are here," said Chase.

"Wait a second. Where's Sig? I don't like that he sneaks around. Why is he not with us?"

"He is not sneaking around. He is probably conveying our request to see a man to Madam the Physical Scientist," answered Chase.

"Can't we just call her Phyllis? She looks like a Phyllis. I'm not comfortable being stuffed in here."

"Well, the door is open, so we know this is not a cell. I believe we are free to walk around, but I would not recommend it."

"How long do you think we were in there?"

"I cannot say, Stew. I was a little distracted . . . by the room full of aliens. Or are *we* the aliens?" Chase stood, walked over to one of the lawn chairs, and stretched out.

"What are you doing?"

"I am going to rest my mind, like *Phyllis* said."

"Seriously, you're gonna take a nap? Now? Here? On Venus?"

"I recommend you do the same."

"Dude. I couldn't nap now if my life depended on it. Besides, I need a soft bed. You're seriously going to nap?"

Chase answered by winking, then closing his eyes.

Stewart began pacing. He should have taken notes. But how could he have? Their packs, along with their cell phones, had been stowed somewhere by Sig. He needed to talk to Sig and try to understand exactly how they had traveled here. The whole thing defied logic. He decided he'd take a few steps outside the room and see if he could spot Sig.

He walked toward the door. The floor was translucent. He

could just make out the stone underneath the glass below his feet. Out in the dark hall, he followed what looked like yellow glow sticks on the walls until he came to another blue glass door. He touched it, then felt around the sides of it. Nothing happened. He passed several more doors of the same type before finally coming to the end of the hallway, where he stood before a purple glass door. This was the room where they had met the other scientists. He thought about how they had each introduced themselves as Madam the this-or-that kind of scientist. They each seemed to have a pretty specific specialty. Madam the Physical Scientist and Madam the Spiritual Scientist were the only ones who seemed to have broader ranges. He concluded that they were at the top of whatever hierarchy existed here.

He was about to turn around and walk back when the purple glass door slid up. Sig stood in the doorway. He was a little ruffled, and he didn't have his suit jacket or vest on. His bow tie was intact. Stewart glanced over Sig's shoulder and saw Madam the Physical Scientist departing the room through a door on the other side. She was wearing Sig's vest. It hung on her almost like a long dress. The door quickly closed behind her.

"Stewart. Good news. Madam the Physical Scientist has agreed to set up an interview with a man."

Either Sig didn't notice Stewart's surprise or he was deliberately ignoring it.

"Before you and Chase sit for another discussion in the conference room, a man will meet with you in your room. I trust this is satisfactory?"

"Yes, that's good," Stewart said, noticing a flush in Sig's cheeks.

"Where is Chase?" asked Sig.

"He's napping."

"Very good. I believe he has the right idea. You should probably join him."

"I have questions."

"Of course you do. We all do. It's quite amazing, is it not?"

"I don't mean for the Madams. I mean for you."

"Yes, of course. You certainly must. I imagine you'd like to chat a bit about how we got here. Let's go back inside."

Sig turned around and headed for the purple table. Stewart followed, looking warily around as he entered, not knowing what he expected to see. They sat.

"Shall I give you all the details as I know them, or would you like the short version?" Sig asked.

"What's your name?" Stewart countered.

"My name? I thought you knew it. My name is Sig."

"What's your full name?"

"Sigmund," he said cautiously.

"What's your last name?" Stewart said.

"Freud."

"Freud?" Stewart repeated.

"Yes. I am Sigmund Freud," Sig said, his face placid, eyes pinching into a slight squint.

Stewart felt his stomach tighten. His heart beat faster. "Where are you from?" he asked.

"Austria," Sig said.

"How old are you?" Stewart said.

"I am fifty-five."

"Have you been to Venus before?"

"Yes, numerous times."

"Of all people, why did you bring Chase and me with you?" Stewart asked.

"I had to share my experience with someone. Chase was the only person I had contact with in New Mexico. Don't be offended, but I didn't exactly invite you. Chase did. Had I known you were a military man, I may not have let you come. The people of Venus value peace above all else. Bringing you here could have disturbed them. Thankfully, it did not," Sig said.

Stewart could tell that Sig was registering his unease behind the rapid-fire interrogation. He needed to calm himself.

"So, how did we get here?" Stewart asked, trying to control his mounting alarm.

"The short story is that we came here by riding on a wave," Sig said.

"That's not possible," Stewart said.

"And yet here we are. An electromagnetic current configured your brain's receptors and transmitters so that you could see the connection to Venus. Once you could see it, you could make use of it. You followed me here. Actually, me towing you here is probably a better way of thinking of it. As if you were tethered by a line to a Jet Ski," Sig said.

"None of this is possible. What was that whole bit in the desert with the drums and the light at the bottom of the arroyo?" Stewart said.

"The drums and 'Yankee Doodle' were Chase's idea. You can think of the location as a portal and staging area where you are prepped for the experience. What is it you are afraid of? Please tell me. I may be able to allay your fears. Fear will not serve us well here," Sig said.

"What about these translation devices? The people of Venus just happen to have these lying around?" Stewart said, grabbing hold of the heavy round object hanging from his neck.

"No, I actually designed those. Madam the Physical Scientist had them produced based on schematics I provided her. I drew mainly from existing language software and gave everything I could to Madam. She had all of Earth's languages translated based on her study of what I provided. It all happened very fast," Sig said.

"Maybe I'm just tired. I think I will join Chase back in our room." Stewart rose to leave. Sig remained seated and looked up at Stewart.

"Don't be afraid," he said, offering a smile.

"Right," said Stewart.

He headed back to the room. He fought the urge to run, glancing behind him as he walked slowly, following the yellow glow sticks. When he was sure Sig was not behind him, his walk got faster.

He stopped cold just inside the threshold of the room. He expected to see Chase reclining on the glass lawn chair. Instead, there was a man—gray, about five feet tall—standing in the center of the room. He was naked and hairless and looked very much like the women of Venus. The man stood looking at Stewart. The face was vaguely masculine; it had slightly less smoothness than the females, providing the most obvious clue as to his sex. His crotch area was smooth. No genitals. Stewart's eyes moved from the crotch up to the chest. He wore a translation device.

"Hello," the man said.

A little out of breath, Stewart ignored all pleasantries, "Where's my friend, the one who was just here?"

"You mean Chase. He stepped out with Madam the Spiritual Scientist. We did manage to talk a little before she came for him. Amiable man. I like him. I am Sir the Worker of Industry. You must be Stewart. It is my very great honor to meet you. I understand you are a scientist."

"I USED TO be Sir the Worker of Maintenance. Before that, I was Sir the Large, and before that, I was Boy the Athlete. Our names change as we change throughout the course of our lives. Before being responsible for all of Venus's industrial output, I was a worker responsible for maintaining all of Venus's residential structures. Before that, I was called Sir the Large due to the size of my reproductive organs. Would you like to see them?" Sir the Worker of Industry said.

Despite a certain curiosity, Stewart responded reflexively, "Uh, no, thank you."

Sir the Worker of Industry continued, nonplussed, "I was told you were keen to see a man. That is why I offered to show you my reproductive organs. Are you sure you do not wish to examine them?"

"No, thank you," Stewart said, holding up both hands as if to ward off an attack. Perhaps Stewart was not the thorough man of science he always considered himself to be.

"There aren't many men in Venus. We are highly valued and honored in our society. I don't know how many men there are. I'm sure Madam the Physical Scientist can give you an exact count. Of the eight hundred children I have fathered, only twenty-five were boys. I was responsible for populating all of Venus. My reproductive period is over now," Sir said.

"I need to speak with my friend," Stewart insisted.

"I'm sure he won't be long. Can I take you on a tour of our living quarters in the meantime? Madam the Physical Scientist said that you were curious to learn how the men of Venus lived."

"I prefer to wait here."

"It won't take long. Please come," said Sir the Worker of Industry, moving toward the doorway.

Stewart stepped aside and let the man pass. He looked around the room. Not knowing what else to do, he reluctantly followed. They stopped in front of the second blue door on the right. They stood side by side in front of it. Stewart was conscious of the man's slight stature, a full twenty centimeters shorter than him. His thinness was a little unnerving. As they stood together, Stewart couldn't help wondering where exactly the reproductive organs *were* stowed. As he pondered, the door slid up, revealing another long hallway with a yellow glow stick railing. Stewart suspected that the ubiquitous railings somehow emanated UV light along with visible light. Sir stepped through the doorway and walked gracefully forward.

After a series of rights and lefts in the dark hallways, Stewart lost his bearings. They came to a stop outside another blue door.

The door slid up. Stewart couldn't figure out how it worked. It wasn't a proximity sensor. Maybe it was specific to individuals. He needed to figure out how to open a door.

Sir the Worker of Industry started to enter.

"Wait," said Stewart. "How do the doors work?"

"I think it best you speak to Madam the Physical Scientist about that," he replied.

"I don't need schematics, just the general idea," Stewart persisted.

"Well, I am not sure how they work. I believe they are programmed to respond to the necklaces," Sir the Worker of Industry said.

"The necklaces?" Stewart looked down at the pendant dangling from his neck. "So you've had these necklaces for a while, then?"

"Yes, as long as I can remember. We use them to communicate with each other. It is said that a long time ago, there were so many languages in Venus that it was hard to understand other people. When the necklaces were created, peace and harmony followed," Sir the Worker of Industry said with a smile.

Eager to corroborate what he'd been told by Sig, Stewart followed up, "I was under the impression that the necklaces were made specifically for our arrival so that we could communicate with each other."

"You'd have to ask Madam the Physical Scientist about that. I can tell you for certain that the necklaces have been around at least since I was a boy. As for the languages contained in the interface, I cannot say. I got my first necklace when I was old enough to have my own cell. Please follow me," Sir the Worker of Industry said.

They stepped into the room. It was very much like the one Chase and Stewart had been stashed in when they first arrived. It was fairly small, made of the same glass walls with stone behind them. Rainbow-swirl glass table in the center of the room. Light blue glass chairs and one clear glass lawn chair.

"Welcome to my cell," Sir the Worker of Industry said.

"Huh?"

"This is my living quarters. I would offer you some victuals, but I am not sure what you eat. Or rather, I should say, what would be safe for you to eat. I don't know how you are able to breathe with your anatomy being what it is," Sir the Worker of Industry said, appraising Stewart.

"You live here in this building, or cave, or mountain, or whatever it is? I thought we would have to travel somewhere else. Where do the other men live?" Stewart asked.

"All the males' cells are in this facility," Sir the Worker of Industry said.

Stewart noticed that Sir responded quicker than Madam. There weren't uncomfortably long pauses between questions and answers.

"So, I guess you could say these are the *mail* rooms?" Stewart attempted a joke.

"Yes, that is what I just said," Sir the Worker of Industry responded, nonplussed.

"No, I was just joking. *Mail* rooms—rooms for males, but also where correspondence gets sorted? Get it?" Stewart said.

Sir laughed a little when Stewart explained, then said, "No, I don't get it. But I am pleased you are amused."

"Forget it. Where are all the other dudes? Do you live here by yourself?" Stewart asked.

"Each male is master of his own cell. One occupant per room. Any more would be crowded," Sir the Worker of Industry said. He seemed to think it silly that he would live with another person.

Stewart looked around. There were a few glass objects, but overall, it was spartan. Just one room. There was not a separate bedroom or bathroom. Just one roundish glass room.

"Where are the other men?" Stewart persisted.

"They are at work, of course," came the reply, matter-of-fact.

Stewart focused his attention back on Sir the Worker of Industry. No matter what Stewart asked, he always smiled with his little round mouth that emitted puffs of yellow mist. This tour of the living quarters did not lower Stewart's stress level. There was deep anxiety behind each of his questions, and he was getting irritated with the regular guy routine. It was all bizarre.

"Listen, Sir. Sir the Worker of Industry. Do I understand correctly that when you are not in this room, you are working somewhere?" he said.

"Yes," Sir the Worker of Industry said promptly.

"Where do you work?" Stewart asked.

"I work in the manufacturing facility."

"What do you do for fun?" Stewart couldn't wrap his head around any of this.

"Fun? Oh, yes. My work is fun. My work is my life."

Stewart tried to detect some hint of sarcasm or exaggeration or irony. He could not. There was little emotion in Sir's eyes to clue him in. The eyes were black and shiny. They didn't lend themselves to expression. Sir smiled a lot, but his eyes always remained the same. Stewart thought the man must be a slave who had made his peace with his situation.

Stewart pushed further. "What do you do here in your cell when you are not working?"

"I rest my mind. I sometimes remember the days of my life when I was young and active. I also sleep and dream. I take my sustenance, and I prepare for work."

"What do you eat?" Stewart said.

"I take my nourishment from the vapors. They are delivered to me at my command."

"You said that you were responsible for populating all of Venus?" Stewart said, his mind bouncing all over the place.

"Yes."

"And you fathered eight hundred children?" Stewart said.

This time, Sir smiled. "Yes."

"Does that mean the population of Venus is only a few thousand?"

"Oh no, not at all. There are many thousands, perhaps as many as fifty thousand."

"But you said you were responsible for populating all of Venus," Stewart asked.

"Yes, I was. Each male, during his reproductive period, is responsible for populating all of Venus. Although few have been as productive as me. Not even close," Sir said, standing the slightest bit taller and straighter.

He continued to explain, "*Each* is responsible for *all*. Take Madam the Physical Scientist, for example. She is responsible for the scientific advancement of all Venus—along with *all the other physical scientists*. Just as when she was a nurturer, she was responsible for growing all the children of Venus. Before a woman becomes a scientist, she is a nurturer. As a nurturer, she is responsible for the care and development of all the children of Venus. She cares for as many as she can effectively handle."

"You said that you were sent to live in a cell alone. Why?" Stewart said.

"To avoid violence. When men get together, there is some-times fighting and discord, especially in the presence of females. We are taught to serve our world. We gain fulfillment through our work. Working for society sustains us and pleases us. We provide for our world, and that is satisfying. We work. The women try to figure out how to make our world better, more livable, and we implement those strategies. It works."

"And you are taught by women?" Stewart asked.

"Yes."

"You can't have a passion for maintenance work," Stewart said, barely containing his incredulity.

"My passion is for people. To do my part, I have helped create life. So, too, I wish to maintain life. I remain in my cell so that I do not disturb the order of life. So that I do no harm. I do not spend much time in my cell, and it is not wasted. I rest my mind and my spirit. And unless I am sleeping and dreaming, I contemplate. Not long ago, there was war in Venus. There was violence. There was terrible pain and suffer-ing. All the people of Venus live in pods located one thousand kilometers below the surface. These pods are spread over a five-thousand-square-kilometer area. We live *in* Venus, not *on* Venus. The pockets are connected by tunnels. I have never been outside my pod. Violence of any sort jeopardizes all life in Venus. The only time I see other men is when I am working, and there are rules for our interaction," Sir the Worker of Industry said.

"If you have been with enough women to father eight hundred children in such a small area, wasn't there conflict with other less . . . ah, productive men? Even if you only encountered them at work?"

Sir's eyes narrowed. "I don't understand."

"If you have been with so many women, weren't some of the other men jealous?" Stewart asked.

"Why would they be jealous? It is not as if I was actually intimate with many women."

"Now I'm confused," interjected Stewart. "You had to have been intimate with quite a few women in order to have fathered eight hundred children."

"Not at all. I have been intimate with very few. During the reproductive period, the men of Venus support procreation by providing biological samples, from which genetic consummation is overseen by Madams the Biological Scientists."

CHASE SAT ACROSS from Madam the Spiritual Scientist.

"I was raised Catholic. It is a Christian religion of Earth. My ancestors believed harmony with nature and with the spirit world was most important. Over time, Christian beliefs were adopted by my ancestors to stand alongside the traditional spiritual practices. Some did it by choice, but many did not. There are many different spiritual beliefs on Earth."

Madam the Spiritual Scientist paused, looking down at the table in front of her, then spoke, "We follow the Word of The Message. There is one Message and one religion on Venus. We believe in Lord the Almighty." As Madam the Spiritual Scientist said this last part, she closed her eyes and dropped her head slightly. "And as you say, some follow The Message by choice, some . . . less so. We all fall short of the purity we are called to."

15

REAL HOME

CHASE AND SIG were already there when Stewart walked into the room. He caught part of their conversation before they noticed him. They were speaking in low voices, and the topic seemed to be returning to Earth. This was a welcome conversation.

Stewart wasted no time. "Are we getting the hell out of here or what?"

They looked up at Stewart. Neither said anything. They sat there studying him as if he were a piece of abstract art that neither quite understood.

Sig spoke first. "This may surprise you, but I do in fact think it is a good idea for us to shorten our stay a bit."

"Thank God. These people are cracked."

"I do not believe they are all that different from us," Chase remonstrated.

"Yeah, OK, we can debate it once we get back home. When do we leave?" Stewart said.

"The question you should be asking is when do *you* leave," Chase said.

"You want to stay?" Stewart said, pointing at the glass floor.

"I do."

"You're crazy," Stewart said.

"I am not."

"Whatever," said Stewart, now regarding Chase as the abstract art. "When do *I* get out of here, Mr. *Freud*?" He stretched out the name *Freud*, then looked back at Chase and raised an eyebrow.

"I take it the earliest opportunity would meet with your approval? Also, you do realize that I am not actually the Sigmund Freud from your historical record? That is simply the name by which you can refer to me. I understood it would be familiar to you." Sig said.

"Mmm," Stewart murmured, looking at Sig. He then turned to Chase and said, "The sooner we leave, the better."

"Very well, then. I shall confer with Madam the Physical Scientist. I anticipate we should be able to arrange for our departure within the next hour or so. I am confident Chase will be welcome to stay longer and am prepared to entrust him to the good graces of our hostesses," Sig said.

"I'm ready to go now," said Stewart.

"Yes, of course, Stewart. You have my humblest apology if this experience has caused you undue anxiety," Sig said.

"No problem. Whatever. Let's just get out of here," said Stewart.

"There are a few things we need to agree on before we arrange for our departure," Sig said.

"Here we go. I'm listening," Stewart said.

"You cannot discuss the contact we have had with anyone," Sig said, his eyebrow raised.

"Why would I want to tell anyone about my trip to Venus . . . on a desert wave . . . where I met Phyllis the Mad Scientist . . . not to mention Louie the Large, or whatever his name is." Stewart's sarcasm was becoming more acute. "By the way, Uncle Sigmund, on the way back, can we swing by Mars and grab some snacks for my buddy?"

Stewart didn't know if he was angry or scared or just plain astounded. For the life of him, he could not understand why Sig —or whatever his name really was—and Chase were treating this whole scene with such nonchalance. There was way too much he couldn't wrap his head around. The bizarre male-female relationship was just the tip of the iceberg. How they had actually gotten here was near the top of his list of mind-bending questions. But even that was not his most immediate concern. Who the hell was Sig really? Why had he brought them here? It didn't make any kind of sense, especially if secrecy was paramount. Stewart had a knot in his stomach and a gnawing feeling that he was going to wake up in the desert sun and realize he'd been drugged.

"I have given assurance to Madam the Physical Scientist that the security and safety of Venus will in no way be put at risk. Divulging the very existence of life on Venus may cause a considerable breach in their security. It would also no doubt cause the authorities on Earth to put our means of transportation under tremendous scrutiny. Scrutiny that I am, at present, unprepared to address," Sig said with finality.

Sig stood and walked to the wall. He looked at it as if he were staring out a window. All Stewart and Chase could see on the other side of the glass was stone.

Sig didn't turn around, but he began speaking again. "I'm afraid our departure from Venus simply cannot be initiated without a serious commitment from you, Stewart, that you will not divulge to anyone what you have experienced here. We will not be able to leave without it, whether we want to or not."

"Is that because you won't take me back or because Phyllis . . . Madam the Physical Scientist has us under house arrest?" Stewart said.

"Both, I'm afraid," Sig said.

Stewart looked at Chase. "Are you hearing this?"

"Calm down, Stew," Chase said.

Stewart was a heartbeat away from completely blowing his top, but a strong desire to have this bizarre dream conclude with him back on Earth kept him in check. An image came into his mind of himself in a pizzeria in California, sitting shoulder to shoulder in a booth with Lucky. They were both laughing and leaning into each other. He missed that time. That fall had been their season of white wine and roses and pizza. The male-female dynamic on Venus had gotten him thinking about the mechanics of his own male-female relationship, the only one that mattered, the one from that fall with Lucky.

His mind went back almost two years. He sat at the kitchen table in his apartment, cool air blowing through the screened window next to him. The air was unusually cool for LA. The thin curtain floated up and drifted back down, like a bride's veil being lifted and gently laid back in place. Outside, leaves tumbled along the ground, then leapt and chased each other.

He remembered reaching over and parting the curtain with the back of his hand. Life was on the move. He took it all in at a glance: sparrows taking steep dives, enjoying the thrill ride before pivoting and winging their way back to the sky, a squirrel flitting from bush to tree to grass as nuts dropped here and there like manna. The leaves didn't seem to be able to catch each other in the wind. Just when the chase appeared to be up, they'd swirl and bound in a new direction.

When he was alone in the quiet like that, he always wondered where she was, whether she thought of him, how she was feeling. He remembered sitting in LA traffic and hearing a song on the radio, his heart swelling with emotion. In truth, his heart ached, the same way it did when he was alone in bed at night and his cell phone vibrated with a message from Lucky.

Her dispatches lit up the dark and brightened his lonely heart. It was at those times that he most wanted to hold her.

He remembered sitting at that kitchen table just before getting ready to meet Lucky for their Friday pizza. The windows at Dominic's Pizza were always fogged, obscuring the burnt-orange vinyl booths inside. The cushions were the same color as the crispy pepperoni with curled edges that Lucky loved. The smells were amazing, as was their time together.

"Stew, you OK? Hello?" Chase asked with a mix of concern and impatience.

Stewart tuned back to reality, or what was passing for it at present. He needed to focus, get control of himself, think of something rational to say that wouldn't torch his only ride back home.

Chase was clearly not going to be any help. He was as peaceful and happy as Stewart had ever seen him. Why wasn't he alarmed? Sigmund Freud? That was just loony. Who the hell was this guy? The question would have to wait. It didn't matter right now. What mattered was getting home, or at least back to the New Mexico desert. His real home was in a small apartment in Southern California where Lucky brightened his days and nights. He decided right then, in that strange room deep beneath the surface of Venus, that he was going to leave the army and go back to LA. He wasn't a soldier. The project he was working on for the government would get on nicely without him. He had never even been told what the propulsion system they were creating was going to be used for. He had his doubts. Being in the desert alone with a bunch of other scientists held a certain intellectual romanticism for him, but it wasn't real romance. That was in LA, in the fall, with wine and roses and the smell of pizza in the air.

Stewart looked toward Sig, who was still looking at the wall. "You told Chase about Venus."

"That was different," replied Sig without turning around.

"How?" said Stewart.

"We developed a relationship built on mutual trust. I knew Chase shared my sense of wonder and would understand the need to hold close the secrets I revealed to him."

"What if I promise to reveal this trip to only one person? Someone whom I completely trust to keep the secret?" said Stewart.

"No one must know," came the immediate and firm reply.

"You had a need to tell someone. So do I. You must understand how unreasonable it is to ask me not to tell anyone. You trusted Chase, and he trusted me, and so far, it's worked out pretty well," Stewart said.

Sig turned around and looked Stewart square in the eye. "And you told no one you were coming here before our departure?"

Stewart thought he might have flinched just a bit. B.O.'s boyish face popped into his head. He didn't think there was any way around it. "I told one person, and he didn't believe me. I needed his help to get off the base. He thought I was completely nutty."

"And is this the person you wish to tell?" Sig took a step closer to Stewart.

"No. But I did trust him. I do trust him. I wasn't even sure about all this myself when I told him. I didn't have any details. I half expected that I'd get out to the desert and there'd be a bunch of Indian dudes sitting around smoking big fat doobies and drinking cactus wine or some such. I won't tell him anything. He'll think that's exactly what happened," Stewart said.

"Who, then?" asked Sig, stepping closer still.

"There's only one person on all of Earth whom I completely trust. I have to tell her."

Chase spoke up. "Let me guess. Lucky?"

"Who's Lucky?" asked Sig.

"Lucky's my girlfriend," answered Stewart.

"*Ex*-girlfriend," Chase clarified. "Stewart dumped her in LA to go play G.I. Joe in the desert. Worst decision he ever made—his words."

"I don't understand. Why would you feel the need to reveal this momentous information to someone with whom you no longer have a relationship? Why do you call her Lucky?" Sig asked, holding Stewart's stare.

"Because I was lucky to have her. She was way out of my league. That and Lucky is an acronym of her name," Stewart said.

Stewart took note of Sig's reaction and continued, "It's like you said. Our relationship was built on mutual trust. The relationship between men and women here on Venus—I mean, *in* Venus—is lopsided, but I guess they make it work, more or less. My relationship with Lucky was lopsided in a different way, and it didn't work out. She wanted me to stay with her in LA, but I felt that would limit me. I wanted to follow my interests. I had the chance to be part of cutting-edge aerospace technology development. I wasn't about to take a subordinate role in our relationship and let her pursue her career in LA while I just sat around. If she wanted to advance in her career, fine, she could do that, but I decided to go to New Mexico. I wanted to send things through space. Well, as it turned out, *I* got sent through space. Coming here fulfilled my dream. But it's not enough. I see that now. What good is pursuing a dream—hell, even achieving a dream—if you don't have someone to share it with? She's the one I want to share it with. And maybe, just maybe, I could still share her dream. I never thought about her sharing her dream with me. What a fool I was. A complete tool. Maybe the whole tool bag." By this time, Stewart was talking more to himself than to Chase and Sig.

Chase stood, nodding slowly and clapping quietly. Stewart and Sig both looked at him.

"How many times in the past year have I tried to get you to talk about your feelings for Lucky? It took coming to another planet for you to be honest with yourself. Bravo. Bravo." He reached to shake Stewart's hand.

Stewart offered a slow, limp hand, his emotional soliloquy having used up his energy.

SIG LIKED WHAT he was seeing and hearing. Two male friends coming to terms with emotion; this boded well for the experiment. But there was still an obvious streak of fear in Stewart. The question for Sig was, how long was he willing to let this extensive vetting exercise continue, and how could he better integrate the Venus aspect of the team's impending Earthfolk experiment? And what of this *Lucky*?

Sig sat down and looked at Chase. "You will be comfortable here alone?"

"I believe so. Although I am not sure what I will eat," Chase said, in his painstakingly complete sentences. He certainly had his own peculiar way of communicating.

"Not a problem. I have given Madam the Physical Scientist an extensive list of suitable liquids and gases that your body should be able to absorb and use for nutrients," Sig said.

"*Should*?" Chase said, raising an eyebrow.

"I meant to say *will* absorb and use for nutrients," Sig clarified.

Chase looked sideways at Stewart, then back at Sig. "You have been here several times before, correct?"

"Yes," Sig said.

"And what did you eat?" Chase asked.

Sig stammered as he searched for a satisfactory answer. "I had some of the very same gases and liquids I just mentioned." He was being less than forthcoming. While he did partake of Venus's sustenance, he wasn't 100 percent sure what the effect of these would be on an Earthfolk subject. He would need to double-check this before leaving Chase here on his own.

"Then there should be no problem, right?" Chase asked.

"Right," said Sig, averting his eyes.

Eager to change the subject, Sig stood and faced Stewart. "Permit me a few moments to consider your request, Stewart, and consult with Madam the Physical Scientist. I should also like to confirm that Chase's dietary requirements can be sufficiently met."

"By all means, Dr. Freud," said Stewart.

With that, Sig walked briskly from the room.

STEWART LOOKED AT Chase. Chase looked at Stewart. This time, there was no chance of the two bursting out laughing the way they had following the conference room meeting with the Madams. Stewart's expression was earnest. His wrinkled brow flattened, and his eyes softened in the way a father's might as he sat his bewildered son down to lovingly explain why getting an F on his report card was, in fact, a big deal.

Chase, for his part, looked at Stewart the way a father might look at a son who, after begging for weeks to go to summer camp, wanted to go home after the first day. There was bewilderment and sympathy in equal measure.

SIG RETURNED TO the room. He was well groomed again with his neatly knotted bow tie, reclaimed tweed vest, and jacket.

"Sig, I have to compliment you on your suit," said Chase, attempting to lighten the mood.

Sig looked at Chase, puzzled. "Uh. Thank you?"

Chase turned to face Stewart. "Stewart, you asked me before why I wear three-piece suits every day. I am going to tell you." Chase paused for a few seconds, then glanced at the glass wall Sig had stared at earlier, wishing there were a real window there. He looked back at Stewart. "I do it because it is timeless, and I often wish time would stop. I am a searcher for truth and meaning. Being on Venus has confirmed things for me that I've always wondered about. Truths I was told to take on faith have been revealed and validated for me. I became a teacher because I wanted to give others the tools they would need in their own searches. History is such a tool. As time goes by, it seems to me that truths get twisted. I believe in tradition and truth—*objective* truth. If I did not wear a three-piece tweed suit every day, I would wear traditional Native American clothes. How weird would that be?

"The fact that the people of Venus have the same basic belief in God that was taught to me as a little boy is life-affirming to me. I have much to learn here."

Stewart understood wanting time to stop. As a physicist, he had wrestled with time once or twice. He was pretty sure it could be sped up, slowed down, maybe even bent a little, but you couldn't stop it altogether. If he could stop time—or even better, reverse it—he'd go back to the fall two years ago, before he chose to leave LA for the desert of New Mexico, before he left Lucky to pursue his scientific interests. He knew now that he should've moved forward with Lucky, in the same direction, not away from her. She had wanted to move to New York to follow her dream, and he should have gone with her. He hadn't been afraid enough of losing her. He had been blindly optimistic about the future. He'd thought then that they would continue to be together somehow. That hadn't happened. Now his mind, a once-neat page, was wrinkled. There was fear. He feared losing Lucky forever. But the fear had come too late, and it coalesced around events he had set in motion. Science had propelled him away from Lisa, and it had brought him to this strange planet. Even if he was able to navigate his way back, what was her trajectory now, and was there space for him in it? Or was he to remain a solitary point on a slope veering toward infinity, alone?

Chase continued speaking over Stewart's thoughts.

"I will be OK, Stew. This is where I need to be right now. I believe coming here is an opportunity no one else has ever had. I am willing to ride this wave, pardon the pun, all the way to shore. How could I possibly leave now if I have the opportunity to stay? My whole life, I have sought understanding of the past so that I could better understand the present and future. Well, the future is here, and I find that I am well prepared for it. I do not know what will happen. I do not know for sure who Sig is. But I know that I trust him. I can see it in his eyes."

Stewart responded in a low voice, darting a glance at Sig, "Let's assume you can trust him, something I'm not ready to do . . . completely. Can you trust these people here on Venus? You are a male. I don't think that will bode well for you here."

"I am willing to risk it. All the great people of history took risks," Chase said.

"So now you're a great person of history? Like Sigmund Freud?" Stewart said.

"I believe that I have the opportunity to play a great role in the history of mankind, absolutely. What happened to your sense of adventure, Stewart? You pleaded with me to bring you here. What are you afraid of?"

"I'm afraid of never being able to get back home and of living like a slave under a rock on a strange planet," Stewart said.

"I think there is a clear distinction between servitude and service. You are a Christian, right, Stewart?"

"Yes," Stewart confirmed.

"Are you not called to serve your fellow man?" Chase asked.

"I don't think *serving man* is a good way to put it, Chase. Serving man around here might mean with a side of fizzy bubbles, for all we know," Stewart said.

Sig cut in, "Irrational fear."

"No. Rational fear," Stewart corrected.

"I am decided. I am staying for as long as I am permitted," Chase declared.

Stewart tried changing tack. "What about your students and your work at the Cultural Center?"

"I'm doing this for all of us. Someday, this experience will be revealed," Chase said.

STEWART WAITED ALONE in a small room. There was a table similar to the one he and Chase had sat at in their original room, but this one was smaller and had only one chair. The glass walls here weren't clear. They were a waxy phosphorescent green. Stewart wasn't sure of the way from their original room to this one. He'd tried to keep track when he was escorted here, but the cavernous rock, the dim glow stick lighting, and a head full of the universe conspired to obfuscate any potential escape route. He concluded that it didn't matter. Retreating to the original room was no escape. There would be no fleeing. He resigned himself to the fact that he was at the mercy of Dr. Freud and his merry band of Madams.

He tried recalling what he could about Venus. He knew

Russia had landed a vehicle on the surface in the early 1970s, and the U.S. might have landed one in the late 70s. He knew that Venus was hot, hotter than Mercury. It was very bright in the night sky. He'd seen it through a telescope as a child. It was similar in size to Earth and probably the closest planet to Earth at any given time. He knew there wasn't supposed to be life on Venus, definitely not human life or anything even approximating human life. But what the heck—theories were constantly being revised based on new evidence. Einstein came to mind. Relativity. Bending time. Slowing it down. There was no friggin' way his body had traveled from Earth to Venus. No way! On a wave? Led by Sigmund Freud? If it had happened, how much time had passed on Earth? Would everyone else be older when he returned? Probably not; Sig went back and forth, and he hadn't mentioned anything about that. But could Sig be trusted?

This entire trip had to be in his mind. It was probably no coincidence that Sig used the name Freud. This was some psychological trip. Stewart circled back to the science of it all: electromagnetism, thermodynamics, wave fronts, light. Energy could not be created or destroyed, only changed. He knew that radiation from the sun was propelled toward Earth and all the planets in the solar system. Most harmful rays were filtered by the atmosphere. Less harmful waves got through and were incessantly hitting Earth; some bounced off, and some passed through it and everything on it. How the heck could his body deconstruct, move, then reform itself? Impossible. This had to be a mind trip.

Stewart's stomach gurgled. He always got hungry when his mind worked fast. A slice of pizza would nice right now. Pepperoni, with curled-up crispy edges.

Maybe . . . maybe it was possible to somehow see an expanded spectrum of light. But that didn't equate to one's mind up and leaving the body, then reconstructing itself light-years away. That was insane.

He thought how the pepperoni at Dominic's looked like craters on a pizza moon. He needed food. He wondered where Lucky was now and what she'd make of his travels. They could share a pie, and he could tell her he'd flashed across the solar system. She wouldn't believe him, of course, even though she believed humans would someday contact life on other planets. She'd recommend therapy. But man, she'd look good doing it, especially moving the blond hair out of her face with one hand and holding a slice with the other.

SIG AND Madam the Physical Scientist sat looking at each other.

Sig considered Madam's figure. He was sure she looked better in his vest than he did. He'd offered it to her as a gift, but she had refused, thinking it unwise to advertise their relationship or the fact that she liked wearing a garment. Sig was under scrutiny for bringing two other-worlders with him to Venus, and Madam felt she should maintain the appearance of detachment. If it were known that she and Sig shared more than diplomatic ties, it could jeopardize her credibility as Venus's ambassador to foreign life.

The people of Venus had taken their initial contact with Sig in stride. There was tremendous interest in him, to be sure. He was a bit of a celebrity. But life did not change. The Sirs went about their work, and the Madams made sure life continued in peace. Perhaps this was because Sig wasn't the first other-worlder to come to their planet. It wasn't so long ago that they had rescued a life from the surface. They harnessed the power of geysers to engulf the foreign vessel into a chemically enhanced and shielded, hollow-rock at the core of a targeted geyser that swallowed the pod and collapsed with it back below the surface. All of this needed to be done before the shell, in which the life was contained, disintegrated. Monitors had determined the vehicle, like others before it, was rapidly burning up. This one, however, was different. Not only had the vessel made it through the atmosphere and onto the surface, but there was life aboard. Madams the Physical Scientists had acted decisively and in unity. They succeeded and were lauded for their achievement.

Vladimir Kontopovic had caused a sensation. He'd been extracted from his shell, and after much trial, error, pain, and discomfort, the people of Venus had found performed novel environmental ministrations that sustained his life. He lived for several years. It was unfortunate that he'd had to be vaporized. Kontopovic had revealed that his mission to Venus was a secret on his home planet. Hardly anyone from Earth knew there was a living being onboard his vessel, and it was to remain so, regardless of what happened to him. He claimed that knowledge of his trip was limited to a very few superior officers. It had been the revelation that he was an officer, a soldier, that had cost him his life. The only reason he lived as long as he did was that it had been difficult to communicate with him. At some point, translation technology made a sudden leap forward, providing for a thorough exchange of information and Kontopovic's ultimate demise.

Sig was acceptable, though. He was the right sort of human, a peaceful sort.

Stewart and Chase, however, were a different matter entirely. They would have to be terminated, just like Kontopovic. Stewart was a soldier, after all. A *soldier*. Unacceptable. He would have to go first. Chase would have to go, too. Madam the Spiritual Scientist spoke highly of him, but he was a spiritual warrior—also unacceptable. They would each father twenty, maybe thirty children. Then they would be vaporized. There could be no risk of another contamination of the Kontopovic variety. Five years of war and many lives lost. Too much violence, pain, and suffering. The near destruction of the planet. The ruination of a progressive civilization.

Madam the Physical Scientist was willing to debate their husbandry. Violence needed to be bred out of the people of Venus, and the science was unclear on whether or not rebellion and aggression were innate genetic qualities that could be passed to other-worlders' offspring. Kontopovic had fathered nearly forty children before he was vaporized, and there did not appear to be any anomalies with them except that 10 percent of them were male, a rather high number. Perhaps Stewart and Chase should produce only five or ten children each. With close observation, there shouldn't be any problems. That seemed a sensible approach. It was a choice that required the wisdom of the full council, though. Madam the Physical Scientist would convene a meeting. But first she needed to speak with Sig. Her small mouth creased into a smile.

After a long silence during which the two simply looked at each other with their hands on the table in front of them, Madam spoke. "Sir, you have something to communicate to me?"

"I do, my dear," Sig replied.

"It will please me to know your wishes," she said, getting up from the opposite side of the table and reseating herself next to Sig. She leaned close to him, her yellow breath dissipating as it reached his face, almost as if they were in a bar and she were blowing cigarette smoke his way.

Sig informed Madam the Physical Scientist of his plan to take Stewart back to Earth with him and leave Chase in Venus. He told her of Stewart's vow to reveal what he'd learned to only one other person, whom he trusted to keep the information secret.

"You understand that this demand must be taken to my personal committee, and likely the full council thereafter. I cannot decide such things alone, Sir. I shall be pleased to convene a meeting with great haste to suit your desire, Sir. Before this, have you any other wishes, which I alone can satisfy?" She moved closer to him.

Sig smiled. "No, my dear. I am afraid I have commitments that require me to travel immediately. I would be most appreciative if you could inform me of your personal committee's decision quickly."

"Very well, Sir. I mean, Sig," she said. She touched him on the arm, rose, and left the room.

Sig remained seated, pondering the circumstances. He needed to get back in touch with Reggie.

MADAM THE PHYSICAL Scientist returned to Sig.

"It was difficult, but I managed to convince my personal committee of the wisdom of your proposed course of action. They have agreed that no adverse action need be taken immediately against the soldier. However, he must remain in Venus. You must travel alone. I could not prevail upon them to permit his egress."

"Madam, my dear. You understand that I can just take him, both of them?"

"That would not be wise. It would put future interaction between you and my people in jeopardy. It would also put me in the untenable situation of being your adversary, which . . . is contrary to your wishes?"

"Of course. I don't wish to have an adversarial relationship with the people of Venus, especially you."

"It pleases me to hear you say that," she cut in.

"But I have an obligation to these Earthfolk, who are in my charge."

"And so, you will take them and go?" Madam asked, leaning closer to Sig.

"I'm afraid I must," he said.

"This is your decision?" she said.

"I'm afraid I have no choice," he said.

"May I appeal to the congeniality of our relationship? I don't wish to oppose your desires; however, I, too, have obligations to my people. Might you consider leaving the Earthfolk in my charge if I assure you that no harm will befall them in your absence? As I have developed a certain affection for you, I pledge myself to honor your wishes in order to demonstrate this affection," Madam the Physical Scientist said.

"I do not see how it can be accomplished. Stewart is already in a state of disorder. If he were to remain here without me, I believe he will act injudiciously. This will force you to take measures that may bring harm to him, even if those measures are in his ultimate best interest. This is not something I am prepared to accept," Sig said.

"I displease you," Madam said, turning away.

"No. On the contrary, I respect and admire your commitment to duty, and I appreciate the affection you just now declared. I have already put you in a difficult position. Might I appeal to the same congeniality you speak of and ask you to accept my pledge that information about Venus will not be revealed to anyone by the Earthfolk? I have means to ensure this. It will undoubtedly result in an abrupt and unsatisfactory conclusion to my work, but I am prepared to accept this if it furthers our . . . congeniality," Sig said, now doing his own leaning in.

"As you wish, Sir. Do you support the lesser threat, Chase, remaining in Venus?" Madam asked.

"Is he welcome to remain?" Sig said.

"No harm will come to him," she assured Sig.

"Then I will not take him with me, if that is what he wishes." In the back of his mind, Sig wondered how many ethical violations he was racking up by leaving Chase in Venus. It afforded the potential for unsanctioned cross-pollination with variables too numerous to be predict.

He looked into the shiny black eyes that peered into his own.

"You trust me, then?" he asked.

"I do. You have affection for me, then?" she responded, rather quickly.

"I do. And it is not contingent upon your acquiescing to my wishes. You should understand that," Sig said.

"I think I do."

"Very well. I will leave immediately," Sig said.

"CHASE, I HAVE arranged for you to remain safely in Venus. I trust you have not changed your mind?"

"Was there a safety concern?" Chase asked.

"No, no. Just some political issues. They have been resolved. You will be well cared for," Sig assured him.

"Great. I look forward to seeing you on your return. Which will be when?" Chase asked.

"I come every few days. Will that be a problem?" Sig said.

"Not in the least. I just want to be sure you will come back for me."

"You have my word," Sig said.

"Excellent," Chase said, throwing up his hands. "It's settled."

"You trust me, then?" Sig asked.

"With my life."

"Excellent." Sig bowed slightly and left the room.

"LET US GO."

It took Sig only two strides to reach the center of the room Stewart was in. "No time for delay. Relax your mind!" he ordered.

"Are we really going to leave Chase here?" Stewart pleaded.

"No time for delay. Are you prepared to leave?" Sig said.

"Yeah, I guess I am," Stewart said.

"Let us depart," Sig commanded.

Stewart didn't know how he was supposed to relax his mind. Alone in the room, he'd been marinating in a simmering pot of concern for Chase, concern for himself, fear of Sig, fear of Phyllis and company, fear of Sir the Possibly Sedated Worker Bee, fear of B-Ball, regret over his lack of a relationship with Lucky, fear he might have ingested drugs, and anxiety that he couldn't remember the last time he'd eaten. Having to relax was just one more ingredient in the bubbling soup. Would his not being relaxed affect the mechanics of his return flight? Ugh.

"OK, Sig, I'm ready," he lied.

Sig walked behind him and placed a hand on Stewart's shoulder. A tingle radiated down his arm and up his neck. He turned his head, not quite enough to see Sig, and just before everything turned white, he asked, "Seriously, can we swing by Mars, maybe grab some jerky and a shot glass from the gift shop—"

PART III

EARTHFOLK

16

MEMORY OR DREAM

W HAT WAS HE thinking? He'd already told Lisa too much, and he was about to tell her everything, more than she could reasonably be expected to handle. He sat in Lisa's office in front of her desk. The emptiness of the room unsettled him a little. The objects around him seemed cold. Even the yellow mug with the waving hands had no life. Lisa had gone to use the bathroom. Her jasmine scent lingered briefly, then faded away. Perhaps she wasn't coming back at all. Perhaps she was getting security or the psychologist as he sat here, thinking fast and seeing too many possibilities.

He shifted in his chair. Were all Earthfolk chairs uncomfortable to the human body? There was such thin padding, and the interlocking chairs were low to the ground, forcing his knees too high above his hips. Just primitive. He looked at the frames on the wall. Lisa Ursula Catherine Kulowski had earned a degree in medicine. Lisa Ursula Catherine Kulowski was confirmed into the Catholic faith. He looked back at the coffee mug. HOORAY FOR DOCTOR K. She had many names. That should help her understand the fact that he used different names. Who was he kidding? It was still deception, pretending to be a local doctor. He *needed* to tell her everything.

Mental exhaustion came quickly with the strenuous thought Reggie had been continually mustering ever since he'd been summoned to ARS-13. His eyelids were heavy, and his mind was wandering. His spiraling failure weighed heavily on him, like the pull of strong gravity. Soon enough, he'd be bound to his body on Mega for the rest of his days. His test subjects, Lisa, the Academy, his team, Zoe, all seemed to pull at him. Zoe . . .

He let his eyelids fall, and sleep came at once. He was back outside the circus tent in that small Earthfolk town so many orbits ago, the heaviness of tears welling up in his eyes. He was alone. He was sad. The unfairness, the laughter, the thickness of the canvas tent under his fingertips overwhelmed him. The tears came, slow and reluctant at first, then fast and determined. His sobs pounded a torturous cadence. His whole body tensed with each gasp. His stomach cramped, his chest tightened, and he fought for air, for life. The world was a salty blur.

After a while, the intensity of his sobbing decreased until it stopped altogether. He had been forgotten. He squatted next to the tent, his mouth open, slowly drawing in air. He tried to voice his sorrow, but no sound came. He flushed with emotion. He was full of sadness and anger. He was disconnected. He was alone.

Reggie opened his eyes and felt a sting in his eyes. He had been crying. What the heck? He was crying in his sleep now? His dream, his memory of the long-ago lesson, had brought on a melancholy mood. *But that's the stupidest thing*, he thought. Emotion was not going to help the present situation. He wanted to remember this lesson in detail but couldn't.

He needed to speak with Zoe. He set off for the lab and was gone with a whirl.

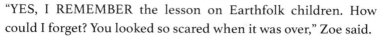

"YES, I REMEMBER the lesson on Earthfolk children. How could I forget? You looked so scared when it was over," Zoe said.

"I don't remember feeling scared. I remember being sad, very sad, but not scared," Reggie said.

"You were scared," Zoe said.

Reggie's eyes wandered, and he stared out past the mist of the lab toward the stars racing away. Zoe hadn't seemed surprised when he'd suddenly appeared. Darned if she didn't always seem glad to see him. "What was I afraid of? Were you afraid? Was the rest of our class afraid?"

"The whole point of the lesson was to look closely at the inherent fear Earthfolk have in their lives. The fear has been well documented by historians, and the class was exploring their research with exercises in how the fear leads to anger and so on. I, too, felt a little afraid. I saw it in your eyes and shared it, I think. I wasn't afraid until I looked at you. I don't know about the rest of the class. You don't know what you were afraid of?" Zoe asked.

"Not for sure, no. I wonder if the rest of the class was even inside watching the circus or somewhere else entirely, getting their own dose of Earthfolk fear. It's unlikely that watching a circus would cause fear. I don't know what I was afraid of. All I know is that it was awful," Reggie said, his brow wrinkled with introspection.

Zoe looked as bright as ever. Her short, straight brown hair threatened to veil her right eye, which seemed a softer green each time she spoke. Reggie wanted to tell her about the Academy summoning him. How it had driven him to hasten his plan to bring Earthfolk into understanding and connection with one another. He wanted to tell her how he felt about Lisa. *Lisa.*

"Don't worry, Reggie, it'll come to you, and you'll be able to sort it out. Relax. You need some sleep. You look tired. Why were you remembering that particular lesson, anyway?" Zoe asked.

"Not sure. Thanks, Zoe. We need to get the team together. We have work to do," he said.

"First rest," she said softly. "I'll leave you in quiet." She dissipated slowly, maintaining his gaze.

Reggie was left alone in the lab. He was tired, perhaps more tired than before. *Just a little rest*, he thought. He closed his eyes and remembered the time long ago at the circus:

A quiet came. His abdomen hurt from the heaving, dry sobs that were thankfully subsiding. He could no longer hear the faint roar of the crowd inside the tent. He lay flat on the ground, his watery eyes gradually focusing on the blue sky above. There was a single white cloud. Puffy. It was at peace all by itself in the sky, without another cloud to keep it company. It was happy, serene. He wondered if it was moving at all. It seemed to just lie there, like him. As he stared at it, he could feel his heartbeat slowing down. His breaths lengthened, and he began breathing through his nose again. He breathed the circulating air deeply. He wondered if he blew at just the right angle, would it reach the cloud? He wondered what it would be like to breathe in the cloud, to float with it. He raised his knees and laced his fingers on his chest, relaxing and focusing on the puffy cloud. He heard nothing— not the circus, not the wind, not the wild thumping in his chest from a moment ago.

He thought perhaps he'd close his eyes for a minute and forget everything when a balloon drifted into view far above him. It rose slowly, high into the sky, on a direct path to the cloud. It must have been an incredibly bright balloon, for even at a great distance, he could see that it was red and had a long streamer attached to it.

Suddenly, the balloon was gigantic. It was shiny red with a yellow smiley face in the center, and it had a long red streamer. For a second, he thought he had somehow flown up to the balloon in the sky, but then he realized it was another balloon, identical to the first. He canted his head in the direction of the streamer and saw a girl standing over him, holding it. She didn't say anything. She just stood there. He recognized her from somewhere.

He looked back up into the sky and saw the first balloon crossing the cloud. The girl looked up, too.

"I was going to give that balloon to you, but I lost it. It flew away," she said.

Reggie looked at the balloon in the sky, getting smaller and smaller as it neared the cloud.

"You're Reggie," the girl said.

Reggie looked at her again.

"I can give you this one," she said, looking at the balloon's smiley face, "but then I won't have any."

Reggie wiped both eyes with the back of his wrist.

"Don't be sad," she said, and squatted down next to him. "Here. We can share this one." And with that, she held out the balloon for him to take.

Reggie sat up, looking at the balloon. He didn't take it. Instead, he turned to the girl, and it came to him.

"You're Zoe."

"That's right. You want to hold it?" she asked, thrusting the balloon closer to him.

"You know, you haven't really lost the other one yet. You can still see it," Reggie said.

He pointed to the now-tiny dot in the sky, and they both quietly watched it.

"Do you think the smiley face turned to a sad face on that one because it's all by itself up there?" Zoe asked, still staring into the sky.

Reggie, now crouch-sitting himself, answered immediately and with confidence, "Nope. It's going to play with that cloud. And that's a happy cloud."

When Reggie opened his eyes, he felt an odd calm. It was

like he'd just had a dream, but he knew it was a memory. He shot back to Lisa's office.

THE SMELLS OF breakfast still filled the air, greeting Lisa and Reggie as they entered Frank's Diner. The aromas of freshly brewed coffee and smoky bacon had a calming effect on Lisa. The morning crowd had thinned out, but only a bit. There was still plenty of dishes clanging and people chattering. It was against her better judgement, but she'd decided it would be best to hear him out. So off to breakfast, again, they'd dashed.

Lisa thought of their breakfast at Frank's. The French toast had been bad, the coffee good. She and Reggie had shared a pleasant, *normal* meal. He obviously liked her. She liked him. He was smart and a little bit odd. They'd enjoyed each other's company. But that was all before she'd found out who he really was—or at least who he really wasn't. Still, there was something about him. Reggie had a more athletic look than Flash, and his light brown eyes would be good for getting lost in, but there was no way they could see deep into her soul the way Flash's penetrating blue eyes had. Flash was a dork. She had a weakness for nerds, though, especially of the stargazing, comic-book-fan variety. She didn't have many guilty pleasures, but one was comic books. It was something she and Flash had shared. While many of her colleagues and associates were reading medical journals or novels, she read comic books and ran an astronomy blog.

Flash was her dork. Emphasis on *was*. She wondered what he would make of this situation here in the diner. He'd eat it up, no doubt, and not just the bacon and eggs. She was pretty sure he still had his old number. Maybe she should give him a call. No, it would be awkward. He would stammer. She wondered if he'd ever tried calling her on her old LA number. Not that she would have known what to say to him. Still, she wondered.

She sat looking at Reggie, waiting for him to explain himself. He didn't seem in any hurry to talk.

The two were interrupted by the arrival of a carafe of coffee and two cups. After placing her order with the waitress, Lisa looked around the diner, thinking how bizarre this whole thing was. Why she was even listening to Reggie, whom she could not bring herself to believe? But maybe this was the best way to get information that would help her patients. This guy had caused their terrible injuries, if he was to be believed.

REGGIE SAT SILENTLY, wondering where to begin and trying to gauge Lisa's capacity to comprehend. He wanted to tell her everything, but she needed context.

"There are some things I need you to understand. Critically important things," he said.

Reggie took the waitress's interruption as a temporary reprieve. He hardly knew where to begin. *Things you resist will persist*, he told himself. He took a deep breath and began again.

"OK. What I'm about to tell you is a bit . . . metaphysical. You might find it disturbing, although you shouldn't. Maybe I should wait until after you've eaten."

"PLEASE, REGGIE. JUST get on with it. I'm a big girl." Lisa could tell he was ill at ease. In the back of her mind, she still thought maybe he was just crazy, or a magician. Here he was, sitting in a diner, claiming to be from outer space. Or maybe he was a crazy man *from* outer space. That would be her luck. How much weirder could this situation possibly get?

Then he started explaining.

"OK. I am human. Agreed?" he asked.

Lisa said nothing. A frown worked its way from the side of her nose down to the corner of her lips. Inside her pocket, she nervously rubbed her thumb back and forth over the glass screen of her cell phone. First he'd said he was an alien from outer space, and now he was supposed to be human. *Just plain crazy* was looking like the best explanation. Damn, she was hungry, again. She sat stock-still, hoping this communicated *don't screw with me.*

HE GOT THE hint. "Okay, Okay. Look. Most of humanity travels the universe and communicates through *the link*, a sort of internet of the mind, and body."

Reggie paused to let Lisa think about what he had just said. She sat stone still. Deadpan. Reggie didn't know how to take it. He poured himself a cup of coffee. All the while, Lisa just stared at him, slowly scrunching the smooth skin of her face into a scowl.

"Ahh!" Reggie exclaimed. His first sip of coffee scorched his tongue and lips. He looked at Lisa. No break in her demeanor. No concern for his pain. He slid his coffee cup as far away from him as his arm could push it.

"All right, let me try again. Time slows for those who travel super-positioning light. Time doesn't stop for you, for Earthfolk. You continue your short journey unawares. Someday, Earthfolk may figure out how to slow time. You may also find *the link*. But it will take a very, very long time if you're left to your own devices. I want to elevate Earthfolk. But this cannot happen while they are so compelled to discord. It would hasten darkness. I gave you and a few others a peek at *the link*. Just a peek. I was rushed, I'll admit. Here . . ."

Reggie reached into his jacket pocket, took out a piece of paper, and slid it across the table to Lisa.

LISA SNATCHED THE note, unfolded it and read:

Information for Travel and Communication

Close your eyes. A bright white light will spark in the darkness, blocking everything. It will swirl, forming a rippling multicolored tunnel that projects through the white light. Follow it with your eyes. When you see the end of the tunnel, move toward it, and out you'll go. Or remain close to the end, and you will be able to communicate with whomever is at the other end without reconstituting yourself. Until you learn your own mind better, you will only know where you are going if you have help pointing you in the correct direction. I will help you locate which wave tunnel to follow. Mapping the universe is an ongoing endeavor. The Academy maintains a database of all mapped locations. It is best to gradually approach your destination until you are sure of it. I will help. Be calm. Think happy thoughts.

"What the hell is this nonsense?" Lisa blurted out. She calmly folded the piece of paper back up and tossed it onto his side of the table. A couple seated across the room looked at her and Reggie. *They probably think we're having some type of lover's quarrel*, Lisa thought. She stared at them until they both looked away. This note was evidence that Reggie was disturbed.

"If I hadn't been rushed, I would have tried to get you to understand this information about *the link* before transmitting to you on electromagnetic waves. It was meant as preparation. But if I'd really been smart, I wouldn't have transmitted to you at all," Reggie said.

Lisa sat shaking her head, simmering.

And still Reggie continued, "Humanity removed time from the equation for speed and suspended itself in a reach for knowledge that was greater than all the questions it knew how to ask. But this didn't inhibit us from the proliferation of *link* usage and expansion. Humility should have warned against chasing dominion over light, because that's what the timeless darkness does. Other Than Human—OTH—is what the greater universe of humanity calls the vague notion of true dark that challenges reason. Administrators of *the link* believe we are perpetually at risk of slipping into darkness. We cannot outpace light if we wish to remain in it. It is a paradox that I'm not sure anyone fully understands. I *am* human. There are humans all over the universe. We just have better tools than you with which to harness the energy that's all around us."

Lisa stared at him, puzzled by his sincerity and by the detail.

"While in *the link,* we do not age. The time that goes by while we are in *the link* is infinitesimal. Our bodies undergo ministrations in stasis to keep them functioning. They lie on planets that have the capacity to care for them. They're all over the universe. There is very little motivation to leave *the link*. In fact, doing so is generally viewed as a punishment."

Lisa considered whether she should wait to call the police or just get it over with immediately. Reggie hadn't shifted his eyes away from Lisa's the whole time he was speaking. He was almost smiling. He seemed to Lisa to be both excited and relieved, like a child.

"I know this is a lot of abstraction for you. But it's the way things really are. It is suspected that something OTH exists past The Beyond, in The Unknowable. The Academy, USC, the people I work for, act as though we have achieved the apex of human knowledge and have no power to reach into The Beyond.

"Sig has probably come the closest to identifying anything in

The Beyond. He is an expert on the subject. The reason I tell you all this about darkness and light is because I may have caused something far worse than allowing your patients to slip into unresponsiveness. I may have introduced something to *the link* that invites darkness. I never really believed in the OTH, but now I'm not so sure," Reggie said.

Lisa wrinkled her nose as if she smelled something bad. This guy was unbelievable. She looked at Reggie, admiring his commitment to his delusions and wondering how he managed the disappearing act.

"Just outside the outer edge of light—" Reggie said.

"How is it we're speaking the same language?" she asked.

"I've been studying Earthfolk, particularly your subdivision, for a very, very long time," Reggie said.

Lisa just shook her head.

"How did you do it? Disappearing in my office," she asked.

"—is what we call The Beyond," he kept on, as if she had said nothing. "It is where darkness actively opposes light, like two armies colliding and comingling at the point of impact. As light expands and rushes forward, so, too, does darkness. Sig detected changes at this point of convergence. He could not understand what caused these changes. He suggested that there may be something—objects, perhaps—in The Beyond. No one had ever before discovered anything of this nature.

"The Unknowable is farther than light can reach, outside the boundary of darkness. We continually move toward it. It is a mystery how anything exists without light. Existence without light cannot be what we would call life. It is the absence of life. The light pushes into the darkness of The Beyond, keeping The Unknowable . . . well, unknowable. Some mystics believe there *is* existence in The Unknowable, that OTH is not only true dark but somehow malevolent. I think the Academy knows more than it has ever revealed on the subject of OTH. Researchers like myself are simply warned off tinkering with *the link* if there are questionable variables involved. Earthfolk are questionable variables," Reggie said.

Lisa felt as though she were looking at an accident scene. So compelling and tragic. Reggie was a handsome, intelligent-sounding man, but everything that came out of his mouth was fantasy.

"Please, stop," she said, gesturing with the palm of her hand. Half of her wanted to keep listening, but the rational side of her needed to exert itself. This man needed help.

REGGIE KEPT ON, "When the light of a corporeal life goes out, humanity suffers a deficit. It is an infinitesimally small deficit. Nonetheless, it is a reduction in our capacity to push the darkness away. Unless a life is transformed within the corporeal period and willingly merges with the great light of the eternal, our light as a whole does not expand, and if it does not expand, we cannot push into The Beyond and The Unknowable.

"We are not all-powerful. We are not gods. We are not conjurers or magicians. We are human. We live our lives that we may join the eternal light. I have spent the better part of my life trying to find ways to connect all the humans in the universe to *the link* in order to expand our light. But there is a risk in bringing online those we do not fully understand. Avarice and violence are part of certain human existences, mainly among Folk. Earth is a good example. If Earthfolk avarice and violence become attached to *the link*, chaos would soon follow, not only on Earth but throughout the universe. Humanity's light would diminish.

"I must find a way to integrate Earthfolk in a peaceful way. If I can succeed with your people, there is every reason to believe I would be able to link many others, because Earth presents one of the biggest problems out there. The Universal Study Collective has studied Earth for a long time. I have studied Earth for a long time. The greed, the avarice, and the violence have all been documented repeatedly. The greatest minds studying Earth have concluded that it would not be enough to offer Earthfolk a way to peace. The evidence suggests they would reject it. Earthfolk cannot have peace with others until they are rid of the fear and distrust within themselves. Every serious attempt I have made to affect Earthfolk in a positive way with respect to *the link* has been met with disappointment. I felt I was close, but failure has been my only outcome."

Reggie paused and reached for his coffee cup. This was the first sign that his monologue might be slowing. It felt good to share his knowledge. Lisa was intelligent, he thought. She must be getting at least some of what he was divulging.

"Lisa, you have a gentle heart and a benevolent spirit. I thought you were the one who was going to provide a model for the introduction of Earthfolk to *the link*. I watched you. I studied you. It's no small thing that I can pass as an Earthfolk. I visited the places you've lived. I came to care for you a great deal. Maybe that clouded my judgement."

She looked from table to table, shaking her head almost imperceptibly. Reggie sipped his coffee. "When I showed you *the link*, you were afraid. Perhaps there was some fear in me, too. At first, I thought it was temporary, an apprehension about the unknown. But as the experiment progressed, it became clear to me that fear was going to continue and that it would lead to misunderstanding. I believe that even if you did not engage in violence yourself, *the link* would cause you to despair, to fear, and therefore it would be of no benefit to you. And if this is the case for a gentle and intelligent person such as you, I can only surmise that others would fare far worse. I didn't account for the sadness of leaving the past, leaving your relationships. You became disoriented, untethered, melancholy. I am sorry for that.

"I know you must feel deceived. I can see now the danger of such close contact. I was warned. There are protocols and safeguards, most of which I ignored in my rush to help Earthfolk.

"I have no choice but to transmit waves to your mind that will hopefully erase this entire experience, or at least make it feel like a dream. For this I am also sorry. If the experience is not entirely erased, you will most likely consider it a dream, one that I hope you remember. And if you remember, I hope the memory of me is touched with kindness. I will be as real as you are willing to believe I am. You should know that dreams are real, but you may not believe this after I transmit," Reggie concluded.

THE WAITRESS ARRIVED with two plates of bacon, eggs, and pancakes. Lisa eyed the bacon dispassionately. If she was going to help her patients, she needed more information about what the heck had actually happened to them. After picking at her food uncomfortably, she finally asked, "On the subject of washing minds . . . it *was* you who hurt these people? The trauma cases? That was . . . uh . . . an experiment of yours?"

"It was me. I was trying to help," Reggie said.

"Why would you continue after the first person collapsed?" she asked.

"I didn't know. I just did my work and immediately moved on. I can cast myself very, very quickly if I choose," he answered.

Lisa knew she shouldn't indulge his delusions, but maybe it could be useful. "You destroyed their lives and disrupted their families. You say you're human, that you're not a conjurer. I'm not convinced. You treated them—and me, too, if you are to be believed—as if we were objects. Did you ask for anyone's consent, or did you just blow their minds with your laser beams?"

"They were unaware that they were part of an experiment. I was rushed. I used theoremifics, and I apparently did not understand the group members' individual makeups sufficiently to make sure the transmissions were completely harmless to them. I should not have sent insufficiently coded electromagnetic waves into their minds. I regret this. I was too focused on what I hoped would happen instead of what could and did happen," he said.

"How did you select these particular people to communicate with?" Lisa felt she was being generous, calling what he claimed to have done *communicating*. She knew she needed to tread lightly, considering the extent of Reggie's obvious dissociative disorder. "There doesn't seem to be any rhyme or reason regarding who you chose."

"You're all connected," he said.

"How?"

"You exchange ideas all the time in your cosmos forum," he said matter-of-factly.

Lisa picked up a piece of bacon and began chewing it nervously. "These people are connected to my blog!?"

"Yes." Reggie shook his head, then turned away. "I am so much worse than Glimmerwac."

"Who?" Lisa said through a mouthful of bacon.

"It doesn't matter. Is there any way your medicine can restore these subjects?"

"First of all, stop calling them *subjects*. They're people. Humans, remember? Helping them is exactly what I'm trying to do, here."

"Of course."

"I don't even know what's wrong with them. My best assessment before your little magic act was that their synapses were cauterized, short-circuiting their brains' signaling."

"That is impossible. I am sure the waves I transmitted had no ability to damage tissue. Synapses would be firing heavily, yes. There could be some psychosomatic reactions, but the tissue itself should not be damaged," Reggie said.

Lisa took a swallow of coffee. She thought about her dreams. The voice in her dream—damned if it wasn't Reggie's. She remembered it clearly. God, was there any way what this man was saying was true? How could he be in her dream? She'd had the dream before she met him... or had she? She couldn't remember the sequence of events. She was getting confused.

"Wait. Were the waves you used on the trauma patients the same as the ones you supposedly shot me with?" she asked, grabbing another piece of bacon.

"With the exception of some different emotion that I coded into your waves, yes."

"What emotion?"

"Well, for the subjects—patients—people, I instructed them to be calm, peaceful," he said, looking off into some unknown distance, his lips pursed almost as if wincing.

"And me?" she asked.

"One of the relationships I have always held dear is with my childhood friend Zoe. You met her. She and I have always interacted very kindly with each other. I recalled one such interaction from when I was very young just before transmitting your waves. So, kindness, I guess, maybe gentleness, and definitely a connection to someone," he said, staring into his coffee cup.

"Tell me—are there really printouts of my brain activity from the sleep center?" she asked.

"Well, I tried to be as realistic as possible, so I did record your brain activity according to Earthfolk measurements just for appearances. But I thought it best not to show them to you, because they might have exposed our intervention in your wave activity."

"Do you still have them?" she asked.

"I gave them to Sig. Why?" Reggie said.

"I have an idea," Lisa said, pushing her plate from her.

"Lisa, I am truly sorry, and I know you must despise me, but you have to understand that I must transmit to you again to help you forget all of this," Reggie said.

"No way. You're not going to just wash away this whole thing. Listen, Reggie, I am not angry with you, and I don't blame you." She spoke as if to a child. "I believe your intentions were good— a bit manipulative and arrogant, but good. You're supposed to be some kind of doctor on your own planet. To be a doctor, you must first do no harm. The Hippocratic Oath?

Reggie shook his head slowly.

"Have you ever heard of Hippocrates? Wasn't he one of your contemporaries, Dr. *Homer*?"

"What?" Reggie asked, confused.

"Forget it. You deceived me, it's true. How do I know you're not deceiving me now?" she said pulling up her phone and pointing it at him.

"Lisa, I disappeared in front of you in your office. What else do I have to do to prove that I'm telling the truth?" he pleaded.

She looked deep into Reggie's eyes. Damn if he wasn't convincing. He certainly believed what he was saying and seemed helpless in the face of her righteous indignation. "If what you say is true, you just gave me a synopsis of the universe and the super, massive, cosmic. . . Wi-fi that runs through it. I'm grateful. I always knew that more life existed out there. This is unbelievable," she said, not knowing if she was talking to Reggie or herself.

She was getting caught up in his fantasy. She acknowledged to herself that she had started really to like Reggie at their first breakfast, before all the crazy stuff emerged. But even then, she had figured he was shaping up to be too good to be true. He'd reminded her of what it was like to search someone's eyes for possibility.

"I think there might be some hope of finding a way to help the trauma patients. I need to look at the scans of my brain from when you zapped me, or *spoke* to me, as you called it. Can I see them?" she asked.

"I gave them to Sig. I'll contact him. Let me step out for a moment," Reggie said.

She wondered if he'd bolt as soon as he was out of her sight.

LISA'S QUESTION OF why he'd continued after the first test subject . . . *person* collapsed stung. Her scolding was justified. His technique had been poor. He'd demonstrated a lack of concern. He'd been too busy dashing from spot to spot, not realizing the devastating effect until he was done with the whole group. He had to do something.

17

THEOREMIFICS

"**G**OOD NEWS," REGGIE said, sliding back into the booth. "Sig has the readings from the sleep study. But I can't show them to you without setting up a complicated electromagnetic wave relay, and I get the sense that you are not keen to experience any more waves than you absolutely must."

"That is correct, Dr. Homer," Lisa confirmed.

"We'll have to wait till he gets back. He's in Venus. He said he'll be back later today. He'll let me know when he's in town. Till then, is there anything we can do?"

Lisa closed her eyes and shook her head. "Sig is on Venus?"

"Yes, in Venus," Reggie replied, sympathetic to her bewilderment.

"Can you share anything more with me about *the link*? Since you're going to turn my brain into scrambled eggs anyway?" Lisa said, with the beginnings of a smile.

"Lisa, I promise that I won't harm you in any way. The waves associated with dream suggestion are mild, and you seem to have assimilated them in a relatively benign manner."

"Benign, my ass," Lisa said. Any hint of a smile evaporated.

"Please trust me when I tell you that you won't be harmed," Reggie said.

"Trust you? Dr. Reginald *Homer*? That's your name? Your colleague, Sig, what's his name?"

Reggie paused. "Uh . . . Sigmund . . . uh . . . Freud."

"Of course, it is. Why not Aristotle or Plato or Socrates?" she said derisively. "What about Zoe?"

"It's Zoe Hypatia, or Delphine. Take your pick. Listen, Lisa. We are . . ." He stopped, trying to think of a way to make her understand their relationship with Folk. "My people are . . ." he tried again, but once more he drew a blank. "My people are your people. I won't say we are more advanced, because I see that in some ways, we may not be as advanced as we once thought. But we certainly have capabilities that you do not. We use our minds in a way that must seem incomprehensible to you. We do not have labels given to us by parents, as is the custom on Earth. We name ourselves. And our names are not easily translated. Even the 'real' names I just gave you—Aurigae, Delphine—are names you can understand. They are the names of stars. For the purpose of research, many of us choose Earthfolk names, just as we use local names when researching other planets inhabited by human beings not yet connected to *the link*. We refer to humans not yet connected to *the link* as Folk. I thought Greek scholars would be appropriate. As for Sig, he had a well-established Earthfolk name already when we began collaborating. His work with Folk predates my own by quite a bit."

LISA'S EYES WIDENED a little. She looked down at her empty plate, then up at him. He was like a new kid in school; he seemed curious, wondering at potentials, but guarded.

"And you admire Homer?" she asked.

"Among many, many others," he said.

"How many planets have humans on them?" Lisa asked.

"Roughly 10 to the 29th power. It changes. It's common for planets not connected to *the link* to destroy themselves. Some planets get colonized and are used for equilibrium and stasis, if the technology supports it. There is very limited space flight. It's not really necessary. What mechanical travel there is occurs mostly within a given solar system. Most planets inhabited by humans are connected to *the link*. Space exploration occurs through *the link*." Reggie said.

"There are people on Venus?" Lisa asked.

"Yes."

"Human?"

"Yes."

"Holy moly," she said.

"Yes. Quite. I'm sure this is the holiest of molies for you. Venusfolk look a lot different from most other humans, though," Reggie said.

"And through *the link,* people all over the universe are able to talk to each other?" she said, a hint of understanding in her eyes.

"*Communicate* would be a better way to describe it, but yes," Reggie confirmed.

"And you can travel through *the link*?" Lisa asked.

"Yes."

"Your body travels through space?" Lisa said, thinking she knew what the answer was going to be.

"No."

That stopped her in the middle of forming her next question, one of the many swirling in her head. "Then how the hell are you here?" she asked.

"I am here because you see me. I choose to be seen, and you now have the capacity to see me. I have reconstituted myself. Everything is light," Reggie replied.

"When you scramble the yolk in my brain, I won't be able to see you anymore?" she asked.

"Correct," Reggie said.

"But we're here in Frank's Diner. These people can see you and hear you. The waitress saw you and spoke to you. When the check comes, that'll be a real check—which you're paying this time, by the way. How do you come to a far-away planet without any cash? Forget it. How can they see you and interact with you if they haven't been zapped like me?" she asked, genuinely bewildered.

"Because I am here," he said, tapping his index finger on the table.

"Is this a dream?" she asked.

"It will be," he said.

"And dreams are real," she said, repeating his earlier comment.

Reggie nodded.

"Holy moly," Lisa exclaimed again, looking around at the other diners.

"Quite."

After a couple of sips of cold coffee, she signaled the waitress, gesturing for more. She was starting to believe.

"Are you afraid?" Reggie asked.

Lisa glanced at him, then turned toward the window next to them. She followed a ray of sun as it sparkled off a napkin dispenser. Light was a mystery to her.

REGGIE WATCHED, CONCERNED. He needed to explain more. "We do not, as a rule, fear the darkness. In fact, we have very little fear, if any. We are content to increase our light. We call the space past The Beyond *The Unknowable* because it forever escapes us. It is not our way to dwell on what is not light.

We focus our attention on what is light, and we welcome it into our minds. Our bodies are weak. They cannot survive the light. Light is not meant for the body. It is only for the mind. The waves of the universe break down the corporeal form. But the mind can live in the light. I do not expect you to understand. It is the way of things for unenlightened planets. You are slaves to your bodies and fail to master your minds."

Reggie could see that he was losing her; her eyes had the same look as his students when they tuned out. There was such a forlorn aspect to her now. Her fair skin was drained of color. Her blond hair, soaked in the sun, showed stressed-out strands floating above the rest. Lovely. He watched her as she looked at the light. The sight of her, the fullness in his belly, the smells of coffee and meats and breads—they brought a wholesome feeling to him. It was pleasant. It almost felt good to be in his body, but this world was dim. He felt he needed to share more with her.

"I am a person, like you. I am not a magician or a conjurer or a god. I am like you, and you are like me. If I were to live among you, I would ponder dark thoughts. If you were to live as we do, you would ponder light. But it seems you cannot live among us. Not yet. I wonder if my looking deep into Earthfolk is the same as looking deep into the darkness. I don't know. I just don't know," he confessed.

LISA SAT AT her desk as Reggie stood quietly looking at frames on the walls. She could hardly process what was happening. She needed to talk to someone normal, someone who could help her process all this. She wanted to call Flash. H wasn't quite *normal,* but no one understood her better and could be trusted to keep things quiet. He would understand.

He would believe immediately. Here she was, waiting for someone named Freud to return from Venus! She started to chuckle.

That's when Sig arrived.

"Sig, welcome back," Reggie greeted him, more animated than he'd been.

Sig wore his usual tweed Earthfolk suit. He seemed older but more relaxed than ever.

"Very good to be back, Reggie, my dear boy," Sig said.

"Hello, Dr. *Freud*," Lisa said, her voice rising. Sig didn't look like a nut. He looked like an old English professor. Lisa wondered how many people were on Reggie's research team. She knew about Sig and Zoe. Maybe there were others.

Nonplussed by Lisa's intonation of his name, Sig smiled and nodded his head. "Dr. Kulowski. I believe you would like these." He handed Lisa a folder stuffed with printouts. She kept her eyes on his as she reached for the folder.

"How was . . . uh . . . your trip?" Reggie asked.

"Not as productive as I had hoped. But not a complete loss, either. One of my friends stayed behind, and one returned with me." Sig spoke slowly in his German accent.

Maybe it was the accent, but it seemed to Lisa that every single word from his mouth had a weight to it. Ostensibly, all he'd really said was that his trip went so-so.

Reggie looked at Sig. "Lisa, Sig and I will step outside your office for a minute. You examine the data in the meantime."

Sig wrinkled his brow.

"Fine," said Lisa, "but don't go far. I'm going to have questions."

"Sure. Sig, a word in the hall, please," Reggie said, heading for the door.

The two stepped out. Reggie folded his arms, took a few steps forward, then a few steps back. "What do you mean one of your friends stayed behind and one came back with you? You transmitted? To more than one person?"

"Yes. I thought immersive exposure and crosspollination, coupled with an established social bond, might yield the result we've been looking for. It went tolerably well. They handled the travel marvelously," Sig said.

"But how? How did it work for you, when I couldn't manage it?" Reggie said, still pacing.

"I'm not quite sure. I used your theoremifics formulas. I infused emotion. I told them to be calm," Sig answered. He was smiling. "Honestly, I didn't expect it to work half so well. But I was calm. Maybe that was the trick?"

"Sig, you know what happened with the social media group in Las Cruces. It was a disaster. I thought you were opposed to taking action without further vetting," Reggie said.

"Just so. This *was* vetting. I transported two subjects who are friends, together, so they could support each other. I did not provide them with an imprint for *the link*, nor did I explain *the link*. They traveled close to me. I used theoremifics and fully intend to use your formula in dream theory to contain the experience."

Reggie stopped cold in his tracks.

"*Intend to?* You mean you haven't wiped the experience from the one who returned with you yet?" Reggie said.

"As I say, I did use theoremifics and a touch of dream theory, but not enough for a full deconstruction of his understanding," Sig replied.

"A *touch* of dream theory?"

"Just enough for him to remember Venus," Sig said.

"Why?"

"Reggie, I believe in you, and I believe in your work. That is why I am here. That is why I'm risking everything. Half measures will not serve the people of Venus," Sig said.

"Venus? We're supposed to be focusing on Earthfolk," Reggie clarified.

"You know as well as I that they are similar in many aspects, very nearly the same. I believe that exposing Earthfolk and Venusfolk to each other may be a good gauge for larger independent exposure to *the link*. My hypothesis was that Venusfolk placidity could soften Earthfolk aggression and that the Earthfolk's need for belonging and basic fairness might stimulate Venusfolk's curiosity and justice. As it turns out, I was not completely wrong. Going into the examination, I had great hope that the Venusfolk would be able to adjust and thus increase the probability of successfully connecting to *the link*. As a result of my examination, I continue to have great hope for Venusfolk connecting to *the link,* much more so than I do for Earthfolk assimilation. I recommend we shift the focus of our energies to Venusfolk. I am prepared to give a full thesis to the team in support my assertion," Sig said.

This was not welcome news for Reggie. Sig was behaving strangely. Why hadn't he mentioned any of this as he was doing it?

"Why haven't you wiped the returned subject completely?" Reggie asked.

"The vetting is not yet complete. The whole point of theoremifics and dream theory is to return the subject to their native environment without harm and study them over a long period of time. That is what I intend to do with this one."

Reggie's shoulders slumped. "Sig. The reason I didn't ask you to participate in this risky trial was because I didn't want to put you or Zoe at risk. You went ahead and grabbed two subjects, when I asked for one, and that one was supposed to be only for vetting and observation on Earth, not travelling the link. Now we have a subject in limbo in Venus and another on Earth who could reveal far too much about *the link*."

"My dear boy. Do not be discouraged. I have some good news. I have made a personal connection with a Venusfolk subject," Sig said.

Reggie leaned against the hallway wall, tilting his head back. "And the revelations keep on coming. *Crosspollination* between Venusfolk and Earthfolk. I can almost accept this. But what kind of connection beyond transmitting to Venusfolk are you talking about?"

"I believe I have established a real relationship with a Venusfolk female. Not as researcher and subject, but as people," Sig said.

"Oh, my stars! Have you lost your mind? Venusfolk aren't even supposed to be part of our study," Reggie said, nearly shouting.

A multitude of warning bells were going off in Reggie's head. Had Sig's judgement been compromised? Was this why he wanted to focus on Venusfolk? At his advanced age and status, getting personally involved with a test subject was inexplicable. But then he thought of the attraction he felt when he was with Lisa; hospital disinfectant would never smell the same again. OK, he thought, maybe it isn't that bad. Sig was levelheaded and mature. He was respected by all who knew him.

"What do you mean by a 'real relationship'?" Reggie asked, hoping he had somehow misunderstood.

"I mean love."

"Holy moly!" exclaimed Reggie, putting his hand on his head in disbelief.

"Quite," Sig replied.

Reggie tried to remain calm. "And what of the Earthfolk test subject?"

"I used very mild theoremifics and dream theory on the returned subject. It seems to have worked well enough. I have no reason to doubt I can do it again at any time. In the interim, I want to see how his experience plays out in his native environment. We have a gentleman's agreement that he won't speak of it with anyone except a friend . . . well, former friend, whom he insisted upon communicating with."

"Former friend? Sig, you're not making me feel any better. You and I and Zoe need to get together," Reggie said. By this time the two were attracting attention in the hall outside Lisa's office.

Fortunately, Lisa peeked her head into the hallway. "Is this a bad time?" she asked, with a smile. There seemed to have been a change in her. Gone was the paleness of her skin and the wrinkles in her brow.

Reggie wondered how much she'd heard. He looked at her grin and knew she had good news. He could use some good news, and darned if Lisa wasn't attractive when she smiled.

"Of course not, what's up?" Reggie said.

"C'mon in," she said, opening the door wide, still smiling.

The two researchers filed in.

"Have a seat," she said.

The two dutifully sat in front of her desk.

"Can you reproduce the exact same waves you hit me with?" she asked the men.

"I'm not sure, why?" Reggie responded.

"Well, I think we may be able to reconstitute the lost synaptic connections in the trauma patients, or at least reroute the connections. The brain has amazing elasticity and adaptability. If you can send them the same waves you sent me, the electric signals may coax the tissue surrounding the damaged areas into functioning normally. The waves seem to have an unusual property that strengthens conductivity. At least, that's what happened in my brain," Lisa said.

"Lisa, I believe the success—or near success—we had with you was due in large part to the emotional content coded in the waves you were exposed to. This is the theoremific effect. I'm not sure I can exactly duplicate the emotion, and there's no guarantee that everyone will be receptive to the same emotion," Reggie said.

"What specific emotion are we talking about?" Lisa asked.

"Um. I'm not sure I know, exactly. There was a mix," Reggie said.

"Reggie, lives are at stake here. Dig deeper," she commanded in her emergency room voice.

"Um, well. There was kindness . . ." he stammered.

"Yes . . ." Lisa coaxed.

"Um, affection . . ."

"Go on," she encouraged.

"Um, well . . ."

"Go on, my dear boy," Sig interjected, apparently delighted by the exchange.

"Well, um, affection . . ." Reggie said.

"Yes, you said that already. What else?" Lisa prodded.

"I don't know. Maybe . . . love," he said finally.

The discussion came to an abrupt halt. Sig raised his chin and spread his lips wide, clearly stifling a smile. Lisa raised both eyebrows and stared at Reggie, who would rather have been somewhere else at just that moment.

Reggie wriggled in his seat, then reached over and picked up Lisa's coffee mug. "Do your patients call you Dr. K?" he asked.

"Just the kids and some residents. Don't change the subject," Lisa said, tilting her head to the side, and considering him.

"Yes. Where was I?" Reggie said.

"Love," she said.

"Um, yes. Love. Maybe love. Maybe."

"So, you love *me*?" she said, perplexed. She asked the question softly, with no small degree of kindness. Her smile from a moment ago was gone, but its memory tinted her aspect. There was a color in her cheeks and neck now, in ascendant opposition to the sallowness of her face earlier at the diner.

Reggie was more confused than ever. "Maybe we should get some coffee," he said. He rose and reached for Lisa's cup, though he had no idea where coffee might be.

"Sit down, my dear boy," Sig commanded. "There's nothing to be squeamish about. You are among friends."

Reggie plopped back down next to Sig.

"You love me?" repeated Lisa, this time lighter, without as much disbelief.

"Maybe," he answered, looking at her.

"Maybe?" she echoed.

"I don't know. I thought I might," Reggie said.

"Is that something that gets infused into your waves? Can you put that into your wave potion on purpose?" Lisa asked.

"Well, it is an emotion. Theoremifics, to work properly, requires emotion. I'm not sure exactly how I did it," Reggie said.

"Can you reproduce your love potion, wave, magic zapper, whatever the heck it is?" Lisa asked.

"I can try," Reggie said.

Lisa rose, walked around her desk, and tenderly touched Reggie on the shoulder. She suggested they talk more about it later. For now, she wanted to focus on the trauma patients, whom she knew were in serious need. She convinced Reggie that he should try to reconstitute the wave concoction.

THEY HEADED FOR the Intensive Care Unit. As they walked, Reggie thought about emotion and how he'd tried to use it. Theoremifics hadn't helped as much as he'd thought it would. He was grateful the experiment hadn't resulted in violence, like Glimmerwac's had so many orbits ago. He wondered how the old researcher had managed to deal with *his* failure. Reggie felt a sort of kinship with the beleaguered academician. He wondered if Glimmerwac had ever developed a tenderness toward Earth-folk the way he had. Why had he started all this? Was it he who had gotten his judgement clouded? He wasn't helping any Folk here on Earth. At least Glimmerwac had shown the good sense not to mess with people.

18

LITTLE MORE THAN SAVAGES

THE RAIN CLOUDS retreated, giving the sun an opening to swarm the dense jungle valley. A thin layer of mist rose and lingered close to the treetops, where it seemed to take a last sorrowful look at the yellow vegetation and hidden animals it was leaving behind.

Dr. Marc Glimmerwac threw open the flap of the largest tent in camp, taking a breath of still-humid air. He sneered. He didn't like spending any more time in close quarters with his captive chimpanzees than he had to. The smell offended him. This morning, he'd had to remain in the tent even after he was finished administering particle bursts to the beasts. He'd hardly begun calibrating his decelerator equipment for cranial attachment to the five chimps when he'd heard the first crack of thunder outside. The storm had moved in quickly and had continued steadily during his circuit of the cages. He detested being wet even more than he disliked the smell of the chimps. So he had sat near the entrance of the tent, listening to the crackling buzz of the fission-powered mini generator as it pushed almost-cool air through clear ventilation tubes that framed the roof.

He'd also listened to the drumbeat of the rain as he looked through the clear sides and ceiling of the tent. Without the sun, he wouldn't be able to lead his Gyrovandi on a collection run. Morning was the best time for gathering new test subjects, as that was when the creatures congregated on the ground. It was also the time of day his Gyrovandi men would be the least drunk. Because of the rainstorm, the chimpanzees would be ensconced in their hidey-holes, or wherever the blasted creatures fled when the thunder roared. Glimmerwac lamented his lack of proper facilities, but it couldn't be helped. It was necessary to remain in the jungle, far away from the Academy's spies, who fanned out across Tecturia Measure continent from their posts at the Guastamo Cavanus Diplomatic Centers, at the idyllic tourist hubs, and at the Refuge for Banished Corporeals.

The Academy had judged him unfairly and imposed on him a torturous life in corporeal form. What kind of life was it to live on a desolate moon, three days away by shuttle, while other Corporeals enjoyed the comforts of GC's resorts and the Refuge? He saw it as an extra injustice imposed upon him. But he would show them that they were wrong. He would show everyone that he knew what he was doing, that it was the advancement of humanity he sought through these dirty beasts. He would be forgiven for disposing of some apes in order to enlighten Folk. If Folk were too dim to accept *the link,* then they deserved to be claimed by the darkness of The Beyond. What were a few hundred filthy primates, including the handful that had gotten him banished from *the link* orbits ago? In the grand scheme, how could they compare to the billions of humans he could force to see the light and *the link*? It was for their own good. He was a hero, a pioneer, a master.

Now that the skies had cleared, he stepped out into the humid air and glanced at the droplets of precipitation glistening off waxy yellow leaves in the surrounding forest. The ground was wet and shiny with little rivulets of water scurrying along the amber earth, trying to escape the sun. He walked briskly to his own tent. Each long stride left a deep gouge in the mud and splashed yellow spatter on the legs of his coveralls. He tried to see inside his makeshift domicile, but condensation had turned its sides translucent. He scowled. One day, the Gyrovandi would realize he wasn't the great prophet they thought he was, and one of them would cut his throat inside his holy place.

He dismissed the thought and looked up at the sun to bolster himself. Its brightness was promising. Perhaps he could trap some chimps today after all. Instead of entering his tent, he reached for a bell hanging beside the entrance. He rang it ten times and waited. Slowly, the native Cavanans stirred inside their group tent. Since there was no air-cooling system inside, there was no condensation. Glimmerwac could see them all. He could hear them grumble as they staggered to their feet. They were little more than savages themselves, he thought. This was the life they'd chosen. They were deniers—or at best, rejecters— of *the link*. They claimed their philosophy required them to live simply without traveling beyond their little world, beyond their little forest. They lived only in the flesh and for the flesh, which was why they were intoxicated most of the time. They let their emotions rule their superstitious existence.

"Come, come. We must replenish our stores. I foresee a great abundance of meat to be had this morning. I have held council with the skies. We shall be favored with good hunting," he said as loudly and as cheerfully as he could. "Quickly! Take your morning victuals, and let us rejoice. We shall set out directly."

He spoke in the guttural Gyrovandi tongue and looked each person in the eye as they emerged from their tent. He was at least a head taller than the tallest of them. Each looked up at him and bowed. A couple of them scurried to excrete their taint at the tree line. *Dirty savages*, he thought with a smile. His was a noble cause, and someday he would be celebrated for the sacrifices he'd made to advance humanity. How many indignities had he suffered? How many savages had he disciplined? Such tedium. There was a perfectly fine covered latrine in which they could relieve themselves. Instead, they squatted, squeezed, and squirted while large leaves and tall grass scratched their legs. And the bugs. . . it was too much for Glimmerwac. He would have to beat one of them.

His thoughts returned to a time when he was in his prime, when he could see and travel the universe through *the link*. The Academy just didn't understand his sacrifices. Even when he had traveled to Earth so many orbits ago, he'd made sacrifices. He was alone, always alone back then. He'd had to observe the vile behaviors of the beasts of Africa. He'd remained aloof from his students. Even though he'd gathered followers, he hadn't revealed the full extent of his research to anyone lest he be shut down.

The Academy and the Universal Study Collective had moved too slowly then, as they did now. They were too cautious. They called it *ethical progression* in Folk research. He called it timidity. They placed too high a value not only on the lives of humans but of these animals as well. As far as Glimmerwac was concerned, the chimpanzees' only value was the advancement they brought to his work and the flavor they brought to his table. But the Academy would come to understand his sacrifice. USC would come to understand. Once he confirmed his sequencing for the decelerator, he would be in a position to use his formulas and equipment on every chimp in the jungle *simultaneously*. And from there, he could move on to the dim Folk of Earth. Soon, very soon, they'd all understand.

Glimmerwac stood at the entrance to his tent and looked around the quiet camp. The half dozen structures were all constructed of thin, clear silane-infused wrap. They were surrounded on all sides by the yellow, amber, and brown hues of the forest. The chimp enclosure was the technological and physical center of camp. Glimmerwac's tent, a holy place, was set apart from the other structures. He was seen as a prophet and great mystic by the Gyrovandi. In actuality, he gleaned his *prophesies* from a spy who sent him information from the Academy's Diplomatic Center, where use of *the link* was permitted. His spy, a former student, had been banished to Guastamo Cavanus. This particular disciple lived in the Refuge and worked at the Diplomatic Center. He sent a courier with messages regarding astronomical occurrences and the weather. Bits of equipment and supplies were procured by other banished student-disciples, who helped Glimmerwac perpetuate his fraud and use the Gyrovandi to assist him in his research.

His students were true believers in his work. *The good of the many outweighs the good of the few* was their shared belief. Though they could not congregate lest they be discovered, they helped their master however they could. They helped smuggle him back and forth from Gatch Moon. One of his students had succeeded in converting a captain in the local Tecturian constabulary. The constable was responsible for safeguarding the insularity of the indigenous inhabitants of the great valley. The Gyrovandi were said to be an uncontacted people who lived in harmony with the primates who also made a home of the valley. The primates were not chimpanzees, strictly speaking— the locals called them barking-climbers—but they were close enough to the chimpanzees of Earth for Glimmerwac. He called them his chimps. Both animals had a physiognomy that was tantalizingly similar to humans.

Glimmerwac watched his Gyrovandi. Their sallow skin was pockmarked with primitive tattoos. They wore only short coverings over their genitalia. He smiled thinly, trying to project happiness from his unshaven, pale face. He didn't like the apprehensive thoughts that forced their way into his head as he stood outside his tent. These thoughts smacked of emotion, which he rejected. He turned, slowly lifted the flap of his tent, and did a quick peek inside. He held his head up and strode in, walking directly to the far corner, where he kept a firm reed. He grasped it and flailed it through the air, testing its action. Good. He sniffed the cool air of his tent, taking in the sweet scent of mint leaves. Yes, he needed to show his strength to these men. His prophetic powers alone wouldn't keep them in line. Even the weekly visits he arranged from mendicant females were insufficient motivation. He swung the reed with a deft snap of his wrist. A buzz sounded in the air.

He walked out of the tent and pulled the cord, ringing the bell three times. An uneasy quiet began to settle over the camp. With the exception of a lone raspy bark from one of the chimps, no one dared disturb the silence. Time for a lesson on camp etiquette.

PART IV

VENUSFOLK

19

A CRUSTY TURD

S TEWART SAT UP with a start.
"Lay yourself back down, son. You must've been half out of your mind, walking out in the desert without water or proper gear."

"Captain Archibald? Where am I?" Stewart looked around. He was in a room with a single bed. There was an intravenous bag hanging from a stand with a heart monitor beneath it. He looked up at Captain Archibald, who'd just stood. He seemed a little concerned.

Captain Archibald registered his disorientation. "You're at the medical facility, son. Apparently, you had some bad meat from the chow hall? MPs found you this morning, wandering ten miles out on the edge of the reservation. Almost had you AWOL. I was a heartbeat away from calling the air force operations commander and having your SCI clearance pulled, hotshot physicist or not. The army is a guest on this base, and we take operational security seriously. Can't have civilians wandering around like nomads in the desert. Doesn't inspire confidence. You know, the Russians and the Chinese have people poking around everywhere, trying to sniff out what goes on in here.

"Now. I've been told it was tainted meat, but I've ordered a drug test for you. It better come back negative. You've been delirious and dreaming, not the usual symptoms of food poisoning, and no one else got sick from the chicken loaf. One of my favorites. I'm a reasonable man, but this detail does not need any drug-related dismissals. Heaven help you if you've been taking drugs. Getting your clearance yanked and getting dismissed from this project will be the least of your worries. Removing my boot from your ass, on the other hand, will be very high up on your to-do list. I'll be back tomorrow morning. Get yourself hydrated, son. You look like a crusty turd," Captain Archibald concluded.

Archibald turned around, folded his chair, and leaned it against the wall opposite Stewart's bed. Archibald held himself upright, a fruit salad of campaign ribbons on his chest twinkling vivid colors against his dark black skin and drab olive shirt and trousers. He must have had important business that day if he was wearing the ribbons. His clothes were pressed into razor-sharp creases. He looked at Stewart one last time, a hint of concern in his eyes, then turned and walked his crisp uniform out the door.

Stewart had never before seen a human side to old B-Ball. He liked the captain better for the flash of humanity in his eyes, even if it was for just an instant. But it had passed quickly, and there was definitely going to be a reckoning with the man at some point.

Stewart was thirsty, and his stomach hurt. There was grit sandwiched between his bare feet and the bedsheet. He lifted the top sheet to see grains of sand scattered around his feet. He looked around the room. It was the infirmary on base. He felt a pinch on the inside of his arm—he was hooked to an IV. Damn.

What time was it? What day was it? Damn. He tried to remember his dream, or his hallucination, or . . . whatever it had been.

That was no freaking dream. He wondered if they'd already taken blood or urine for the drug test Archibald had ordered. He was as curious as Captain Archibald what the results would show. He spotted his pack leaning against the wall in the corner of the room. He threw the sheet and thin cover off and swung his legs off the edge of the bed. The gown he had on exposed his back to the air, a little cool.

He stood and shuffle-stepped toward his pack, IV pole in tow, hoisted it, and walked it back to the bed. He searched it for half a minute before finding what he was after: his cell phone. He thumbed through the contacts and called Chase. It went right to voicemail. He thumbed back to contacts and tapped the Cultural Center.

After three rings, a woman answered. "Hello, Cultural Center."

"Hi, is Chase there?" Stewart asked in his best businesslike voice, which actually came out as if he were asking if Chase could come out and play.

"I'm sorry, who?" the woman said.

"Chase," he said with some uncertainty.

"Do you mean Pinkerton? Dr. Deerchase? Dr. Pinkerton Deerchase?"

"Um, yes," Stewart answered, his mind racing, mostly trying to think of ways he could torture Chase about the name Pinkerton, which his friend had somehow neglected to ever mention.

"Dr. Deerchase hasn't been in for several days. Is everything OK? Who is this?" the woman asked.

"This is his friend Stewart. I'll try reaching him at the school, thanks. Everything is fine. Goodbye."

Before he could hang up, the woman quickly asked, "Mr.

Stewart—you're his camping friend, right? Is Dr. Deerchase OK? Someone else called a couple of days ago, a man with a German accent. He said that Dr. Deerchase would be out of town for a long time and that he might not come back to Las Cruces at all. We're all a little worried. Dr. Deerchase is a character, for sure, but we'd miss him terribly if he left. It's not like him to just disappear. Should we reach out to his emergency contact? Are you sure everything is OK?"

So, Sig didn't think Chase would be back. What happened to returning for him in a few days? Stewart wondered who Chase's emergency contact was. His brother lived too far away. He didn't expect the woman to give him a name, but it couldn't hurt to ask.

"Can you tell me the name of Dr. Deerchase's emergency contact?"

"I don't think I can give out personal information over the phone. I can tell you that it is a military friend, and Dr. Deerchase just changed his emergency contact a few days ago," the woman said.

"You can't give me the name?"

"I'm sorry, I can't," she said.

"I understand. Thank you."

"Mr. Stewart, please call us back if you're able to get in touch with Dr. Deerchase."

"Will do, thanks."

Stewart hung up. This was no dream. As for drugs? Still a possibility. There was no doubt in his mind that the contact was B-Ball. The fact that Chase had just made him his contact might mean B-Ball knew a lot more about Chase's activities, and Stewart's, than Chase had admitted. He was going to have to confront the captain.

~

"YEAH, I KNEW you and Pinky were going someplace."

"Pinky?" Stewart repeated as he stood in front of Captain Archibald's desk.

"Deerchase," Archibald clarified.

"Captain, did you know *where* we were going?" Stewart asked, keeping his hands in his pockets so as not to fidget and show his nervousness.

"I thought so," Archibald said.

"And you were the one who allowed us out onto the missile range?" Stewart asked.

Archibald said nothing.

Stewart took that for assent. "Why?" he continued.

Again, Archibald said nothing.

"Let me guess—it's classified. You mean you're not the only one who knows where we went?" Stewart said, trying to come to grasp the scope of the establishment's understanding.

"Classified," Archibald said.

"You've been tracking disturbances out on the range, haven't you? Big flashes of light that blast out of a depression in the desert?" Stewart said.

"Classified."

Stewart kept at it. "Did you track us?"

"Classified."

"So you did," he said, allowing himself a smile.

"Classified."

"Did you know that we actually got to our destination?" Stewart said, smiling even more broadly.

"No," answered Archibald, lifting his head a little.

"Did you know that Chase—um, Pinky—is up there right now and might not be able to get back?"

Stewart figured that if Sig hadn't been honest with him about when Chase would return, their deal to not tell anyone about Venus was off. Besides, Archibald clearly already knew about the trip.

Archibald shifted his eyes to the cell phone in his hand. He looked up at Stewart for a second, then back at his phone.

"Which operations have you been read in on, Mr. Gordon?" Archibald asked.

"Sorry. You know that even operation names are classified. I can tell you I've been read in on Operation Sat-Strat, because you were the one who gave me the briefing. Outside of that? Classified," Stewart said, with no small measure of satisfaction.

Archibald stood. Very slowly, he interlaced his fingers across his lean midsection. He reminded Stewart of a priest about to pray—if the NBA had priests in battle dress uniform.

"Do not give me a reason to chew your face off, young man," Archibald said, in a calm voice.

Stewart leaned back a bit, as if he'd been shoved. The captain wouldn't really chew his face off, would he? He was pretty sure that was against regulations.

Father B-Ball smiled and continued his sermon. "What operations have you been read in on? Keep in mind that if you don't answer me, I will pull the larynx from your throat and beat you with it. I'll give you a minute to form a proper response, one that places value on your upper respiratory system remaining inside your body and your face out of my spit bucket."

Stewart didn't need a minute. "Operation Sat-Strat and Operation Piggyback, sir."

Stewart had no way of knowing whether Archibald was part of Piggyback. He didn't know much about it himself, other than that it involved a daisy chain of specially outfitted satellites and experimental radar. The only reason he'd been partially briefed on it was that his work on Sat-Strat had to be summarized each week and presented to the Piggyback cadre.

Archibald walked around from behind his desk and closed

the office door. Stewart remained standing the way he saw soldiers stand when they were at ease. He was anything but at ease with B-Ball behind him.

"Sit down, Stewart," came Archibald's voice. It sounded like more of a mild suggestion than a command, especially since the captain had used his first name. Stewart took it as an order nonetheless.

Archibald sat on the edge of his desk, close in front of Stewart.

"Stewart, I have some things to tell you that you may find hard to believe."

"With respect, sir, I doubt it," he answered, glancing off to the side.

"How much do you know about Operation Piggyback?"

Stewart, sensing they were through dancing around classifications, told Archibald everything he knew about the operation. It wasn't much.

Archibald said he was hoping Stewart knew more. That it would have saved time. He spent the next half hour summarizing the government's effort to follow and record wave movement that defied the known laws of physics. Operation Piggyback was one of the most secret military-run scientific endeavors in history. Anomalies had been detected in the desert more than two years ago, Archibald explained, on land that was already secured by the government for guided weapons and aerospace testing. The best and the brightest were brought in. Civilians, like Stewart, were hastily recruited. They were instructed to blend in so as not to arouse suspicion. It was all done very quietly. Unfortunately, all the expertise and equipment could only track the light but so far. Once it got deep into space, it was lost. More money and resources poured in as the anomalies occurred with increased frequency.

Archibald continued, "Initially, it looked like there was an extraterrestrial aspect to the wave movement from and especially *to* this area of desert. But aeromagnetic mapping and ground testing pointed to naturally occurring radiation with some type of reflection, and the big brains lost interest. They still weren't able to explain the bounce-back or the concentrated force of the waves, but the focus of study shifted to how to use these naturally occurring bursts to support satellite communication and weaponization. That came from Washington. Your piece, a very small piece, was to help propel a power relay receptor to a special satellite that would be positioned somewhere"—here B-Ball put his long fingers up in air quotes—"'on the vector of the obliquity of the ecliptic,' whatever the hell that means."

Stewart nodded. He knew exactly what that meant. He'd traveled along it.

"The part of this whole thing that you might find hard to believe is that I am trying to protect you and Pinky from the asshats in Washington who, as we speak, are looking to launch weaponized satellites into this *obliquity*. I'm thinking that's a bad idea, if this really is some sort of portal. There are those in Washington who want to exploit the positioning of these satellites for political gain, grandstanding our progress in space domination or whatever talking points will make them look good. The spooks see an opportunity for massive overt signals intelligence gathering, due to the speed of the waves.

"I knew what Pinky was going to do. He came to me when he was first contacted by this Austrian scientist, Sig. What he told me was unbelievable, but it also fit with everything we were learning about the disturbances. He convinced me to check out Sig's claims on the off chance that we really had contact from aliens. I wanted to find out just as much as Pinky. I didn't know he was going to drag your sorry bag of bones into this. Plus, I thought it had to be bullshit," Archibald said, getting up and going back to his seat behind the desk.

He took a sip of coffee, then continued, "All Pinky could tell me was that the dude was Austrian, his name was Sig, and he was very smart. Not a whole lot to work with. I couldn't find anything on the guy. I followed him myself. Once, I tailed him to a tavern, but I swear he just disappeared. I thought he might be a plant, so I rolled with it. I figured I could find out what he was after, but he never asked Pinky any sensitive questions, and I could never place him in any restricted areas. I got some surveillance photos, ran them through the Agency's facial rec system—Nothing. If Pinky was going to meet him somewhere, I figured I could track him, see who his contacts were. And if the story was true, I couldn't let the ignorant bastards running things from their luxury SCIFs in DC know about the potential contact. I used every bit of technology I could muster here to try and find this guy.

"I know you probably can't believe that I was doing things outside of regulations, but there is more at stake here than compromising classified information. This thing is about being human. If we really can travel to Venus and the living beings there are human, or even if they aren't, we need to tread lightly. Have you ever heard of the of Pauhalimo?"

Stewart shook his head.

"Good. They're indigenous people who live on an island near Bangladesh. They were supposedly the last *uncontacted* people in the world. Not long ago, some dude decided to make contact. Completely illegal. He knew it. They're a protected culture. He wanted to bring salvation. He knew there was risk. Poor bastard got himself ventilated—by blow darts and arrows."

Stewart shook his head. "I don't follow. Are you saying we should prepare for a hostile encounter?"

"No. Just the opposite. Who's to say the Pauhalimo needed saving? If there is life on Venus, we can't just go crashing up to these mother-loving aliens without a well-reasoned analysis. And I don't think the military higher-ups are much into cultural and spiritual thought. What if the people of Venus don't want to be contacted? Look, if we can't even deal with a culture on an island in the Bay of Bengal, how're we supposed to say hello to Venetians or Venusians or whatever they're called—"

"Venusfolk," Stewart offered, trying to be helpful.

"What?"

"Not important," said Stewart.

"Listen, I trust Pinky to give me a no-bullshit assessment. When I get his take, I'll decide what needs to be done or not done and how," Archibald said.

Stewart had more questions than answers after listening to Archibald, but his sense of urgency was mounting. "I trust Chase's judgement, too. But here's the thing—neither one of us may ever see him again." Stewart went on to relate his entire trip to Venus, from Organ Mountain to speculations on how large Sir the Large really was and where he stowed his junk.

Captain Archibald was too astonished even to take notes.

Stewart took pleasure in dazzling the man who'd just threatened to have his face for lunch. He concluded by describing his tense and abrupt departure from Venus and the fact that Sig knew Chase wouldn't be back.

"What do you make of that, *Birdy*?" Stewart couldn't resist saying.

Archibald seemed to snap out of his trance at the name Birdy. "We need to find this wing nut Freud forthwith," he said. "Also, if you ever call me Birdy again, I will beat your ass into a small pile of pulp, stick you in a blender, eat you, then shit you out and flush your stinking turd of a carcass into the sewer. Clear?"

He might have miscalculated how stunned Captain Archibald was. At least he had an ally in trying to help Chase.

20

CHASE IN SPACE

C HASE WATCHED HIS host as he carefully placed a clear glass tray holding four cigar-size vials of liquid onto the table. There was a white liquid that looked like watery milk, two clear liquids, and some sort of black potion that was fizzing and smelled slightly of rotten eggs.

"Thank you, Sir. I believe this should be sufficient. One of these drams fills me quite nicely, particularly the clear one," said Chase.

"If there is anything I can do to make you more comfortable, please let me know."

"I shall. Please tell Madam the Spiritual Scientist that I am most grateful," Chase said.

Sir the Worker of Industry nodded and headed for the door. At the threshold, he turned back to Chase. "Madam the Physical Scientist"—he paused for a quick flourish of his hand—"will see you in the Think and Talk Room when you are sufficiently refreshed. I believe you know the way?" Sir said.

"Yes."

"You may proceed whenever you are ready. There will be

others waiting for you upon your arrival. They will notify Madam the Physical Scientist," Sir said.

"Thank you, Sir."

Sir the Worker of Industry nodded and left.

Chase sat pondering the vials in front of him. He'd tasted the clear liquid earlier. Madam the Physical Scientist had insisted he try it in the presence of a team of scientists. He'd been led to a small room with many tubes protruding from the glass walls. The tubes were part of a network of glass pipes through which gases and liquids flowed into and out of the rock behind the walls. Phyllis and six additional Physical Scientists had stood by while he tentatively placed a vial of the clear liquid to his lips, gave a broad grin, and downed the contents. Fortunately for Chase, there had been no ill effects. But that hadn't stopped him from grabbing his throat, bulging out his eyes, and making a gurgling sound. There had been a collective gasp. Chase had burst out laughing. "Just kidding." None of the scientists had smiled. Tough crowd.

The liquid itself was not particularly palatable, ranking somewhere between pure vegetable oil and water with an antacid dissolved in it. It did, however, satisfy his hunger almost immediately. On reflection, he realized the joke had been a bad idea. He wouldn't make light of serious issues again.

He sat and considered trying the fizzy, bubbly liquid for his second meal in Venus. He concluded that he wasn't that adventurous. He knew the clear was safe but thought the watery milk might taste better. He lifted it with his thumb and index finger. He found himself growing less optimistic as he raised it to his mouth. It had a chlorine odor, slightly different from the chlorine odor in the air and the chlorine odor of the clear liquid. It wasn't that different from the chlorine odor of Sir the Worker of Industry's breath. He decided he wasn't really that hungry or thirsty. He could eat again later. He delicately placed the vial back in its spot on the tray. He was eager to see more of Venus, anyway.

Chase did some quick stretches and headed down the hallway to the purple conference room. The door slid up as soon as he stood in front of it. Cool. Inside, there was silence. About a dozen Madams were seated around the table. All had their thin hands flat on the table and were looking straight ahead—meditating, maybe. No one moved when he entered. He saw that there were two empty seats. Wanting to be respectful, he quietly made his way to one of the chairs and gently sat down. He looked around. Nobody moved. No acknowledgement of his presence. He looked at the Madam seated directly across from him. He thought he'd be able to tell if she was focused on him, but without a focal point in the eye, it was hard to tell for certain. She could be looking at him. She could be a million miles away.

He looked from face to face, noting the subtle differences in contour, severity of angles, depth and length of their cheeks. Their almost-flat noses were hard to distinguish. Where did the nose begin? Where did it end? It was a bump on the surface of the face. The shade of their skin was all the same. The size of their heads was different, but the overall shape was consistent.

Chase thought he should meditate, too. He closed his eyes and imagined where he was: inside a rock in a galaxy, positioned somewhere in the universe. He pictured himself without anything else around him, just sitting in this point in space. In the infinite universe, here sat a speck that was infinitely small, yet to him, his life was immense, epic. The people in the purple room with him were also infinitely tiny. He wondered how they saw themselves in relation to the universe. Maybe they were contemplating the vastness of space as well. They were together with him, and that meant something. Were they bigger when they were together? Did their lives amount to more when lived together?

He thought of the Cultural Center back home, with all its history and meaning. He'd always felt connected to the past. He felt a sense of spiritual solidarity with his ancestors. They too had contemplated the sun and the stars. They were humble before the mysteries of life. They made their own sense of things. They accepted the shape of their own footprints. He wanted to share that tradition with the people of Venus, who, after all, were also human. So far, he saw no reason to believe they were anything less or more. He felt he had at least as much to offer them as they had to offer him.

When Chase opened his eyes, the room was empty save for Madam the Physical Scientist and Madam the Spiritual Scientist. Upon seeing him awake, they both nodded from across the table. Neither said anything; they merely continued looking at him. He sensed they would stay silent until he spoke.

"Hello," he said after clearing his throat.

"Greetings, Earthling. We come in peace," said Madam the Physical Scientist mechanically. The two Madams continued to stare at him, immobile.

Taken aback and suddenly very alert, all Chase could get out was, "What?"

The two Madams turned toward each other, and then the creases of their mouths arced up and they squeaked, yellow puffs of mist emanating from their mouths. Their heads vibrated and rocked back and forth. Were they laughing? The air around their heads was turning into a cloud of yellow mist from their heavy breathing.

Chase sat wide-eyed.

Gradually, they settled down, and their heads stopped shaking. They looked at him.

Madam the Physical Scientist, her thin lips still upturned,

nodded and said, "A joke. Sig instructed us to say that—he thought you might find it amusing. We certainly did. Sig explained to us that alien life was frequently depicted on your home world as similar in appearance to us and that there was much speculation about exactly what 'extraterrestrial life' would look like and if they could communicate."

Chase cracked a smile and couldn't help laughing.

"Touché," he said between chuckles. "Please allow me to apologize for making light of a serious situation earlier. It is common for the people of Earth to process tense situations with humor. I should have realized that your concern for my well-being and my ability to survive on your food were not sources of comedy."

"No apology is necessary," said Madam the Physical Scientist. "You were simply trying to lighten the mood. We are grateful for your consideration of our temperament."

"Was your meditation satisfactory?" asked Madam the Spiritual Scientist. "We dared not disturb you, sir."

"Yes, it was," he answered.

"I am pleased that you have elected to accept our invitation to remain in Venus. I should very much like to continue to explore the contours of your"—Madam the Spiritual Scientist struggled for a word—"beliefs."

Chase nodded. "I could not miss the opportunity for this exchange. I would very much like to explore your contours as well." He thought about what he'd just said. They were talking about spirituality, right? He had no interest in Madam's anatomy. Well, maybe as a curiosity. He compared the two Madams sitting across from him. They didn't appear to be that different from each other, or from Sir the Worker of Industry, really. There had been something in Madam the Spiritual Scientist's voice that hinted at a double entendre when she'd mentioned contours. Their private conversation when he and Stewart had first arrived in Venus had been exhilarating. Chase had come away thinking the people of Venus were very spiritual and not unlike the people of Earth. He could not judge her body language well, but she had ended their discussion by saying it had been "most stimulating." Hmm.

"Madam the Physical Scientist informs me that your friend has returned to your planet. How does that make you feel?" Madam the Spiritual Scientist said.

"I will miss him, but it's what he wanted. For that, I am glad," Chase replied.

"You are wise, sir . . . Chase," Madam the Spiritual Scientist said.

"Madam the Spiritual Scientist has offered to take you on a tour of Venus," Madam the Physical Scientist interjected. "I think it is the best way for you to gain perspective on how we live. It will also serve to remove you from this environment, which may become uncomfortable as word of your friend's departure spreads among our people."

"What do you mean, uncomfortable?" Chase said.

"Allowing Stewart to leave with the knowledge he has gained of Venus will be viewed by many as a security risk. This might lead to your isolation or other uncomfortable treatment. If you travel, I believe we can minimize the potential for negative interaction."

"I am not certain I understand. I thought I was welcome here."

"And so you are. But likely not by everyone, at least not once the full council learns of your friend's departure. It may have been better if he had not come here. It was Sig's judgement to bring him here, and I sanctioned it, but I did not know he was a soldier."

"I do not wish to be the cause of upset. If my being here is a problem, I will, with a heavy heart, agree to leave."

Madam the Spiritual Scientist spoke up. "That ship has sailed, to put it in Earthfolk terms."

It occurred to Chase that Stewart may have been on to something, but he didn't flinch. With the widest grin he could manage, he said, "I defer to your good judgement. I will be happy to see more of Venus."

CHASE FOUND HIMSELF in a cavern a short time later. There was no glass—not on the walls, not on the floor. There was no furniture. It was empty and quiet save for the delicate sound of trickling water. There were stalactites hanging over his head like rock chandeliers. The stalactites were different colors. Some were very pale aqua. Others were like large sponges of burnt umber. The place smelled of wet earth. There were thin rivulets of water creeping down the walls, hugging them all the way down to the ground, where they disappeared into narrow crevices. Chase could hardly fathom what deep recesses the water sought out. The only light in the chamber was from a ring of yellow glow sticks affixed to the lower part of the walls. The passageway leading into the cavern was lit the same way. Opposite the entryway, there was another much narrower passageway leading down and out of the room. It didn't appear to have any lighting.

Chase took a breath. Somehow, the air seemed purer down here than it had in the glass rooms he'd been in. Madam the Spiritual Scientist had deposited him here with instructions to await her return. She told him it was a good place to meditate and that he should avail himself, if he was so inclined. She would return shortly, and they would commence their tour.

He looked down at his feet. The ground was solid stone that had a naturally smooth texture. He sat on his heels and touched it with his fingertips. He closed his eyes and breathed deeply. He listened to the melody of the trickling water. Before long, it was massaging his temples and stroking his hair. Wait, what?

Chase opened his eyes. An aqua-colored stalactite stared down at him from far above. Somehow, he was on his back with his knees up. He was looking at the ceiling. His hands were on his chest. His temples were being rubbed. He tilted his head back, and there was Madam the Spiritual Scientist, her elegant fingers gently tracing circles on either side of his head. He closed his eyes. Long fingers firmly plowed through his thick hair, slowly feeling their way along his scalp.

He fell asleep.

When he woke, everything was completely black. Had he opened his eyes? He wasn't sure. He made a conscious effort close and reopen his eyes. Yes, they were surely open. The trickling water had stopped. The air was cooler. There was a very strong chlorine smell. It filled his nostrils, and he tasted it. It was like the aftertaste of the clear liquid. He was still on his back with his knees up, and his hands were on his chest. He turned his head left and right. He moved his right hand up in front of his face. Total darkness. He moved his hand closer until it touched the right side of his forehead. He'd been aiming for his nose.

As he had earlier, he tried to picture himself as a point in the universe. He couldn't. He felt he was in a black hole and there was nothing around him. He needed light to see himself. If this was what it was like in space, he wanted no part of it. He needed light. Everyone needed light, right? But there was more to him than his body, he told himself. What made him . . . *him*? The length of his legs, or the color of his hair, or the shape of his face, or the clothes he wore . . . He gave himself a quick pat down. He wasn't wearing any clothes. No wonder it was cooler.

He was in a predicament. What had happened to him

while he slept? The last thing he remembered was drifting off to sleep as Madam the Spiritual Scientist stroked his hair. This was an odd way to treat a guest. What about the tour of Venus? He could feel his cheeks flushing. Despite the cold, there was a drop of perspiration on his forehead. He was uneasy. It was the same way he'd felt when, as a child, sleeping under the stars like his ancestors had done, a small rattlesnake had slithered on top of his sleeping bag and settled in.

Now, as then, he wasn't sure what to do. Should he try meditating and just wait for Madam? He wouldn't be able to relax. Should he try mapping out his surroundings by feel? Too risky. His one consolation was that Stewart could not see him now. Hell, no one could see him now. He couldn't even see himself.

"Are you uncomfortable, Sir?" Madam the Spiritual Scientist's voice broke the silence. She spoke so softly it didn't surprise Chase. Her question was soothing, natural.

"I am fine," he said, trying to will himself so.

"Your forehead is wrinkled, and the muscles of your abdomen have contracted," Madam the Spiritual Scientist said.

"You can see me?" he asked, turning his head in the direction from which he thought her voice was coming.

"I can see you better now than at any time since we first met," she said.

He turned his head a few degrees more, trying to zero in on the sound of her voice. Was she moving? He felt her fingertips on his knee. They slid slowly up his thigh. His stomach tightened more, and his cheeks grew warmer. Having no other sensory stimulation other than the cool, powerful smell of chlorine, her touch was electric. The hair on his legs and arms stood up. He had goose bumps everywhere. Her beath reached him. It reminded him of scented laundry detergent.

"I cannot see you," he said.

"What is it you wish to see?" she asked, her lush and quiet voice filling the air.

"What about our tour?" he said.

"Sir, if you wish for me to discontinue our exploration and commence touring the confines of our planet, I shall respect your wishes and do so immediately. You have only to declare it."

Silence returned.

CHASE WOKE AGAIN. He was wearing clothes this time, and that was a good thing. But he must have fallen asleep again. He couldn't remember, and that was not a good thing.

He remembered Madam the Spiritual Scientist touching him—definitely a good thing. That was it, though. It was still dark. It occurred to him that Madam might be there, watching him.

He turned his head in the darkness. "Madam? Are you there?" he asked.

There was no response.

"Madam," he called out in a louder voice.

This was absolutely no way to treat a guest.

Had they been intimate? He'd thought things were going that way. He hardly knew her. He had no idea how it would even work. He rationalized that he had no such interest, but he hadn't objected when she had touched him. Her voice was soothing, and she had showed such deference, such respect. She had quite charmed him.

A touch of anxiety snaked its way back into his thoughts. OK. He had clothes. He was physically fine. There was no immediate threat. What to do?

He stood slowly. He had a sense that he could fall over at any time. He tried bending his knees and crouching a bit, as if he were on the foul line in a basketball game, dribbling low and getting ready to take a shot. OK. Now what?

He took a step and stopped. He took another step, then another, then another, his arms out in front of him like a hunchbacked sleepwalker. He expected to hit a wall any second. Should he count steps? He'd already taken five or six. He took up counting from there. He figured he could always retrace his steps to the area where he'd awoken. He somehow deemed that a safe spot.

When he reached thirty-five steps, he stopped. The place was bigger than he'd imagined. Maybe he should go in another direction—maybe a right angle to his current course. No, he would lose his bearings, wouldn't be able to get back to the safe spot.

"I do not understand," he said out loud. He swiveled his head up and down, left and right. Blackness.

He thought he heard something behind him. He did his best about-face, spinning what he hoped was 180 degrees. He clung to the hope that his safe spot was still safe and that he could count steps to get back there. When he got to forty-one steps, he stopped. For lack of a better idea, he squatted on his heels.

"Madam?" he said into the cool air.

"I am here, sir," came her immediate response in a soft voice.

"You left me," he accused.

"Only for a moment, I assure you. You are quite safe here. You need not fear the darkness," Madam the Spiritual Scientist said.

"Madam, I am not afraid of the dark. But I do need light to see. Do you understand that? I need light. Where exactly are we?" Chase asked.

"You are with me in the Quiet Caverns. Can you trust me that you are safe?" she asked, her voice seeming to float around him.

"You left me," he repeated.

"I left you so you could rest and so that I could consult with Madam the Physical Scientist," she said.

"I have a question. If all of those who are responsible for the scientific advancement of Venus are called Madams the Physical Scientists, how do you distinguish the exact one you are talking about when you speak with others?" Chase asked. In the back of his head, a crazy thought was elbowing its way forward: if he couldn't see her, maybe it wasn't Madam the Spiritual Scientist at all. It sounded like her. But . . .

Madam the Spiritual Scientist spoke up. "There are no secrets here. When I ask one of the Madams the Physical Scientists about an issue, they either know of it or they do not. If they know, they will offer a satisfactory response, and if they do not, then I continue to ask until I reach the one Madam who has not yet shared the information I seek. We are a community. Do you understand?"

"No," he said, still looking around at the dark.

"I told you just now that when I left you, I went to consult with Madam the Physical Scientist," she said.

"Yes," Chase answered, noting that Madam's voice seemed to have moved.

"What does that mean to you, sir?" Madam the Spiritual Scientist asked.

"It means that you went to ask her how things were going out there with the Earthling debate," Chase said.

"And who do you think I asked?" Madam said.

"Madam the Physical Scientist," Chase answered.

"Precisely," Madam said.

Chase thought he could detect a smile in her voice. He was more confused than ever.

Madam the Spiritual Scientist continued, "I spoke with Madam the Physical Scientist, but not the same Madam with whom you and your friends have been meeting. Does that help?"

"A little, I think," said Chase. "But how would another Madam know about my situation?"

"As I said, we share all," Madam the Spiritual Scientist said, her voice definitely right in front of him now.

"I think I am starting to get it. Why is there no light here?" Chase said.

"Sir"—Madam's voice got lower—"here we make our own light. You are a wise man. You will see. You will see the light."

Madam the Spiritual Scientist drew near to Chase. He could sense her directly in front of him. He could smell her earthy breath. It was not unwelcome.

CHASE WOKE IN the dark again. He lay on the stone floor recalling his very first conversation with Madam the Spiritual Scientist:

"Billions of souls. How many were lost before they departed? How many did not have the opportunity to find their way to the light? Billions of particles colliding, diminishing each other as they plunge like a waterfall. How many rose from the depths? How many were submerged, never to rise again? How many joined the light? How many became darkness?

"Soldiers. War. My country, your country. What does that matter when you are gone? Your descendants may honor your sacrifice. They may not. What does it matter? What is a triumph of the human spirit? Triumph over what? Subjugation? Despair? Victory is war avoided.

"Billions of souls have the chance to be nourished. Victory of the human spirit does not mean victory in war. Can this victory of spirit in the individual result in ceding your Earth to the warlike? Maybe.

"Chase. Is it evil you fight? Or your own propensity toward violence and bloodlust? Or maybe that *is* the evil you fight? You cannot peacefully coexist with others until you have peace in your own heart. I wonder if you can have peace in your heart," Madam the Spiritual Scientist had said. She'd said it plainly, as though they were talking about trivial matters rather than of billions of souls, of good and evil.

"If I am attacked and I defend myself, am I warlike?" Chase had countered.

"Yes."

"Am I to do nothing and be ruled by evil?" he'd pressed, sure the strength of his conviction was evident.

"Maybe," Madam had answered just as sincerely.

"If evil rules, how can we see the light? Where will our nourishment be? Where will my soul be if I am shown nothing of light? You do not have to be a soldier to kill. You do not have to be a soldier to be killed. We must fight for the light. We must fight evil. We must fight . . ." Chase remember how his words had trailed off. The conversation was so abstract, he remembered wanting more time to think.

"You are warlike and will live in darkness," Madam had said matter-of-factly

"I live in a world of light *and* dark. I must struggle toward the light," Chase had said. And that sentiment seemed prescient now as he lay in profound darkness, recalling the exchange.

"War is living hell," Madam had said.

"Life is both darkness and light," he'd countered.

"True life is light," she'd said. He had thought, at the time, that he understood what she meant. Now he wasn't so sure.

"In my world, life is both light and dark. It is a struggle to oppose darkness," Chase had said.

"You cannot join the light, because you bring the darkness with you," Madam the Spiritual Scientist had replied. And that had made sense to Chase. It still did.

"I am not evil. But I will defend myself," he had said.

"From whom?" she had wanted to know.

"From my enemies."

"And who are your enemies?" she'd asked.

"Those who would do me harm. Those who bring war."

"As long as you hold violence in your heart, you will always have war," Madam had said. He remembered her drawing closer to him, almost expectantly, when she'd said this.

"You have no war here?" Chase had asked. He remembered hoping the answer would be affirmative. What an interested world Venus was.

"Correct," Madam had confirmed.

"You have only light?" he'd said.

"Not exactly. We have not extinguished all the violence in our hearts. But we manage it."

"Then you will not enter the light either," he'd said. It had been a shallow rhetorical victory, he thought now.

"Maybe not," she had conceded.

"Do you fear me, Madam?" Chase had asked.

"Maybe. Do you fear me?" she'd countered.

"Absolutely," he'd answered. He smiled now, as he had then. Did he still fear her? After pondering it, he found that the answer was still *absolutely*.

"Fear brings out the violence in your heart," Madam had said.

"I am a scholar. I love peace and understanding," he'd said, seeking the high ground.

"You are a soldier, or your people are soldiers. You use weapons to deter violence. But what happens when the weapons do not deter? You use them. You kill and create misery," she'd declared.

"I am not a soldier. And I do not create misery. Misery is part of being alive. It cannot be extinguished," Chase had said. Of this, he was sure.

"I do not accept this," she'd said.

"That does not mean it is not so," Chase had replied.

"If you fear me, does that mean you wish to deter me from violence against you? Or can you accept that I do not have the violence in my heart that you have?" she had asked.

"You said that you have not extinguished all the violence in your heart but that you manage it. That is not a comfort to me. I don't know that you wouldn't get rid of me to preserve yourself."

"Perhaps your fear is of the unknown and not of me," she'd said with finality.

As Chase lay on the dark floor, recalling the conversation in his mind, he remembered the long silence they had shared and then the last things they'd said:

"Can you see the waves?" he'd asked.

"No. Can you?"

"No. Have you ever seen the waves?"

"Yes. Have you?" she'd answered.

"Yes."

"Were you afraid when you saw the waves?" she'd asked.

"Yes. Were you?"

"Yes. So, we both have fear. What were you afraid of?" Madam the Spiritual Scientist had asked.

"I am not sure," he'd confessed.

"I am," she'd said. "You, like me, were afraid of the unknown. And that is precisely why you fear me. I will concede that I fear the unknown. You are unknown to me. That is why I fear you, perhaps. But this does not have to lead to violence. Fighting is only one response to fear."

It dawned on Chase, as he lay in the cavern, that Madam the Spiritual Scientist had experienced *the link*. But when? And where had she gone?

Chase drifted off to sleep again in the quiet darkness, nebulous thoughts of light and peace padding his descent.

21

REFLECTION

C HASE HELD A spear with both hands. The weapon was heavy and smooth and long. The point was razor sharp and ready. He was wretched for want of something or someone to pierce.

He'd skewer it where it stood. It was a destroyer of peace.

Chase stared into the dark. He began walking fast, then faster, until he was running into the dark. He smelled the water. He heard it. He ran alongside the gurgling whooshing. He didn't fear the dark. He only sought someone or something to plunge his spear into. He needed to pierce the enemy of peace to the core.

His pace slowed. He stopped. Sweat seeped out of him. Fatigue and desperation seeped in. The smell of the moist damp rock was strong. He listened. There was only a faint drip, no whoosh and bubble. The water's flow had ceased. And then the drip ceased. No sound. His legs were like dead weights; he could barely lift them. He tried to drag the weight of his legs toward the water, first one foot, then the other. His legs refused.

He lowered himself to the ground and began to crawl, one hand on the spear, the other clawing the smooth, stony ground.

The odor of moist air grew stronger and was mixed with . . . what? The smell of someone! He grasped the spear tight in his damp fist. He vowed he wouldn't throw it. He'd thrust. He'd stab it till it was dead. He wouldn't let go of the spear, no matter what.

His sweat-soaked hand slipped on the moist rock, and he fell into a pool of water facedown. His head submerged. He couldn't breathe. His spine locked. He couldn't get his head out. He pushed a weary arm against the slippery rock. His head emerged; he gulped the watery air. Too much water. Too little air. He gasped several times, and then he saw the enemy.

It had the eyes of a destroyer, seething in wretched anger. Hungry, wild. Chase stabbed for the heart. Then he dropped the spear and collapsed. Before him in the water lay the bright, shiny image of himself and Madam the Spiritual Scientist in an embrace. Like tangled vines, they clung tightly to each other, rhythmically climbing one another toward the light.

The darkness hated its reflection. It only came with the light.

PART V

FOLK

22

A REASONABLE ASSUMPTION

WHEN REGGIE LECTURED from his classroom at NGC 6543, the space had seemed small. Surrounded by his students, he'd felt secure. His connection to each of them had held him fixed. There was little distance between them, at least until they dispersed for the term. Then a lonely divide seemed to open up in the space around him. Now, back at his lab though Sig and Zoe hovered close, he felt the same isolation he had when his students left him. How strange.

"All right, I have to tell you the whole story," Reggie said to Sig and Zoe. "I conducted my own field experiment on multiple subjects simultaneously. My target group consisted of six subjects, adult male and female Earthfolk. I transmitted waves infused with instructions for emotional preparedness. The trial did not succeed. All six subjects lost consciousness, failed to recognize any pathways, and suffered traumatic brain wave interruption. I chose my test group because of their connection to each other and their interest in space and life beyond Earth. My reasoning was that their collective interest and preexisting bond to one another would serve as a platform to support an emotionally stable identification of at least a few incoming wave corridors. I erred in my assumptions.

"As we speak, all six subjects' normal functioning has ceased. They are not dead, and they have not been removed from their environment. There is a serious investigation on Earth regarding the circumstances that caused the subjects to malfunction. The Academy is not aware of any of this, yet they've already summoned me to Mega. I have three rotations left before I need to appear, at which point I am done for. Questions?"

The space was silent. Sig had one eyebrow raised and the other eye squinted as he looked at Reggie. Zoe's brows tilted into a V low over her eyes, slightly perplexed. Reggie took measure of her. Short brown hair, pale white complexion, and green saucer eyes—altogether lovely, despite the hint of perturbation.

The silence was starting to unnerve Reggie. "Comments?" he said.

There was silence.

"Zoe?" he prompted, thinking she'd be the more sympathetic of the two.

"Well, Reggie"—Zoe's measured tone hinted at the challenge it was for her to control her emotions—"you know my position. But for Sig's benefit, I'll give it again. What you did was irresponsible, unscientific, unethical, and illegal. Furthermore, you did it using our data and research but without including us in the planning or execution. You sent us off on a convoluted mission to distract us from what you were planning. You misled us. And worse, you failed. Failure is not an option when conducting experiments with live subjects. Isn't that what we always said? That we would not be like the scientists of old? That we would hurt no one? I thought we were a team. Together, we may have succeeded. Instead, you pulled a Glimmerwac to the nth degree."

The space was silent again. Reggie was stung.

After an uncomfortable pause, Zoe resumed, "I have been calculating probabilities and making observations to vet a subject as fully and as thoroughly as the Academy demands, while you've been haphazardly blasting any Earthfolk that moved, traipsing around with your *Lisa* friend. But it doesn't matter now how carefully any of our targets were selected, because you've probably spoiled any chance we might have had to advance Earthfolk integration. Your conduct is incomprehensible to me. I've nothing further to say, except on a personal note. I can only hope these transgressions won't compromise our relationship."

Reggie was reeling, on the verge of becoming emotional. He was worse than Glimmerwac. He had a thought to flee. Odd. He looked from Zoe to Sig and back to Zoe.

Finally, the green in Zoe's eyes seemed to grow lighter. "Were our target acquisition and vetting assignments nothing more than cover for your solo performance?" she asked.

She was offering Reggie an opening to explain himself. He seized it.

"Absolutely not. The work you did was no less valid than anything I've done. But when I suggested avenues of inquiry for you to pursue, I hoped we wouldn't have to proceed to active trials. It's true, I used everyone's prior research and data stores to inform my experiment, but you must believe that my intention was to protect you from the consequences. I thought if I was successful with my group experiment, I wouldn't have to ask you to do a risky exercise with your targets that could end up costing you. I was already in trouble with the Academy. I thought I could build on any success in my group experiment with what you discovered while vetting your subjects. I deliberately conducted the experiment without your knowledge so you would be innocent of collusion in anything the Academy might deem unethical. I take full responsibility for my failure," Reggie said.

"*Might* deem unethical?" Zoe mimicked with a smile.

"There are some gray areas," Sig offered sympathetically. "In any case, the Academy will shut us down whether or not we knew what Reggie was doing. Our careers are over."

Silence asserted itself yet again.

"Excuse me for a moment," Sig said, and twirled off.

Then it was just Zoe and Reggie suspended in the clear space of the lab.

"Zoe, I don't know where I went wrong," he said.

"I think that's exactly what Marc Glimmerwac said just before he was exiled to Gatch Moon after his experiment failed," Zoe said. Before Reggie could respond, she closed her eyes and turned away. "I'm sorry. That was unkind."

Reggie's shoulders hunched. His light brown eyes looked off into space. He should have at least told Zoe about being summoned to Mega before he'd executed his experiment. He said nothing. Lisa's face popped into his head. She was smiling, and her face brought him a glimmer of hope. Her part in the experiment had gone well. Maybe there was hope for the stricken test subjects. Maybe they could be restored.

Zoe moved closer to him. "I'm sorry. What I just said was hurtful. It was meant as ironic humor. Isn't that how Earthfolk jest? I'm sorry. I see that the situation affects you deeply," she said.

She reached out to touch his forearm. In all the many orbits they'd known each other, she'd never touched him, not once. Tremors of emotion welled up in him even though it was a mere intermingling of their images. He raised his eyes to meet hers and saw sadness in them. He shared it. He became sad that she was sad, and she was sad because . . . just because she was, he thought.

She withdrew her hand before touching him. "I have to speak with Sig," she said, and she too was off.

A SWIRL OF light and Zoe appeared. When she came into focus, she didn't say a word. She hovered, taking in the scene. Sig's cool, deep blue eyes were earnest and contemplative as he stared out over some sort of camp situated in an area cleared of the leafy yellow trees that surrounded it. There was lots of activity. There seemed to be one central figure who stood at the center directing others who scurried from tent to tent. Zoe thought there was something familiar the central figure, but from their distance upon a hill, she couldn't pinpoint it. Sig was evaluating, trying to grasp something. She had no idea what she was looking at. She knew only they were on Guastamo Cavanus.

There was emotion in Sig's face. Zoe dared not speak. But to channel it, that was the challenge. That's why she'd followed him, right? She needed to do something.

Zoe thought back to her early study of emotional philosophy. Most emotion sprang from deeply ingrained memory from early developmental years or from dreams, maybe from both. Emotion was to be controlled. It was to be examined for usefulness. There were some doctors of philosophy among advanced humanity who held that emotion was the catalyst of all evil. The most respected of her teachers held this view. Without dispassionate observation of the self, one could not understand what it meant to be human, he had argued. She had bought it at that time. But after many orbits of independent study, research, and living, she wasn't so sure anymore. Yes, dispassionate study was key to *scientific* advancement. The question was, did that equate to *human* advancement?

What to do? She'd not seen Sig like this before. He was a

thoughtful person, given to introspection before speaking, but he was staring inwardly and said nothing. Sig always said *something* after searching his thoughts, even if it was a non sequitur. Something. This time, he had nothing.

After a time, Sig seemed to let go of his mental clench. They stood on a rock, jutting out from one of the hills encasing the camp, with swaying limbs around them. The amber earth of the clearing on which tents stood provided some relief from the bright yellows of the forest. He turned to her, but she spoke first, "You are upset over what Reggie has done?" Zoe said. "I contacted Earthfolk too."

"That's not important right now. There is danger, and I don't mean from the Academy," Sig said.

"But it is important. This whole thing is tied to emotion. Humanity has suppressed it, and for good reason. But it is still part of us. Maybe it's not as integral to our existence and daily lives as it is for Earthfolk, but it *is* still present," Zoe said.

"I can't discuss philosophy right now. There is a lot you don't know, Zoe," Sig said.

"Enlighten me."

"I've seen things in The Beyond," Sig said.

"Well, we're on the edge right now. Show me," Zoe said.

"There is danger from a great darkness, a darkness vaster than we have ever known or even imagined," Sig said.

Zoe paused to think. Warm humid air pulled on her face. "You believe that darkness is getting closer. Where might this darkness first penetrate *the link*? Would it be logical to assume that the entry point would be at the edge of what is known? Near the very spot where we stand?" Zoe said.

"Yes," Sig said.

"You're afraid. You fear for Reggie and me?" Zoe said.

Sig continued to stare at the waves of grain as he spoke, "It's not just you and Reggie. Although, I do care for you both."

"Fear is an emotion like any other. It can be destructive, but it can also temper other emotions that threaten bad outcomes," Zoe said. She pictured Reggie's Earthfolk friend, Lisa. "Think about what Reggie is trying to do. Wouldn't the introduction of Earthfolk energy to *the link* increase the intensity of the light, which we believe strengthens us against the darkness? Even if they are relatively few in number, adding them could help," Zoe said.

Zoe circled around to look Sig in the eyes.

"You don't understand. You haven't seen what I've seen, Zoe," Sig said.

"I see you. I really see you, Sig. You yearn for expression, for understanding, for love and respect. You are a great person, perhaps greater than all of us. You are at your noblest and belong most to our community when you put others before yourself, which is exactly what you did when you brought Reggie and I together and gave up your own work. I say we go back to the lab and help Reggie sort out this mess, share what we know—which is substantial—and look to do another experiment. One that will succeed, with all of us working together. What do we have to lose?" Zoe said.

Sig began sobbing, almost uncontrollably. Zoe watched him cry. She was astonished, too moved to offer words.

"I am in love with Madam the Physical Scientist of Venus. I have been for a long time. Venusfolk subjugate the males on their planet, but I love her anyway. It is irrational. It is a problem. It is passionate. I am ruined," Sig said.

"Holy ferrous fissures!" Zoe said.

23

FOLLOWING THE RULES

"I S THERE NOBODY on this team who's following the rules?" Reggie asked, shaking his head.

Reggie's confidence had returned after Zoe and Sig returned to the lab filled him in on their respective transgressions. His visage became more vivid than ever. The burden of acting alone had weighed on him. The sense that he had betrayed them had weighed on him. But these weights were lifting. Zoe had much more depth of character than Reggie had ever imagined. And Sig—well, Sig was human after all. He loved a Venusfolk. Reggie understood. It wasn't that different from his feelings for Lisa.

"OK. We need to meet with Lisa again. There has to be a way to undo the effects of my wave transmission. But first, let's see all of your current findings. Zoe, you go first. Sig looks like he needs a minute." Reggie glanced at Sig, whose face was blotchy and red. Had he been crying? The old boy needed to get a grip.

Waves of light and dark spaces alternated in the examining glass the three hovered before. Sig moved forward and said, "No. I will speak. Thank you, Reggie. I am . . . First, I must apologize —" Sig started to say.

Reggie interrupted, waving him off, "I said we're not going to do that. I think it would take too long for each of us to apologize to each other."

"—for my emotional outburst," continued Sig, ignoring Reggie. "It was unbecoming of me. I shall give my data along with recommendations. I will see our experiment through to the end, and then I will terminate my commitment to USC and my commission from the Academy."

"Sig . . ." Reggie started to object.

"It is the honorable thing to do," Sig kept on. "And I need to do it before I am forced to do it. Right, then. I elected to physically remove two subjects from the desert of New Mexico. They are friends in direct proximal contact with one another. I further elected to introduce them to Venusfolk, a decision I now realize may have been influenced by my own emotions and desires. At the time, I reasoned that it was done for the potential softening or expanding of the Earthfolk's understanding of community and their receptiveness to the broadness of human life. Both subjects have an abiding interest in space, and one of them is a man of science, while the other is quite spiritual. In keeping them together and observing their dynamics, I sought to augment my study of Earthfolk by including Venusfolk. I have prior experience with Venusfolk as well as Earthfolk, and I believed the two different Folk could support each other, much as Reggie hoped for with his group experiment. I believed Venusfolk dynamics would blend well with the Earthfolk need for belonging. Based on my observations, I formed the opinion that Venusfolk were better candidates for connection to *the link*. I came prepared to recommend that we shift the focus of our efforts to Venusfolk. I see now, however, that my judgement was impaired. Therefore, I shall report only my observations of the Earthfolk subjects, as prescribed. In summary, based on the documented fear quotients, I am comfortable with one of my subjects being exposed to *the link*, but not both. I hold my recommendation on Venusfolk in abeyance. They may in fact be viable. I am not sure why my experiment was successful when your experiment, Reggie, was not."

Reggie felt the gravity of Sig's uncertainty. He sympathized, and his respect for Sig grew. He was a man of integrity and inspiration, illicit affairs with Venusfolk aside. He made a mental note to express this to Sig, but he had a fire growing in him now. He looked at Zoe. "Zoe, let's have it. I have to get back to Lisa," he said.

The three researchers hovered in their lab in Earth's galactic neighborhood. The visual acuity was intense as Zoe prepared to communicate. The red clouds surrounding the lab seemed deeper to Reggie, almost angry. But of course, that was silly. The red of anger shouldn't and couldn't be associated with Zoe.

She lightly bit her lower lip and began, "I believe our fundamental approach is a bit off. We all recognize the role of emotion and fear in the Earthfolk paradigm, but what we fail to appreciate is the change that takes place in Earthfolk as they age. I would argue that this holds true for us as well, but that's a whole other topic. Why have we focused on adults? Is it ethics? Do we feel that interacting with children would somehow invalidate the integrity of the data? Why? My research points to a purity in children that fades over time in Earthfolk. This slow fade culminates in the thoughts, memories, and behaviors that we all agree make introducing them to *the link* problematic.

"I have been studying a family unit. Initially, this was to gauge a target adult's support element needs. Metadata from Academy archives show a ratio of eleven to two, male to female, in terms of the sex of historic target subjects. They have been 100 percent adults. Why have we historically weighted toward males in our studies? Why do we choose only adults? I believe it is because traditional scholars have always considered children undeveloped. That may be true, but they are also untainted. My research indicates that the placidity inherent in *the link* is mirrored in the mind of my Earthfolk child subject. I recommend we target a child. More specifically, a female child. This won't resolve the issue of male Earthfolk violence, but it may get us closer to understanding the true capacity of Earthfolk humans."

Reggie considered Zoe in her entirety. She was remarkable not only in appearance but in substance. Like Sig and him, she continued to project in Earthfolk attire, which emphasized her delicate frame. What she was saying made sense. She seemed to gather magnetism as she spoke. He was drawn to her. "Go on," Reggie encouraged.

"I have developed an emotion filter that I believe is very accurate at parsing Earthfolk emotional communication. It should help enormously with the theoremific instruction infusion during wave transmission. I retrieved a set of data from the Academy archives that you may find interesting. It relates to an isolated Earthfolk transmission that passed near—or some say passed through—*the link*. I'm referring to the data from an anomalous signal that first led to the discovery of Earth and Venus. It was the sound of a human laughing, one of the most fundamental human communications. It exists in humans prior to learned behavior. It is similar to the innate need for belonging. I took this extract from the Earthfolk signal and used it alone as a baseline in my study of the family unit. I discovered that the laughter of the child is unrestrained and evinces a purity that is lacking in the adult. Why would Earthfolk intentionally submit a laugh into the universe? The golden record, they called it. I suggest that it is a defining *human* characteristic, not limited to Folk. Also, they connect with a higher power, especially as children."

"Enough! There should be no experiment," Sig broke in. "What if the reason for Earthfolk violence is unknowable? What if what lies out past The Beyond is a soulless reflection of humanity and we just can't see it—yet? It moves closer to us, perhaps to dominate us, if we haven't let it in ourselves already."

Sig loosened his bow tie. Not getting the relief he sought, he undid the tie completely and slid it slowly from his neck. With one hand, he crumpled it into a ball and stuffed it into his jacket pocket. Still not getting relief, he removed his jacket. Looking around the lab in an almost confused state, he slowly folded the jacket in half, then flung it like a disk without looking where it flew, the image of it disappearing in space. First the revelation that he was in love with a Venusfolk, and now his image disrobing in front of them. What was going on?

Sig continued, "I believe the possibility of self-destruction goes unaddressed, not only in our research but by the Universal Study Collective and the Academy. It is metaphysical, to be sure, but prescient. What is the moral rubric that guides us? If others, beside myself, have seen into The Beyond, they have ignored the philosophical implications and relied on an age-old ethic, which smacks of complacence."

"I think we have to stay focused on Reggie's Earthfolk experiment," Zoe said.

"Agreed," Reggie said.

Zoe smiled and said, "My vetting of Earthfolk has convinced me of the need for emotional support among the subjects. Reggie was on to something in using a group; the bond just needs to be deeper, though. And I believe we have that same need for support. Sig, as long as you are thinking of your Venus love, you are distracted. I think you should go to her and bring her here while we formulate emotional waves. That positive energy could help us."

Sig said nothing, only shook his head in frustration.

"I'd like to check something out, myself. Then we can meet back here and hopefully find a way to jump-start these poor

Folk. Reggie, you should go to Earth and . . . your Lisa. The Earthfolk group needs you there. It is where you want to be," Zoe said without looking at Reggie.

Reggie tried to discern her temperament. The way her words tapered off, it was as if she expected him to say something. She turned to leave.

"Wait," Reggie said.

She turned back quickly, a hint of a smile forming on her face.

"Where are you going?" he said.

The almost-smile flattened immediately. "GC. Something about it has been troubling me," she said, and was gone.

The surrounding space had indeed turned crimson.

24

NOT MUCH TO SEE

"I WANT TO watch you do it," Lisa said.

"There's not much to see," Reggie said.

"I'll be the judge of that. Let me watch, and I'll tell you whether or not there is something to see," Lisa said.

"There's really nothing," Reggie said.

Lisa lowered her eyebrows, and the left side of her mouth curved into a frown.

Reggie, anxious to get started and perceiving intractability in Lisa's face, acquiesced. He asked Lisa to show him to the rooms where the trauma patients were being observed, then gave her instructions. She was to arrange for privacy. She was to say and do nothing once they were alone. She was not to move, not to say anything, not to do anything. She agreed, and off they went through the labyrinth of the hospital.

The patients were in the intensive care unit in a special section that was surrounded by a clear plastic tent. Inside, they lay in beds surrounded by accordion-style curtains that didn't go all the way around, so those on the outside could watch them carefully. There were six patients in all. It was late, but there were still some family members at the perimeter of the clear plastic tent, keeping an eye on their respective loved ones.

Reggie pulled Lisa aside. "We need to be alone with the patients."

"I got it," she said.

Reggie stood back while Lisa approached one of the three people camped outside the tent and introduced herself. The others, sensing the potential for precious information, quickly gravitated toward her. Once she had greeted each relative with a handshake, Lisa buffeted them with procedural jargon and medical nomenclature. By the looks of the scraggly bunch, they were too tired to process what she was saying. She could have been giving instructions for how to make crusty macaroni and cheese, for all they knew. What they did understand was that they needed to leave the ICU floor for a bit. The lovely doctor was going to do some tests. She assured them she would contact them herself the moment she was done. She promised to do everything possible to diagnose and treat their loved ones.

Even from a distance, Reggie could tell she was good with them. There was touching and lots of eye contact. She even got them to smile, which was remarkable, under the circumstances. Reggie could sense their emotional upheaval. He felt a pang of guilt as he watched Lisa at work. There was no doubt her priority was helping these people. It was clear everyone had confidence in her, especially Poonam Murthy's husband. He was sufficiently moved to hug Lisa before leaving the area. Reggie heard the man say, "Thank God for you." Reggie hoped he could back up the confidence they had in Dr. K. He was eager to get zapping.

After the last of the family members left, Reggie went to Lisa.

"OK, now we need the nurses to take a walk."

"Got it," she said.

She marched over to the nurses' station. There were two

nurses and what appeared to be an intern or another doctor. Within a minute, the little crowd was chuckling. Lisa was amazing. Then, one by one, they left the area. Remarkable.

She trotted back to the tent, all smiles. Beautiful.

"Good to go," she said.

Reggie took her in for a second. She was in her element.

He composed himself. "OK, you remember the deal? You don't move. You do nothing. You say nothing. Clear?"

"Yes, sir," she said, saluting, still smiling. She was optimistic, certainly more optimistic than Reggie. She thought this is going to work. He hoped it would.

"OK, shall we?" he held the crinkled plastic flap of the tent open for her. There was a yellow balloon with the words GET WELL SOON in red script tied to a chair where one of the family members had been sitting. It was the last thing Reggie looked at before entering the tent.

Reggie closed the flap behind them. Lisa looked at him and nodded. He understood this to mean that she was now on her best behavior. The pressure in Reggie's mind mounted. He wasn't used to all these feelings. He was going to have to calm himself before he could start the process. He'd already decided he was going to try a female first. A female, he reasoned, may have just a hint of an advantage over a male for the reversal. He hadn't told Lisa this, but he was going to use dream theory, engaging the posterior cortical region of the brain, along with theoremifics in such a way that if it did work, anything they might have seen when Reggie had first transmitted to them would seem like a dream they had after passing out. He and Lisa both knew there was small amount of brain activity in the comatose patients, though Lisa had said it wasn't anything that would sustain functioning. Reggie was reasonably sure they were experiencing a kind of dreaming completely new to them. He was confident the dream theory part of the wave formula would work. If the theoremifics part, the emotional part, held up, perhaps they wouldn't get overwhelmed again.

The more he was around them, the more sympathetic Reggie became to Earthfolk fragility. Before this experiment, he hadn't really had an appreciation for how mind-blowing the exposure to multiple new waves could be. He had understood it intellectually, but he was starting to feel it viscerally now that he was in his corporeal form so much and thinking almost entirely in Earthfolk terms.

Gradually, he eased his mind into thinking in cool, scientific, unemotional terms. He loosened himself from Earthfolk constructs. He wasn't sure how long this took in Earthfolk time, but he was fairly sure it wasn't long enough to jeopardize their privacy. He was getting to where he needed to be. He considered Lisa, her rosy cheeks as she'd trotted over from the nurses' station. Was she a distraction? He didn't think so. He would use her for inspiration, to summon the requisite emotion.

Reggie stood rigidly still.

LISA TOOK REGGIE'S instructions seriously. She tried to stay perfectly still. She thought she detected a twitch in her left index finger. Then she felt that she had tilted her head just a fraction. She was coming to the conclusion that she wasn't very good at staying perfectly still. She watched Reggie, hoping her eye movements didn't count. She was waiting for him to reach into his pocket and take out a device, which he would tinker with. He'd point it at Mrs. Murthy, the one he seemed to have settled on, and an electrical current would shoot into her cranium like a low-intensity lightning bolt. She had it all worked out. Only none of that was happening. Reggie was just standing there. The professional and moral risk she was taking in believing this man, this spaceman with his wave frequencies and tunnels, was irrational at best.

Lisa continued to watch him. She wondered if her balance was a bit off. It wasn't. She wanted to take a step. She didn't. Reggie just stood there looking at Mrs. Murthy. Then he looked at Lisa. She looked back. He was considering her. She wondered if she was allowed to smile. She opted for caution and didn't. Then he turned back to Mrs. Murthy. Lisa thought about his look. He definitely liked her. Did he love her? Heavy. Didn't he know that intergalactic romances never worked out? She suppressed a chuckle. She couldn't even make an interstate romance work. But seriously. This was heavy.

Reggie seemed to relax his whole body. He stepped closer to Mrs. Murthy, walking around to where her head rested on the pillow. He hunched over and whispered in her ear. Lisa couldn't hear what he was saying. Damn. She wanted to move closer, but she was committed to remaining frozen. For the sake of those in her care, she wasn't going to move until Reggie said it was OK.

Mrs. Murthy began to wriggle. She sprang up, eyes wide open. She said something, probably in Hindi, then collapsed. Lisa hadn't thought to unhook the monitors. She was going to need to get to the nurses' station quickly if they were going to do this undetected.

Reggie shook his head. He stood and whispered, "It didn't work."

Lisa unfroze, flipped a switch on the monitor, and bolted for the nurses' station, where red lights were flashing from a console and an annoying buzz was coming from somewhere. She worked some controls, and all seemed restored. The two nurses from earlier came strolling in. They each had a cup of coffee and were quietly talking. Lisa stood and chatted with them for a few minutes, then returned to the tent. Reggie was sitting on a stool, looking at Mrs. Murthy.

"You zapped her?" Lisa said.

"I did," he answered.

"There should be a recording of her neural activity. I've had these folks hooked up to monitors since they came in. Let me download the readings. I'll need the laptop from my office. I told the nurses to let the patients rest and that you would be observing them. Put this on—you'll look less suspicious."

She pulled a scrunched-up surgical mask from her pocket, handed it to him, then left.

REGGIE SAT CONSIDERING his options. He could cut his losses if he used dream theory on Lisa now. She would most likely be able to live a normal Earthfolk life. The longer she was exposed to him and his contaminating ideas, the harder it would be to get her awareness back to where it was before he started tinkering. These patients, on the other hand, seemed like a lost cause. But he'd vowed to do all he could. He was conflicted. All of his ethical training didn't mean much once he'd gone down the slippery slope of experimentation on live subjects in violation of Academy protocol and law. The Academy would punish him harshly, and he would welcome it. At this point, all he wanted was to get these Earthfolk back to functionality.

He briefly considered if there was anything the Academy could do to help these people. Sadly, he knew the Academy would do what it had done numerous times before: isolate the breach, neutralize the contamination, and assign these Folk to the historical archive of failed field experimentation. Lisa would be designated as one of the contaminated. Part of him knew this was the correct course. He didn't have to like it, and he didn't have to submit to it just yet. But the reckoning was coming.

· · ·

REGGIE WASN'T SURE how long he'd been sitting with his eyes closed, when he heard a collective chuckle coming from the direction of the nurses' station. He took it Lisa was back. The laughter got louder. It was still going strong when the tent flap peeled open and Lisa walked in. She wasn't smiling. She pulled a mask from her pocket, covered her face, and went to work. She connected a cable from her laptop to a machine that sat atop a wheeled cart. The machine had wires running to little round electrode patches stuck to Mrs. Murthy's head with conductive gel.

After pecking a few keys, Lisa slid another stool close to the machine and sat watching her laptop. The voices from the nurses' station died down, allowing for what passed for hospital quiet. Reggie noticed the low beeps coming from heart rate monitors attached to the other tent patients. The sound of air flowing through ducts all around them was interspersed with an occasional thump or click. The percussion provided backup to the heart rate beeps in a low-key rhythmic tune common in hospitals everywhere.

Reggie pushed himself up off his stool, still listening to the hospital room sounds. He looked at Lisa. She was fixated on her laptop. He walked to the tent flap, turned, and looked at her again. She glanced his way. All he could see were two hopeful eyes over the surgical mask. Pretty.

He stepped outside the tent. As he closed the flap, he ran his fingers down the thin plastic. The smoothness of it struck him. This material wasn't meant to keep anyone out but to contain what was inside. He looked toward the nurses' station. Two nurses were seated there, both writing something. Reggie sat down and watched them. They had no idea what was going on here. No one did. They had put up their tent to contain what was unknown to them.

He listened. He could still hear the faint beeping and thumping. It had a familiar sound. Sad. He replayed the electromagnetic transmission he'd given Mrs. Poonam Murthy in his mind. Why hadn't it worked? Lisa's theory was sound. He had zapped her, and she was more or less fine. It should have worked again. He had attached his feelings for Lisa to the wave. They were tender. He thought of her face, her blond hair. Beautiful.

The faint hospital tune continued. He wanted to get in there and save these Earthfolk. His shoulder and neck muscles were tight. He was experiencing fatigue. Corporeal form was having an effect on him. He tilted his head back. As he did, his eye caught the GET WELL SOON balloon. It had come loose and was bumping around on the ceiling. In his mind's eye, he saw another balloon. It was the one Zoe had given to him long ago during the Earthfolk exercise at the circus. That's what he had in his mind when he'd zapped Lisa—the feelings he had from that time, that gesture from Zoe. It was pure. It was *love*. He'd infused love into the wave he'd zapped Lisa with. Not love for Lisa, but for Zoe.

His heartbeat quickened. That's why the Murthy wave had failed. It wasn't complete. It had affection, but it didn't have the right genuine selfless emotion. Sig had a *relationship* with a Venusfolk female. That's what he'd been thinking about when he'd transmitted to his test subjects. *That's* why it had worked so well. It made sense that Folk would need a strong emotion to stabilize them. *The link*, as used by wider humanity throughout the universe, worked because emotion was removed from all, transmitter and receiver alike. There was an equilibrium. But with Folk, emotion pervaded essence. Love was a balancing factor. But what was it exactly?

If Reggie had been hooked to a monitor, the red lights and buzzers at the nurses' station would have overloaded their circuits.

Reggie burst into the tent. "I need you to leave."

Lisa looked up from her laptop. "What?"

"I need you to leave. Please," he said.

"I have to look at these readings. I'm sure I can figure something out, identify an anomaly. I'll be darned if I don't see an excitation in the posterior cortical area of her brain," Lisa said.

"Please leave," he said again. Reggie didn't look at her when he said it. He was concerned that looking her in the eyes would stir up emotion that would confuse him. He would get distracted from the powerful emotion he was feeling. He knew it was love, and he didn't want to lose it, not one bit of it. It was a feeling he couldn't describe to himself. It made him warm and tingly. It joined him with Zoe, even though she was . . . he knew not where. He wasn't connecting to her through *the link,* but he *was* connected to her. It was amazing.

"What are you going to do?" Lisa asked.

"I'm going to try again, and I need for you to not be here."

"I didn't move. OK, maybe just a twitch. But I did everything you said."

"It's not that, Lisa. I just need you to leave. Don't talk to the nurses. Don't make them laugh. Leave the ICU entirely. Come back in about twenty minutes."

Lisa didn't say anything. She began disconnecting her laptop, and not in a graceful way. She yanked the cable from the machine, practically slammed the laptop shut, kicked the stool out behind her, and stormed out of the tent. Reggie refused to look at her. She marched directly to the exit and was gone.

Reggie walked slowly to Mrs. Murthy's side. He looked at her face. He wondered if she loved her husband. He wondered if it was her husband's balloon that was flitting around the ICU ceiling. He was sure this time he would be able to restore these people. He walked around the tent, looking at each of the subjects. He knew them by name. He knew the names they used in the Cosmos forum. It was Lisa's forum username, MindOvr-

Matr, that had first caught his attention back when he was monitoring test subjects for transmission. There was OdysseyLady2001—that was Poonam. Reggie recalled her sitting alone behind her motel when he'd transmitted to her. She'd spilled her juice. There was Profesora_Erg, also known as Mariluz Ramos, and her friend Starwatcher424, Paulina Fernandez. They had been having such a delightful time at the coffee shop before he'd transmitted to them. Then there was StarSurveyor, George 'Fitz' Fitzhugh, and AlienWheelman, Edwin Figueroa, along with Martino "Tino" Martinez, who used his own name on the forum. Reggie had nearly missed transmitting to the men by the bridge. As it turned out, he had messed up, but by nearly frying their brains, not by missing them. They all seemed to be in a strange state as they lay in their beds. They were the same people they'd always been, but there were no smiles, no laughing in a coffee shop about silver foxes or chuckling inside a truck about cold water. They were a sad sight. They didn't deserve this.

In a surge of confidence, Reggie made the decision to do all six at once. He was sure they wouldn't be able to respond. It was a calculated risk. If they were able to respond, *his* mind would become overwhelmed. He looked toward the nurses' station—three nurses and two orderlies. He wouldn't need but a minute. He'd risk it. They would probably think he was praying, standing there with his arms stretched out over the patients.

REGGIE PAUSED OUTSIDE the half-open door of Lisa's office. He could hear the squeak of wheels rolling around and a drawer sliding open. He peeked inside. Lisa was sitting in her desk chair, which she had rolled across the room to a filing cabinet in the corner. She was fingering her way through files in the cabinet.

"I hope you're looking for Mr. Murthy's phone number," he said, triumph in his eyes.

Lisa turned her head. "What are you saying?"

"I'm saying there are six patients sleeping downstairs. They're OK, not comatose, just sleeping," Reggie said with a smile.

He waited for a reaction. Lisa sat staring at him. He watched her closely. There were shadows under her eyes that he hadn't noticed before. She was tired.

Finally, in a low voice, she said, "So you did it? You woke them?"

"Not exactly. They're still asleep and should wake up naturally."

"And they are OK? They have all of their cognitive function?" she asked.

"As far as I can tell, yes. You will have to evaluate them yourself, but I'm fairly certain they are all fine. Also, you'll have to talk to the nurses in ICU; I'm pretty sure they've called security on me. Apparently, there's no Reginald Homer in any of their medical practitioner databases, and my USC ID card doesn't seem to have much authority here," he said with a smile.

Lisa stood and slid the cabinet door closed with her hip. "Well, I guess you did it, Reggie. I'd give you a big hug, but I wouldn't want you to get the wrong idea."

Reggie looked back at Lisa and said, "I'm afraid I must once again apologize. I don't love you. I didn't mean for you to fall in love with me—"

"Whoa, whoa, whoa, there, space cowboy! Who said anything about me loving you?"

Reggie felt heat rising in his face. "I assumed that since I developed strong affection for you—something . . . in the vicinity . . . of . . . love—that you quite naturally felt the same."

"It doesn't really work like that, Reggie," she said, approaching him.

He took a half step back, thought for a moment, then stepped forward again. "Lisa, how does it work? Love—how does it work?"

"Damned if I know, Reggie. The love I had, I lost. I was too stupid to make it work. I can tell you how it doesn't work—you can't make it work by being apart from the one you care about most in the world, or the universe, as the case may be."

"So, it is something you must *make* work. You've been in love?" Reggie said.

"Yes. I think I still am," Lisa said.

"How can you still be in love? You said it was lost. You couldn't make it work. I'm confused."

"Welcome to my world, Dr. Homer. And I mean that quite literally," she said, reaching out to shake his hand.

Reggie was reluctant to take her hand. He didn't know what he would feel. Instead, he asked, "What should we tell them when they wake up? Certainly not the truth."

"Let's get them moved to regular rooms so we can have some privacy with them. We'll just tell them they passed out. I'll need to evaluate them individually anyway," Lisa said.

PAULINA LOOKED TO her right, and there was Mariluz, asleep. There were two people, a man and a woman, sitting in the corner of the room near the doorway. The woman wore a white lab coat. They must be in a hospital. The woman's hair was long and blond, the man's dark and curly. They were young. Paulina didn't move except to eye her surroundings. The last thing she remembered was having coffee with Mariluz and talking about a new school administrator, the one Mariluz described as a silver fox. She remembered telling Mariluz that there would be no silver foxes in her future. They'd made plans for their visit to the Very Large Array, where Mariluz was excited to meet AlienWheelman from their Cosmos Forum group. She remembered leaving the coffee shop. Mariluz had said *hasta luego* to the barista, and they'd gone outside. Then everything went white. That was all she could remember.

FITZ OPENED HIS eyes. He was lying on his side. The first thing he saw was Tino in a hospital gown, sitting on the side of the bed across from him.

Tino blessed himself and smiled. "*Jefe*. Thank God. I thought you were never going to wake up."

"Tino? Where are we?" Fitz said, feeling rested but confused.

"Hospital," said Tino.

"What happened?"

Tino laughed and shook his head. "I don't know. I just remember being in the truck and joking with Edwin about the *agua fría*. Then I passed out and thought I was going to hell, because everything was red, but then I didn't, and then I was behind the truck on the ground, and that's it, *jefe*. Weird, huh?"

POONAM MURTHY OPENED her eyes. She blinked several times and rubbed her eyes. She yawned, but she didn't feel tired. She was hooked up to an intravenous tube. She was in a hospital. There was a small plastic cup of water on a small table next to her. That reminded her of the orange juice she was sipping as she sat behind the motel. She remembered checking her email, being drawn in by the static on her screen, and then . . .

In the middle of her thought, she noticed her husband sitting at her feet. He stood.

Poonam half sat up, looking at him. He was smiling. She frowned.

"That laptop you gave me is garbage."

25

HUMAN UNDERSTANDING

"I'M HEADING BACK to my apartment, unless you need me somewhere else?" Lisa asked.

"That is fine," Reggie said, lost in thought.

"Everything OK?" she asked.

"Yes, fine," Reggie answered. He looked out of the sixth-floor window of the empty hospital room in which they'd convened. "What will you do now?"

"First order of business is to take a shower. Then I need to evaluate my patients for residual damage. What about you? Should I schedule a press conference to announce that you're here? The amazing Dr. Homer's Road Show comes to Earth!"

"Not quite," he said.

He shook his head and became quiet again, looking out the window.

"Didn't think you'd go for that," she said, joining him at the window. "So, what? You're going to leave now? Just like that, after all this? I have so many questions about the universe, about how the link works, about life. What do we do now?" she said, continuing to look out at the sky.

He stared down at the flat land outside. He thought of Zoe. It occurred to him that he loved her and had for a long time. He wanted things to slow down so that he could be with her. But how was he going to rein things in now after all his passionate calls to action? Should he continue the experiment with Zoe and Sig's targets, now that he had the elusive element needed for a proper transmission formula? Time was short. Should they continue with Zoe's Earthfolk child? He needed to see Zoe and Sig. He would ask them, let them decide what to do. It's what he should've done before. He didn't have the heart to tell Lisa that he still needed to scramble the eggs in her brain. It could wait.

"You are a woman of faith? Is that the expression?" Reggie asked, turning to Lisa.

"Yes, that's the expression. And yes, I am. Why do you ask? What do your people believe?"

Reggie looked out the window again, up at the sky. He knew he had to deal with correcting Lisa's mind; but the thought of this troubled him. Lisa's interactions with her fellow Folk flowed naturally from her faith. This had become apparent to Reggie when he was first considering her for inclusion in his grand theoremific wave experiment. He'd become invested in her almost from the beginning because of it. One of his first observations of Lisa came to his mind. He recalled the scene in this very hospital that had drawn him to Lisa.

"THERE IS NOTHING you can say to justify the suffering. Life is a misery. I only want it to stop, and it never does. Why? Why is this allowed to happen? They give me medicine that numbs the pain and numbs my mind. Yeah, the drugs allow me to sleep, but I suffer in my dreams. When I wake up, my mind is dense like a block of firewood. I feel like I'm holding this wood, my mind, in my hands. I can measure the weight of it, feel the thickness of it. Slowly it heats up, then burns to ash and slips through my fingers, and I'm left with nothing but gray-black soot. My thoughts return, and they're dark, and I despise myself for being a miserable creature. I dislike other people because they don't suffer and because they continue to enjoy all the simple things that I can't. I hate them all. I hate you. Now, tell me, Doctor, what you came here to say," the patient said.

Reggie had stood in the doorway of the hospital room, listening to the conversation between Lisa and a patient, who had apparently suffered a stroke resulting in painful nerve damage.

"You know, you are not alone. There are many *good* people who suffer. Some of them find a measure of meaning in it, even peace," Lisa said. She was patient and kind, sitting close to the man.

"Wonderful. They must be insane. And knowing that good people suffer just proves my point. It's a miserable world," the man said, staring at Lisa, an implacable scowl chiseled into his jowls.

"They're not insane. You told me you used to be a man of faith. Some people find comfort in knowing that they do not suffer alone and that their reward will be great if they suffer in humility and in faith. It is at the time of their worst suffering that they are closest to the divine," Lisa said.

"Are you telling me they choose to suffer to be closer to God?" the man said.

"It is not that they choose suffering. They merely accept it as part of being human. Just as they accept the providence of the nearness of God and, because of their burden, dependence on Him. Do you think you suffer as punishment or for no reason at all? No. It's just the opposite. Your suffering could be an opportunity for deeper meaning in your life," Lisa said.

Quiet took hold as the man pondered. A low beep from a

depleted intravenous drip going into his arm was the only sound until the man rolled over with a sigh.

"Please go. I despise you and everyone else," the man said.

"No, you don't," Lisa said, shaking her head dismissively.

"I hate everyone," the man said, turning his head back toward Lisa and chuckling.

"No, you don't. You said you despise yourself for being miserable," Lisa said.

The man held tough. "Everyone, everything, is ugly."

"No, it isn't. Especially not you," Lisa said. She tucked in the sheet at his side.

"It's all a lot of hot air, Doctor. You don't know. Why aren't *you* suffering? If suffering is such a gift, why aren't you doing it?" he said.

"I am suffering right now," she said.

The man smiled broadly. "Very funny."

"We all have our crosses to bear. I am not God. I cannot presume to think like God. I just want you to know that you are not alone. I will pray for you. I hope you can find meaning in your low time. The Lord is with you and waits only for you to welcome him in and fill your heart. Please let me know if there is anything I can do for you," Lisa concluded.

Reggie had watched from the doorway as Lisa placed her hand on the man's bed, closed her eyes, presumably in prayer, and walked out.

Reggie had hustled out of view so Lisa could walk past without noticing him. He followed her to the elevator. Once the doors closed, he dashed for the stairs, reaching the lobby just as the elevator doors slid open again. Lisa walked out with her head down, clearly contemplating her conversation with the miserable man. She made her slow way to the coffee station in the hospital cafeteria. He remembered how it seemed to him that she was carrying a heavy burden.

. . .

NOW, LOOKING UP at the sky, having Lisa near to him, he wondered why she had taken on the unnecessary anguish of talking to the man about pain and suffering and faith. Did she really believe what she'd said, or had it just been an attempt to ease the man's pain, part of her duties as a physician? In either case, it was an eminently rational position that she'd espoused. He could see how it would help these Earth humans make sense of bad things happening, including violence.

Lisa had been trying to enlighten the man, in her own way. But why hadn't this particular form of enlightenment come up before as a mitigating factor in the risk of Folk connection to *the link*? Why hadn't the spirituality of Earthfolk been addressed by the Academy or USC? Arcane mythology, false hope. Surely that was it. But then it should have been addressed as a pitfall to avoid. It was rarely mentioned in current treatises on Folk suitability for *the link.*

The Academy represented the apex of human understanding; that's what everyone was taught from an early age. He turned the phrase over in his mind—*human understanding.* The apex of *human* understanding. Lisa had said she was not God and could not think as God. Maybe all humanity got were hints, clues to follow. Who was to say that pain and suffering weren't totally necessary? Maybe he and the researchers of USC had misinterpreted the violence and fear in Earthfolk. Maybe Earthfolk's true flaw was a lack of understanding of their own emotion, their own meaning. If this was true, then the Academy, USC, and he possessed the same flaw. Was trying to extinguish emotion and therefore pain and suffering truly noble? It seemed advance humanity needed to get its own act together before expanding, before *elevating* Folk.

Was *the link* a gift from God? Here they were riding a wave of human understanding. But was it a pathetic apex, this understanding? According to what Lisa had said, the spiritual and the emotional were intertwined and directed toward the divine. Yet the suppression of emotion and spirituality was promoted, institutionalized, throughout greater humanity in the universe in order to minimize suffering through *the link*. A worthy goal, to be sure, but what were the side effects of life without pain?

How could he approach the Academy with this arcane wisdom he seemed to have stumbled upon? Even in the most liberal corners of USC, it would be a tough sell. The Academy would think his work was fringe, and USC had caved to the Academy's oversight. This understanding of Folk spirituality would certainly be deemed pseudoscientific conjecture by even the most sympathetic of scholars. The Academy would be pleased he meant to pull back on integrating violent Earthfolk into *the link,* but they would have much consternation over his reasoning. He might fare better with USC if he slowly revealed his insights, over time. But each scenario he came up with ended with him being banished from *the link*. He knew that was inevitable, based on what he'd done. But it was hard to countenance.

Scaling back on enlightening Folk would nullify everything he'd ever worked for, everything his team had done. His team was now sold on integrating Earthfolk, and he was the chief salesman. They must cease their work with Earthfolk immediately. He needed to meet with his team.

Reggie stared out of the window. What exactly was it he was correcting in her mind? The blue sky offered no answers. What *did* his people believe?

26

GUASTAMO CAVANUS

R EGGIE WAITED ALONE in the lab. The deep red of the surrounding nebula did little to improve his mood. He thought about what Lisa had said regarding love. How if one person loved another, it didn't necessarily follow that the other person would love them, too. *It doesn't work like that,* she'd said. What if Zoe was simply a dear, sweet friend who had affection for all her friends and he had misunderstood her many kindnesses? Gloominess dimmed his presence. He needed to see Zoe alone, regardless of what they decided as a team.

Just then, there was a whirl of particles. "Really? Now?" he said to no one, preparing himself for reception.

His mother's eyes materialized.

"Reginald. Why so glum?" his mother said.

"My project has had a couple of setbacks, that's all. What are you doing here? The Collective doesn't like unauthorized people in its sensitive Folk research labs," he answered.

His mother hovered, eyeing all the virtual instruments.

"Oh, no one is worried about an old lady seeing her son for an instant. I'd like to speak with you. Your father and I have discussed it, and we strongly believe you should petition for a partner. You have been spending too much time alone. You were too distracted to have a meaningful discussion when I saw you in your classroom. I was hoping we could talk now," she said.

"Mother, if you think I was distracted in the classroom . . . I have much more pressing concerns now. Can we talk about this another time?" Reggie said.

"Reginald, you can't keep putting your own life on hold for the sake of Folk."

"Mother . . ."

"It's not healthy," she insisted.

"Mother, we can talk after my project is complete?"

"Oh, very well, dear," she said.

Slowly, she started to fade out.

"Mother, wait!" he said.

She materialized in full form again. Never having taken her eyes off of him, she was concerned and continued to peer deep into him. "Yes, what is it? Is everything all right?"

"You've been partners with Father for a long time," he said.

"I should say so, dear," she said, looking at him quizzically.

"And you love him?" Reggie asked. The question had been forming in his mind from the time his mother had first asked him about petitioning for a partner.

"Your father and I have been very well suited these many orbits," came the terse reply. She was clearly uncomfortable.

"And you love him, right?" Reggie insisted.

"Our petitions were matched perfectly, and we have lived in harmony ever since. We had you, and we prospered. Our bond deepened."

"What about love?" Reggie said.

"Love? Why do you ask about love? Reginald, you really have been spending too much time in the archaic." She eyed him closely. "It's just as I suspected. You really need to petition for a partner, and soon. I can help you. Your father can help you. Won't you let us make some inquiries on your behalf?"

"Is love too extravagant an emotion for us? Does it really lead to disruption, as Academy wisdom tells us? I believe that you love father, and I don't know why you are hesitant to admit it. I understand your apprehension about its power and the stigma placed on it, especially in academia. But surely you can tell *me*," Reggie persisted.

Her eyes bounced around the lab. She smiled and focused back on Reggie. "What does love mean to *you*?" she asked.

"That's just it—I don't know. But I want to learn. I hoped you could show me," he said.

"If I do love your father, so what? It's just a word. Peace and harmony are what we strive for. We have each other's best interest in mind always. Is that love? Call it what you want. We control our emotions, and we prosper together," she said.

"Spoken like a true Academician."

"Don't be cross, Reginald. I am trying to help you. Don't get caught up in the savage notions of Earthfolk or Venusfolk or any other Folk, for that matter. Corporeal pleasure is fleeting, and the mythology of love has been discredited by the Academy many times," she said.

Reggie wasn't sure he knew his own mind. This was unfamiliar territory for him. One thing he could always rely on was his ability to produce clear, cogent hypotheses. When emotion was removed from decision making, better decisions were made. There was no question of this. But a strange sort of clarity was creeping into his mind. As he looked at the image of his mother, she seemed the same as she had ever been, but for the first time, this didn't seem quite right. She hardly moved, only present before him as an image. He had never thought of her as an image before. She cared for him. He didn't doubt that. But why?

"Mother, I have seen deep spiritual love in Earthfolk. One

person in particular has had a profound influence on me. I observed firsthand a powerful noncorporeal love while I was vetting this test subject. Lisa has demonstrated for me a depth of altruistic potential in Folk. This is a contradiction of everything we thought we knew about Earthfolk. There is no violence in Lisa's heart—"

"Oh, my stars. Lisa? Who in the universe is *Lisa*? Have you been ensnared by one of the savages?" his mother said.

"Mother, do you know nothing of Earthfolk? They are not savage. Have you read any of my work? There is a prodigious amount of violence and suffering on Earth. That is all well established. But the capacity for peace and, yes, love is tremendous. I think it rivals our own *peace*, in its way. Maybe we are the savages, flitting around like masters of the universe, poking and prodding undeveloped worlds."

His mother scowled. "You seem to be the only one poking and prodding, Reggie."

Reggie thought through what was troubling him by speaking aloud, ostensibly to his mother. He circled her, not really looking at her, and continued, "We are not gods. But we try to think like gods. How like gods we must appear to Folk. And what sort of gods are we? Do we really have their interests in mind, or are we merely concerned with maintaining and expanding *the link*, our precious *link*? What is *the link*? I think there may be a big difference between what it's supposed to be and what it is. It is supposed to be the means by which humanity connects with each other without need for corporeal form, a natural expression of our humanity. It is supposed to be the means for shared consciousness, the propagation of knowledge, and advancement. It is supposed to represent unlimited opportunity for progress, but in its framework is the understanding that humanity has already reached the apex of its knowledge. If that is true, then what are we really doing? Have we ceased to explore our own selves because we have become gods who poke and prod others? I haven't been *ensnared*, although I can tell you truthfully that I have feelings for Lisa. That's right, *feelings* . . ."

"Oh, my stars!" his mother cut in.

". . . but I have even stronger *feelings* for someone else, someone whom I think, whom I believe, also has great depth and understanding of emotion."

His mother stopped shimmering.

"This other person, she is one of us?" his mother asked, raising an eyebrow.

"Does it matter who she is?" Reggie pleaded.

"It's not a Venusfolk, is it? They're such dull Folk. You wouldn't be able to connect with them properly through *the link*. You wouldn't be happy for long, plus they have strange notions of order—"

"I think we should talk later, Mother. I'm expecting my colleagues," Reggie said dismissively.

He was having a difficult time holding in his emotion. He thought it best that his mother leave. The last thing he wanted was for Zoe to appear while his mother was around. He didn't trust himself not to melt into a puddle of affection upon seeing Zoe for the first time in the new and tender light which he now held her. *Zoe.* The name was like a smile rising out of the pond of his mind, causing ripples in his soul. He could feel her presence when he thought of her. It was like the twisting of a velvet ratchet somewhere in his chest. Her short brown hair, straight and neat, slightly longer on one side, where it slid occasionally over a striking green eye, shading half her delicate face. Exquisite. He knew he'd been searching for her.

His mother squinted at him. She had the wisdom to say only, "Goodbye, Reggie." She began to fade, but before she disappeared, she added, "We just want you to be content, dear."

"There's more to life than chasing contentedness. Goodbye."

And she left. Reggie was now by himself again, but he didn't feel alone. Zoe's smile kept him company.

A GREAT FLOURISH of particles dusted up, without the usual advance swirl that signaled someone's approach. Sig literally popped into the lab. His pupils were almost entirely dilated. Something was wrong.

"Guastamo Cavanus is in peril!" Sig said, heading for an examining glass.

"What?"

"Guastamo Cavanus is lost," Sig said.

Sig's movements were furtive, he swirled from screen to screen, not addressing Reggie directly.

"What do you mean lost?" Reggie said.

Sig turned his head and fixed a stare at Reggie. He scowled the spoke, "I mean, there is no contact with anyone on the planet. And further, there doesn't seem to be a planet!" Sig said, turning back to the screen before him.

Reggie turned that over in his head, immediately making the connection with Earthfolk's exposure to *the link*.

"Is this us? Did we do this?" Reggie asked. "Did *I* do this?

"I don't know, maybe," Sig said.

"What communications are there?" Reggie said.

"None. As I say, there is no one who can project themselves there or establish a connection," Sig said.

"Impossible," Reggie said.

Sig shot a look at Reggie. "There is no communication," he said.

"GC doesn't appear on any of our examination glasses," Sig

said, staring into a display. "There is darkness where GC should be shining."

"There are several thousand souls on GC. Was this *me*?" Reggie asked again.

"I don't know!" Sig said.

"Has the Academy issued a statement?" Reggie asked.

"Yes. All Folk research has been suspended. All theatres of operation are to submit their research data for review immediately. The Academy has convened a meeting of the Security Council. It is anticipated they will issue a directive ordering mass reconstitution. All planets signatory to the Universal Way shall take measures to conceal themselves and inhibit transmissions," Sig said.

"They're worried about being seen? By whom?" Reggie said, a sense of foreboding rising in him.

"I think you know by whom," Sig shot back. He moved quickly around the examining glasses.

"OTH?" Reggie said.

"OTH!"

"Where's Zoe?" Reggie asked.

"Don't know."

"We need to find her," Reggie said.

"Damn. The Academy just shut down *the link*!" Sig said.

Sig stared at the examining glass before him. There was nothing but a puffy frame. There were no images inside it. It was as if he were looking through a clear glass at the nebular mist in the distance.

"I didn't know they could do that," Reggie said in disbelief. "How can everyone, everywhere, reconstitute themselves at the same time? It will overwhelm the stasis stations and food supplies. Basic needs beyond maintenance will have to be met. It won't work. Not for long. What about those who haven't yet reconstituted?" He thought for a moment. Then it occurred to him. "What about us?"

Reggie moved beside Sig and stared into the nebula. It appeared that the Academy considered the risk of everyone simultaneously being fully present in their bodies to be less than the risk posed by the destructive nature of whatever it was that had consumed Guastamo Cavanus.

"Try transmitting," Sig said.

Reggie concentrated. He got nothing.

"Damn," was all he could say. "I didn't know they could shut down *the link*. The entire *link?* How is that even possible?"

"They can, and they did. Travel will be impossible. Connecting to *the link* is not an option," Sig said.

The apparent emotion in Sig's voice affected Reggie deeply. The pain in his frantic tone differed only slightly from the stab of guilt Reggie was feeling. He saw himself as responsible, and it made him irresolute. He didn't understand how he had done it. Yes, there had been warning from the Academy, but they worried over everything. It wasn't possible for a planet to just disappear. It was still there, no doubt. It just couldn't be seen. The Academy was overreacting. But what if Guastamo Cavanus was the start of a contamination of the fabric of *the link?* Reggie felt weak.

"So, not only is research suspended, but all *link* activity, including travel, is suspended?" Reggie said.

"Looks like it," Sig responded.

"We're stuck here? In the nebula? In the lab? How do we get back to our home planets to materialize in our original corporeal forms? How do we minimize our light if we can't use *the link?*"

"I don't know." Sig said. He concentrated on the examining glass as though he were actually looking at a transmission, but there was nothing, just the silence and distant light of space. "They'll have to open *the link* after they've secured it."

"They've been securing it for eons," Reggie offered. "They'll have to open it. But wait, how are you and I able to communicate out here if *the link* is down?"

~

REGGIE AND Sig grew more and more frustrated as they tried to calibrate and recalibrate their thoughts, concentrating, trying to communicate beyond themselves. After a while, they just hovered.

Sig began to fade then swirled off. Reggie tried to follow but couldn't. After what seemed an eternity, Sig returned.

"There are a limited number of emergency portals. I've just been to Mega. I convinced the Academy we had research that may help. They're allowing waves through our lab's nebula, and have authorized our team to travel to Mega to personally brief the Security Council. We have to leave immediately. They won't leave *the link* open long, and we need to get to Venus before we go to Mega. Zoe's on her own on GC?"

"Oh, my stars!" If Reggie had been in his body, he would have collapsed. It dawned on him that Zoe said she was going to GC.

~

"LISTEN TO ME, Reggie. Let us take what information we have and go to the Academy. We'll reveal to them the violations we've committed. But first, we need to go to Venus. One of my test subjects may know something of the OTH."

"We're not going anywhere without Zoe," Reggie said.

None of the men had ever experienced anything like the feelings they were having. A profound quiet came over the two of them, and for a short time, neither moved or tried to communicate.

Reggie looked over Sig's shoulder as he tried to see Guastamo Cavanus. "You said your subject may know something," he said, turning his head toward Sig. "What?"

"There was a disturbance with one of my subjects in Venus," Sig replied. "We need to go."

"What kind of disturbance? And what happened with the one you brought back?

"We cannot worry about Stewart right now. We must get to Chase. He may have seen the OTH. And if that's true, he may be able to explain something of our present situation."

Reggie turned to Sig. "When you looked into The Beyond, what exactly did you see?"

"I've already told you. Movement," Sig answered.

"Yes, but what kind of movement, exactly?" Reggie asked.

"Just movement."

"You *saw* it? Or you deduced it from calculations?" Reggie asked.

Sig thought for a moment, then responded, "I saw it."

"What did you see?" Reggie asked again.

"Movement," Sig said.

"You're not helping," Reggie said.

"There was a shift in the darkness, a shadow," Sig said.

"How did you conclude that it would seep into *the link* with the introduction of Earthfolk? And exactly what was it that moved?" Reggie asked.

Sig suddenly looked confused, almost alarmed. He shifted his eyes left and right.

"I thought I saw a *link*," he blurted out. "A solitary pathway. But it disappeared instantly. I wasn't sure. It was so unexpected

—a flash, really. But in that instant, I thought I saw a person. A human person. And . . ."

"That's impossible," Reggie interrupted.

Sig stared past Reggie, then closed his eyes, breathed deeply, and looked at Reggie again. "The person I thought I saw at the other end of the connection was myself—in The Beyond! Fear gripped me. There was malice in my face. The whole thing was instantaneous, almost like a glitch. I never told the Academy any of this. It was bad. I believe this was the movement I saw. It makes little sense, I know."

The words struck each of the men like a splash of cold water. They looked at one another, each registering doubt.

"Sig, you must go alone to Venus? You can decide for yourself whether it's a good idea to bring your lady friend along with the Earthfolk, but you should do it immediately, while you can still travel. I will stay here. I don't accept that the entire population of GC is gone. It's . . ."

"Impossible?" Sig finished. "Like seeing yourself in The Beyond, or shutting down *the link*?"

27

JUST BEGINNING

C HASE WOKE IN darkness for the last time.
He was clothed and very warm. His face and armpits were damp with sweat. He was on his back. He felt rested and at peace. A slow drip of water was the only sound. He could smell chlorine on his shoulders. He thought about Madam the Spiritual Scientist. They had definitely been intimate. She had said something: *I am to respect you, and you are to . . . love me?* There had been an inflection in her voice on the word *love*. She'd said it just before they embraced. He smiled.

"Madam?" he said, trying to imbue the word with the tenderness he was feeling.

No response.

Chase remembered their closeness. The sweat, the smell, the heat. It was the most erotic, most sensual closeness he had ever felt. He was slightly giddy from it. Her arms were smooth passion. She had been silent. He had not. He was pretty sure he had cried, joyful tears and gasps. He remembered that for an instant, he had been scared of his own primal instincts, and then there had been light, and the fear had gone away. Then there was only gentleness.

Chase heard footsteps. "Madam?" he said softly. "Madam?"

"I am afraid not, dear boy," came a strongly accented voice.

"Sig?" Chase said.

"Yes. I have come for you, Chase. We must leave now."

"I cannot leave now. There are some things I am just beginning to understand here, not only about Venus, but about myself," Chase said.

"Sorry, old boy." Sig's voice was right behind him.

Before he could say or do anything, Sig had him in his arms, and they were moving.

28

THE ACADEMY

NOTHING LIKE THIS had ever happened before. There were catastrophes, of course—collisions of planets and objects, natural disasters—but never before had an entire planet simply gone dark without warning. There should have been some indication of energy transfer. Guastamo Cavanus had to have gone *somewhere*. There had to be some indication of a cataclysmic event. But there was nothing.

Despite his resolve, Reggie could gain no further understanding of what had happened. He was in the midst of quadruple-checking their instruments when everything in the lab came to a standstill. The lab became suspended in a gray haze, and four pairs of eyes appeared: representatives of the Academy. There was none of the usual formality or advance preparation. The eyes emerged without any faces or bodies attached. They just observed. For a few moments, there was an uncomfortable silence. Then another pair of eyes approached in the usual way. A human form took shape around them. It was a female.

"I am Melephatia. I have been sent to retrieve your research and obtain all information related to your experimentation with Earthfolk and Venusfolk. You will provide me with this information immediately and communicate with no one until I direct you to do so. I make this request of you on authority of the Security Council of The Academy. Do you understand?"

Reggie simply nodded.

"You wish to comply?" said the representative.

"Of course," Reggie said.

"Your authorization shows a team of three. Where is the remainder of the research cohort?" the representative asked.

"One is gathering additional findings, including a witness, so that we can give you a complete report. I believe the other is on Guastamo Cavanus. We can't reach her," Reggie answered.

The eyes of the representative searched him.

"Maybe you can help us reach her," Reggie said. "All our instruments show no sign of Guastamo Cavanus."

"I am only permitted to tell you that there is a great darkness where the planet of Guastamo Cavanus once shone." The representative said this with no more emotion than if she were reporting atmospheric conditions on a vacation planet.

Reggie didn't understand what had happened, and he was getting the sense that the Academy didn't either. He thought about Zoe disappearing. It clouded his mind. The thought that pushed its way to the forefront, though, was that he had made this happen. But how? He formed a list of events as he understood them.

1: He showed Lisa a glimpse of the link. She came through it fairly well.

2: Sig took two Earthfolk from New Mexico to interact with Venusfolk. It went well.

3: Zoe observed a family of Earthfolk in New Mexico. The family was not exposed to the link.

4: He showed the social media group a glimpse of the link. It went wrong. The six Earthfolk were injured by the exercise. He was able to reverse the effects, and they appeared whole again. No harm done.

6: Zoe was dead.

He needed to clear his mind. What did it mean that Sig had seen himself in The Beyond?

Reggie then considered Sig's activity. Sig had taken two Earthfolk males through *the link*, one of whom was back on Earth, fully cognizant of the experience. How had this Earthfolk coped with the experience? What capacity did he have for using *the link*? Had he attempted to connect to *the link* outside of Sig's supervision? Unlikely, but not outside the realm of possibility. Had he disturbed some wave balance, signaling the OTH? Possible. And what of the other Earthfolk, the one still in Venus? He had been exposed to *the link* and then been left unsupervised within in it. Had Venusfolk also been exposed to *the link*? Sig had proposed that they prioritize experimentation with Venusfolk. Had he gone ahead and done his own experiment out of love or some other misguided notion?

And then there was Zoe. Dear Zoe, whose biggest weakness, it seemed, was him. She had paid for her emotional attachment with her life. The pain Reggie felt caused him to waver. He couldn't concentrate. He saw only her face as she spoke, the light in her, the gentle caress her words had been to him over many orbits, going back to when they first met. How had he been so blind for so long? How had he not seen her for what she was? And now, she was gone. Gone. It didn't matter where her stasis was if she couldn't reconstitute herself. Still, he wanted to see her body, even if it meant looking into vacant eyes. He would have to bear it. Regret and self-pity vied to strangle him. Emotion fought reason for control of his thoughts now.

He looked at Melephatia. She was communicating with the Academy, obtaining instructions. What would they do if he broke down in an emotional heap? They would not allow him to travel. He needed to travel. He had to find Zoe. It was completely irrational. He knew it. It didn't matter. Her body would be on Mega.

"I think it best we go to Mega immediately with what information we have and wait for your team from there. You won't be able to travel on your own," Melephatia said. She moved close to him.

Melephatia nodded toward Reggie.

"Wait!" he cried.

"Yes?" she responded with infernal equanimity.

"My colleague Sig will be here very soon. We should wait for him. He will have an Earthfolk with him—a potentially very important Earthfolk," Reggie said.

"Am I to understand that you have introduced Earthfolk to *the link*?" she asked.

"Yes. You didn't know that?" Reggie said.

"I need a list of every Earthfolk with whom your team has had contact. Now," Melephatia commanded.

Reggie went into as much detail as he was able, recounting all his steps, naming names, locations, pulling up wave signatures on multiple screens. He communicated techniques used, results, errors, everything. It felt good to come clean, but it wasn't enough to extinguish his guilt.

AS REGGIE UNBURDENED himself to the amazed Melephatia, Sig appeared. He was alone—no Earthfolk in tow. He had neither his bow tie nor his vest. He appeared younger without the full suit. The tweed jacket over a white shirt gave him a casual look. His expression, however, was far from carefree.

"Sig, where's the Earthfolk?" Reggie asked.

"He is on Mega already. At the moment, I think this is the

safest place for him, and for everyone. The less time he spends connected to *the link*, the better, at least for now. Madam the Physical Scientist refused to leave her home world and come with me," Sig said.

"Explain yourself," demanded Melephatia.

"Chase, the Earthfolk, came into contact with an OTH while connected to *the link* in Venus. The OTH pursued him, attracted by . . . I do not know. His nearness, maybe? The point is that the OTH had no power over him. It saw him. It definitely saw him. He saw it. But I believe it could not penetrate *the link*," Sig replied.

"Did you just say that the OTH saw an Earthfolk while he was connected to *the link*?" Melephatia asked.

"Precisely," Sig said.

Reggie took a small measure of satisfaction in Sig's unemotional response to the Academy representative. She was obviously processing a lot of confusion.

"This is disconcerting. You are aware of the prohibitions against introducing Folk to *the link*, are you not? This must be connected to Guastamo Cavanus. The extent of your transgressions is troubling. I think I understand," Melephatia said, looking at Reggie.

"I am not sure that you do," Sig corrected.

"Doctor, I do indeed. You opened a window for the darkness, for the OTH. It may not have been able to control the dim Earthfolk, but it could have turned from him to the most exposed, those closest to the darkness, those on Guastamo Cavanus. There is no time. We must retrace your steps. Come," she commanded.

∽

SIG AND REGGIE sat in full human form in a large hall. They sat next to one another on the same side of a long table. Each ruminated in silence. They might as well have been alone. Their thoughts were heavy. Neither felt much like talking. Reggie looked at the high vaulted ceiling, following the wood joists from angle to angle. He admired the ornate carvings that capped each terminus. Mega was a colossal planet with a terrific number of climates and landscapes and seascapes and atmospheres. It was the heart of universal administration, and it was the height of corporeal amenity and culture. The great hall in which they waited was constructed mostly of wood from the Deep Woods region of Mega, or possibly imported from Greenworld. Reggie thought this an interesting choice to project the power and authority of the Academy. The smell of Tallwood filled the hall. The only noise was the crackling of a fire that roared in a stone hearth. Perhaps the point was not to project power and authority but to convey warmth and community. The community of humans.

Reggie had been subjected to an intense interview. He had been required to answer question after question about his individual research and activities as well as the research and activities of each of his colleagues. His data and the team's data had been displayed and referred to again and again. Reggie had patiently answered every question thoroughly and honestly, over and over, looking each authority in the eye. He had willed himself to show no sign of fatigue or frustration. These were luxuries he had no right to. He was now a public menace. Who knew what would happen to him? His thoughts vacillated between desperation and emptiness at the loss of Zoe. Why should he fear a fate he freely had chosen? He decided he didn't care what happened to him.

Reggie looked up from the fire. He turned his head toward Sig. From the look of him, he'd been put through the same question grinder. He didn't need to say anything. The weight of tragedy, both personal and public, buckled their spirits.

It occurred to Reggie that they had each lost someone very close to them—Zoe, Madam the Physical Scientist. But it was more than that. The loves they had lost were new and—at least for him—unformed and unspoken. Sweet and sorrowful was the mystery of their new loves, their new losses. His guilt over his Earthfolk work was great, but it lacked the depth and finality of losing Zoe.

Sig was the first to speak. "I do not believe we caused the loss of Guastamo Cavanus," he said, looking straight ahead.

Reggie turned to him, but said nothing.

"The Beyond and The Unknowable are effectively the same. None of us can know, by its very definition, The Unknowable. I cannot see how giving Earthfolk and Venusfolk a glimpse of *the link* invited OTH from The Beyond to overtake a planet. The Academy's concern has always been that Earthfolk would bring their malice and discord into *the link*, not that a gateway into *the link* would be opened for The Unknowable, the OTH, whatever that is," Sig said, turning to look at Reggie.

Reggie stared at Sig's wide eyes.

Sig continued, "Why GC? If the OTH had access to *the link*, why would they take GC? Through *the link*, one planet is as close as another. Why not Earth or Venus, the sources of the supposed contamination? The evidence we *do* have shows that the OTH could *not* penetrate *the link* through Earthfolk or Venusfolk. Chase is evidence of this. Madam the Spiritual Scientist is evidence of this."

Reggie stirred, trying to process what Sig was saying.

"Think about it," Sig kept on. "What is it about Guastamo Cavanus that attracted them? A short trip? Nonsense. Or was there something else about the planet?"

"There aren't many people living on GC," Reggie offered,

warming to the line on inquiry. "A few thousand maybe, and a good percentage of these are diplomats from other places. Everyone lives on the largest continent. It is an average-size planet for its solar system, and it has four moons, which are each exactly one-eighth its size—Hatch Moon, Thatch Moon, Patch Moon, and Gatch Moon. The only *link* activity comes from the Academy Diplomatic Centers and, to a lesser extent, from the tourist locations."

Reggie sat up straight after naming the moons. He continued his description, "It's a beautiful planet in terms of atmospheric conditions and natural wonders. GC is best known for its high-volume falls and constant low thermal fissures. In addition to humans, there is an abundance of animal life, with primates being the most dominant species. They number in the many thousands."

Reggie drummed his fingers on the smooth wood table. He talked over the taps, "Humans from Mega began a colony on GC about a hundred and fifty orbits ago. Dispatches from GC at the time of colonization reported a remarkably smooth assimilation into the rhythms of the planet and its ecosystems. The colonists inhabit coastal locations, all south of the equator on a peninsula of Eastern Tecturia. The climate is tropical. The main occupations are agriculture, zoological research, and intergalactic sociological planning. It essentially hosts long-term gatherings of interplanetary representatives, as well as tourists in search of an exotic vacation spot. It is basically a spot for scientific conferences, cultural exchanges, and various other Academy boondoggles. People are drawn to it because of its natural beauty and proximity to The Beyond. The majority of inhabitants are visitors, but there is a small indigenous population."

"Thank you," Sig said.

Reggie continued to tap, now with both hands, and faster.

"I saw myself in The Beyond, or at least a dark reflection of me," Sig said. "I wasn't sure it was me. For a long time, I didn't believe it was. I've since come to believe it almost certainly *was* me. I suppose it's theoretically possible that I exposed *the link* while I was looking into the dark."

Reggie responded immediately, "No. Absolutely not. you followed Academy protocols. Didn't you?"

Sig took a moment to consider this. He nodded slightly without saying anything. Then he stood and stretched. "Well, then. The only other unauthorized exposure to *the link* was by you with Earthfolk, and me with Venusfolk."

Silence resumed, and Reggie continued to tap a rapid cadence.

29

CONNECTIONS

A WOMAN, DRESSED in a fuzzy, white, thigh-length sweater with tiny colorful sequins glistening from it, entered the hall, followed by two younger women. She looked familiar to Reggie. Sig stood immediately.

"Sit down, *Freud*," the woman said with a wave of her hand.

Sig sat down.

The two young ladies used handheld devices to project large displays at the head of the table. There were four in all. The woman in the white sweater sat directly across from Reggie, eyeing him in a friendly way. She was older, around Sig's age he guessed.

"Do you know who I am, Dr. Aurigae? Or should I say, Reggie . . . Homer, is it?" she asked politely.

"You sit on the Governing Council of the Academy," Reggie responded, clearing his throat and sitting up straight.

She smiled. "That's right. I am also sister to your colleague. I believe he uses the academic name Sigmund Freud. I am the one responsible for approving your Earthfolk study."

Reggie folded his arms and nodded. His first inclination was to offer an apology for deviating from the study's parameters.

But he knew they were well past that. He continued nodding and said nothing.

"I wanted to meet you before the Security Council issues its next set of proclamations." She waved her hand. "Isn't that how the Earthfolk greet one another, with a wave?"

Reggie pursed his lips and raised his hand. She let her hand fall but held his eye.

Then she waved at Sig. "Hello Freud."

Sig rolled his eyes.

"We're ready, Dr. Eridanis," announced one of the young ladies standing by the displays at the head of the table.

Everyone looked. The first display screen showed a pink-and-yellow planet. The second display showed the same planet from a greater distance. It was situated in the center of four equidistant moons. The third display appeared to be a close-up of one of the moons, a rocky moon with many craters. The final display was larger than the other three and held scrolling lines of equations, lights and darks, and ever-changing density functions, line graphs, and vectors.

"What are we looking at, Dani?" Sig asked.

"Well, *Siggy*," she responded. "I thought you would recognize—"

"Guastamo Cavanus," Reggie cut in.

"That's right," Dr. Eridanis confirmed.

Reggie stood and went immediately to the screen with the scrolling data. He put his face close to it and searched every inch. He looked it up and down and then did the same second time.

"There's something very weird going on here," Reggie said to the display.

Dr. Eridanis gestured to one of her assistants. "Display the current view of GC."

The young lady made gestures waved her device, and a fifth

virtual screen appeared. It was all black with only a dark gray crescent at the center, barely perceptible.

"What's this?" Sig asked.

"This is what's left of Guastamo Cavanus. No *link*, no human life detectable."

Indignant, Sig held his palms out. "And yet you smile?"

"I smile because there is hope," she said, gesturing toward Sig, as if offering it from the palm of her hand.

Reggie noted that she didn't touch Sig. She'd tried an Earth-folk wave with him, but it was awkward. Earthfolk often embraced or shook hands in greeting. Touch was important to the humans of Earth. He wondered if it made them more human than those who eschewed it.

"There is hope, brother," Dr. Eridanis said again. She with-drew her hand and stood, walking to the head of the table beside Reggie. "Tell us what you see, Aurigae."

"I'm not sure, but there appears to be way too much electro-magnetism bouncing back and forth here," Reggie said. He pointed to a spot on the data screen.

"Precisely," Dr. Eridanis said. "And can you tell from where this anomaly is originating?"

"No. I need to see a corresponding coordinates display," Reggie said.

"I'll tell you. It's the space between Gatch Moon and Guas-tamo Cavanus," Dr. Eridanis said.

Reggie was jolted but said nothing. He sensed what was coming.

"Follow me, gentlemen," Dr. Eridanis said. No room for discussion. The two young ladies, who could be twins, rushed to the door and held it open for the group. Dr. Eridanis led the way.

Reggie trudged behind. They walked down a long corridor with a dark hardwood floor. There were pieces of holographic light-art lining the green walls of textured metal. So much for hominess. Dr. Eridanis paused before a set of double doors at the end of the corridor. She looked at Reggie, then at Sig. She held Sig's eye for a moment, then waved her hand and the doors opened.

Light shone from inside. A mild breeze escaped the room as soon as the door was open. Reggie caught a scent. Was it jasmine? Hospital disinfectant?

Reggie bound toward the doors, then came to a halt in the doorway.

"Glimmerwac!?" he gasped, peering inside.

Seated in the center of the room was a tall man. He was bald but for a little bit of fuzz above his ears. Pictures of the man that Reggie had seen always portrayed him as dignified if no-nonsense appearance. But too much time in laboratories had turned him into a cadaverous old man with no hair. He wore baggy pants and soft loafers. A white stiff-collared shirt was the only thing crisp about him.

"Professor Glimmerwac?" Reggie called into the room.

"Reggie?" came a female voice off to the side.

"Lisa?" Reggie said.

Reggie walked into the room. That's when he noticed the others standing around the perimeter. There had to be a dozen people.

"Reggie?" came another familiar voice from the other side of the room.

"Zoe!?" Reggie was overcome with a wave of emotion.

Reggie kept his eyes on Zoe in disbelief. It was as though the lightest of air gathered in his chest, then danced through his whole body, leaving his cheeks flushed. He opened his mouth wide to draw in more air while at the same time trying to smile.

A door on the opposite side of the room opened, and another group of people filed in.

.   .   .

AFTER SEEING REGGIE, Lisa looked at the first person through the door on the far side of the room.

"Flash!" she exclaimed. She scrutinized the familiar contours of his face as he scanned the room looking for the source of the greeting.

Stewart tracked the voice.

"Lucky?" he shouted back, locking eyes with Lisa.

SIG SHOULDERED HIS way into the room beside Reggie and surveyed the crowd. He saw a familiar face to his right. "Chase."

Chase stood along the wall and calmly nodded. "Sig," he said evenly. Then he looked at Stewart. "Why did that woman just call you Flash?"

"Because of my last name, Gordon," Stewart answered, still soaking in Lisa's countenance.

"Huh?" Chase didn't understand.

"Flash Gordon, from the comics?" Stewart said, without taking his eyes off of Lucky—Lisa Ursula Catherine Kulowski.

Reggie broke his concentration from Zoe long enough to see a woman and a man shuffling in on the far side of the room.

Poonam? Reggie thought.

Poonam Murthy was about to say something when the man behind her called out, "Tino?"

"Jefe!" Martino said, standing along the wall with his two co-workers. He began laughing, slapped his thigh, and pointed at Fitz.

The chatter rose, everyone talking and shouting over each other.

Then the room suddenly went completely silent.

All eyes followed two slight metallic-gray figures with shiny black eyes, no clothes, and petite little mouths with no teeth as they glided into the room from a side door. A thin line of yellow mist trailed each of them.

"Madam!" Sig approached Madam the Physical Scientist, took her hand, and began weeping softly, and everyone went from being stunned to being stunned and moved.

"*Diablos*," whispered Tino to his friends, raising an eyebrow.

PAULINA PRESSED CLOSE to Mariluz, staring at the two slight figures who had captured everyone's attention. She glanced at the other side of the room. A tall man with silver-gray hair was talking to a younger man. The younger man looked familiar. She was fairly sure he was the parent of one of her students. Martino Martinez—that was his name. He went by *Tino*. Martinez said something, and the tall silver-haired man laughed. Mid-smile, the tall man glanced at Paulina. She felt a jolt of excitement and immediately looked away, then slowly, self-consciously looked back.

FITZ NOTICED THE woman on the other side of the room. There was a younger woman clinging to her arm, clearly frightened, but not the lady with the big brown eyes. She was composed. He liked her immediately.

MARILUZ SCANNED THE faces in the room, trying to make sense of things. What the hell was going on? She recognized Poonam Murthy, the substitute math teacher. She was supposed to go with them to the Very Large Array. Beside the two extraterrestrial-looking creatures, there was a bedraggled, wild-eyed older man seated in the center of the room, like the object of some weird hazing ritual. The walls of the room were made of rough-cut wood. The last thing Mariluz could remember was sitting at the coffee shop and then a hospital room. And now, inexplicably, she was here in this room with a bunch of other people. She was scared, unlike Paulina, who seemed more interested in a man across the room than the two ETs. The man *was* handsome. The curly-haired man standing next to him wasn't bad either, and much closer to her own age. He looked vaguely familiar. She might have seen him somewhere before. She couldn't quite place him, though. She reached out and gave Paulina a squeeze. Mariluz looked back at the young man with curly black hair. He was talking with two other men. One of the others also looked familiar—maybe a parent.

"He looks like the picture on AlienWheelman's profile," Paulina said.

"Huh?" Mariluz said, keeping her eyes on the men.

"The guy standing next to Martino Martinez and the man with silver hair," Paulina said. "The one you're staring at."

"That's it! It's him. It's Wheelie. I knew I recognized him!" Mariluz exclaimed, squeezing Paulina's arm tighter. Despite her uneasiness, a smile creased her lips. *"Es guapo."*

ONCE THE INITIAL shock of seeing the two Venusfolk wore off, everyone began speaking freely and rapidly again. It took some time for Dr. Eridanis to restore order. She motioned for Reggie to join her. He was reluctant to leave Zoe but obediently followed to the next room.

Dr. Eridanis sat him down and explained why she'd assembled everyone. She was exploring responses to the breach in *the link*. This gathering of Earthfolk and Venusfolk, had all been influenced, directly or indirectly, by theoremific waves.

"We focused on the anomalies emanating from Gatch Moon, which led us to Dr. Marc Glimmerwac. We were able to determine that he began his research anew almost immediately upon settling on Gatch Moon. Somehow, he managed to recreate transmissions simulating *the link* even though he'd been reconditioned. No one has ever been able to reconnect themselves to *the link*. We think he used proxies and artificially generated waves, crude but transmittable. He targeted a large population of animals living on Guastamo Cavanus. He wasn't able to travel through *the link*, but with the assistance of several other exiles, he managed to get to GC," Dr. Eridanis said. She gave Reggie a moment to process.

Reggie couldn't believe what he was hearing. Glimmerwac hadn't been able let go of his desire to elevate Folk. Reggie was convicted by the thought.

Dr. Eridanis anticipated him. "He was warned to stop his Folk research. And like his first experiment on Earth, this one went terribly wrong. So wrong that the primates he practiced upon experienced a violent psychosis. Without warning, the entire primate population aggressively attacked each other. We suspect that the psychosis spilled over into the human population. Your team member Delphine—or, what do you call her?" Dr. Eridanis asked.

"Zoe," Reggie said.

"Yes, Zoe. She had already left the planet when it happened. She went to Earth to retrieve something or other from an Earthfolk family. We have the family here in another room. The timing was fortunate. We believe there is chaos on GC now. *Before* we imposed a shutdown of *the link*, the planet went dark —zero electromagnetic signatures. *The link* has been compromised. But whatever, whoever, it is, could not completely negotiate *the link* before we shut it down. There are complications. Things you're not aware of, Reggie. The question now is how to contain the spread of contamination. To that end, we must figure out if there is any way to restore GC," Dr. Eridanis said.

Reggie had suspected something as soon as he'd said the words *Gatch Moon*. He knew Glimmerwac was in exile there. Glimmerwac just couldn't let it go. The old Folk researcher was obsessed with his work. He had never learned the right mix of emotion. It was all sounding very familiar to Reggie. He retraced his team's steps again. Something Zoe had said leapt out at him —a higher power is with them.

30

THE MESSAGE

ZOE HANDED REGGIE a black-and-white marbled notebook. Dr. Eridanis requested quiet, and the din subsided. Reggie began reading aloud from the notebook:

"*Cicadas and birds and squirrels and frogs, cows, horses, flies, and people. All give voice to the day. Clicks and chirps and bellows and croaks, grunts, whines, buzzes, and yells herald the march out of night's nervous keep. The scent of grass and leaves and trees and a stream, the cool mountain air. It all fills the senses. But there is a special time in the thick of the forest, at the height of day's beauty, when sound fades. The animals rest. The burble of the stream becomes a distant memory, and the wind alone speaks to the soul. Humility embraces all. The compassion of silence, which calms all disquiet, is offered as a gift. It is quietly received and understood to be the joy of simply being alive. A man lets fall his defenses, and a gentle heart knows peace. The voice of God is met with gratitude and praise and a single life-affirming tear.*

"*Today, I looked up and saw above me a way through the trees. I saw a bright star behind the blue sky. A shining, brilliant star. I saw rays of light that marked the path before me. As I looked, I listened. And I heard the quiet, the calm of life. And I heard a voice. It was the soft voice of the One who walks with me through the woods. His words showed me what lay beyond the sky. It was home. The way through the trees was the way home. I sat and rested in the woods, and I knew I was not alone. Through the quiet, I heard a whisper in my ear. The soft voice told me the meaning of life. And it was this— movement. Moving closer to the light. That was it. It was simple, and it was brilliant, like the star shining behind the blue sky. Just as the light from the star was racing wildly toward me, life was moving toward the eternal light. I understood the way. I needed to follow the path, and I would see and hear and be led home. Mine must always be a quiet and gentle heart to feel and follow the path of light, and I will know peace and love forever."*

Reggie nodded. "They have the chance to move toward and connect with . . . God. Folk do not need *the link* to be connected," he said.

"You don't have all the information Aurigae. And the souls on GC, they're connected?" Dr. Eridanis asked. "What of them?"

Zoe slowly rose and motioned for Mike, Isabella, Mike Jr., and Elle to stand by her. The family exchanged confused looks but rose together and went to her.

ZOE TOOK A moment, smiled at everyone in the room, then walked close to Elle and gently took her hand. The girl wasn't afraid. She beamed. The beauty of life radiated from her.

"What does this mean?" asked Dr. Eridanis.

Reggie answered. "It means that Earthfolk, and Venusfolk, and all the other Folk we call unenlightened may not actually be so. They have within them a child's peace. I don't know if the people of Guastamo Cavanus are lost forever, but I believe that the struggle for their souls is an individual one. The darkness is a reflection of us. We must examine our own movement toward light."

Dr. Eridanis shook both of her hands. "You don't know what you are saying," she said.

Reggie ignored her, and spoke to everyone in the room. "I have made elevating Earthfolk my life's work. Yet, it seems I am the one who was in need of enlightening. We have lost touch with our humanity because of *the link*. I don't expect the Academy or USC to accept what I'm saying. But I hope you will at least consider it. Why God gave us *the link* I don't know. Perhaps there is a way to use it as a tool and not as a way of living.

"I regret the part I played in all this. I regret my hubris. I thought that connecting Earthfolk to *the link* would be my greatest achievement." Reggie looked at Zoe and continued, "But perhaps my only real achievement is the realization that true wholesome emotion has found me. I achieved this not by exposing Folk to *the link* but by exposing myself to the feelings I have toward the one whom I care for most, and have since I was a child. I look forward to sharing myself with her as children do, as this child does with her family."

Zoe, tears threatening to spill from her eyes, reached out her hand, and Reggie took it.

Dr. Eridanis moved forward, hands now at her side, her face betraying no emotion. "That may be well and good for you, but *the link* is in jeopardy, and the potential for cataclysm has not abated. I'm afraid *the link* will be shut down indefinitely while we deal with what has happened. The stakes are too high," she said, putting no more emphasis on *cataclysm* than if she were speaking about a canceled appointment. She turned toward Sig, who was holding Madam the Physical Scientist in his arms, the picture of serenity.

"You haven't shared what you know of *the link* with them I see. I thought for certain you had. You are a true and noble Academician, brother," she said.

Sig shook his head slowly, and the serene smile that hung so well upon his face darkened.

Reggie wasn't sure what was going on between Sig and Eridanis. There seemed to be something beneath the surface being communicated between them.

Dr. Eridanis turned back to Reggie. "Come with me once more, Aurigae," she commanded, and headed to a side door.

Reggie shot Zoe a glance and let go of her hand. He followed Dr. Eridanis.

Inside the next room, Dr. Eridanis turned to Reggie. "You no doubt believe *the link* simply exists, that it is an energetic fabric that humanity channels naturally. This is partly true, but it is not the whole story."

What Dr. Eridanis said about *the link* was precisely what Reggie believed. It was what all of advanced humanity believed, not just Reggie.

"*The link* is a network, and not simply one of minds tapping into the energy waves around them. It is also a *physical* network of antennas, relays, and reactors, linked together to form a large generator-receiver-repeater array located . . ." She paused, walked over to the doorway, and looked back into the room where everyone was standing. Reggie joined her and followed her gaze. Conversations continued; hands gesticulated and voices rose and fell. No one saw them.

"The array is distributed throughout The Beyond, just outside the expanding universe of light. We have the technology to reach it. The Academy controls the array's functioning through portals. As the ultimate security measure, this has never been revealed to anyone outside the Academy. Advanced humanity's ability to use the mind to connect is natural enough, developed over eons—that much is true. Theoremifics is unnecessary. The essential thing is . . . What I'm trying to say is . . . *The link* itself . . . is artificial. The waves are controlled for human access," Dr. Eridanis said, then breathed a deep breath.

With these few words, everything Reggie thought he knew about the universe was upended. He looked around the simple room to which they'd repaired. It was as if Dr. Eridanis wasn't standing right next to him. Of all the scenes he'd witnessed in his life—the strange planets, the swirling lights and tunnels, the streams of consciousness—none of it compared to the surreal sensation he felt now. The smooth silver walls, the artwork suspended around the room, all seemed incredibly ordinary. The holograms on pedestals, even a holo that depicted intersecting light beams from multiple suns with dramatic color shifts seemed too ordinary a backdrop for this paradigm-shifting news. The revelation was meant to magnify his awareness but had only succeeded in stupefying him. He caught his reflection in a shiny part of the metal wall. It was the same expression on Lisa's face when he told her about advanced humanity and *the link*.

Dr. Eridanis moved into his field of view but said nothing, only stared into his eyes. There was perhaps a trace of concern in her. She said nothing.

Reggie shook his head in disbelief. "How is the Academy able to bring Earthfolk and Venusfolk to Mega without problems? What about the violent tendencies and fear? You broke your own rules, bringing them here. They seem fine. How did you manage to get the wave sequence right? How were you able to do it without the necessary theoremific emotion . . ."

"What? Because we have no love?" Eridanis interjected. She cocked her head slightly, scrutinizing him.

Reggie nodded.

She raised her voice slightly, "Love has nothing to do with it. Frankly, it's an absurd notion, to think that love can transport humans. Preposterous. Technology, Reggie. Technology."

"We . . . What about their bodies? Are they in comas back on Earth?" An image of Lisa lying prostrate flashed through his mind.

"Probably. They're nowhere near ready for *the link*. It's not important. They'll be back on their home world soon enough. Most of them are being cared for. Those who aren't, well. It was a necessary risk. They should be fine. Did it not occur to you that they'd actually made it into *the link* when you transmitted to them and revealed its pathways? They *were* in it. But it wasn't love that brought them back to their hospital rooms. It was us. We found it expedient to coordinate their return with your activities. We knew immediately once you transmitted to the Earthfolk that you had breached protocol," Eridanis said, turning her head and looking away.

Reggie doubted they knew *immediately*. They would have intervened sooner. Sig must have told Eridanis after he found out about the Earthfolk group and what Reggie had done. The summoning to appear at the Reconfiguration Station had nothing to do with it.

Eridanis' voice softened again, "*The link* makes no concession for emotion. The Folk of Earth are human, capable of the same mental acuities that we are capable of. They need no coddling. That was all your creation. A mysticism you attached to an emotion you know little about. How would love mitigate violence? If anything, it leads to more of it. But the OTH. The OTH are real. We were prepared to vaporize all of the Earthfolk at the first sign of trouble."

Reggie circled a holographic display, a globe spinning on its axis with tiny lights twinkling from deep within it. He presumed it represented a planet locked in Mega's gravitational field. He stared at it, his mind calming as Dr. Eridanis spoke. His life's work was a fool's errand. He'd been chasing an illusion, like the holo in front of him.

Dr. Eridanis slowly came around next to him and stared at the globe as well. "As I told you, we brought them back to examine them for any connection to the disturbance and to be certain of their ignorance of the events *you* initiated. We are confident they have no understanding of where they have been. And we have a high degree of confidence that they had nothing to do with the anomalies surrounding *the link's* functioning. We can bring Folk into *the link* any time. We don't do it because they must be sufficiently rid of their ridiculous ideologies and violent tendencies. You understand this much or you would not have pursued your misguided theories."

Reggie walked to the other side of the globe and thought about what she said. He talked through the globe, "But my dream theory. It must work. It does work, doesn't it? It's the reason the Earthfolk don't remember anything as reality? And you used it?"

"Correct," Eridanis said.

So, the Academy had watched over his shoulder as he developed his Folk dream theory. Then they made use of it once he'd tested it on Lisa.

"You were too caught up in your own romance to consider, rationally, all the possibilities," Eridanis said.

Reggie walked around the globe yet again, staring at the tiny white lights. *Technology*, he thought. He craned his neck, peeking over the display. "If there are antennas and relays in The Beyond, how are there no electromagnetic signatures coming or going from it?" he said, focusing on Dr. Eridanis.

She looked away, then moved in front of a nearby hologram. It depicted an inside view of an exploding sun. She appeared to appraise it.

"The universe expands and contracts like the beating of a heart," she said. "We have the technology to manipulate the energy this creates. The array is at its most essential during expansion, when energy moves away. The array keeps us bathed in reflected waves during the expanding loss period as we wait for the contraction. The wave signatures of these reflections are cloaked until they are well inside the boundaries of common observation.

"The technology is incredible. It has been around for so long; I dare say very few, if any, understand it entirely. Even fewer are entrusted with its use. Only those who have been indoctrinated with the profound responsibility inherent in it are worthy of the sacrifice of dedicating their lives to its maintenance. Only those born to serve the awesome power of *the link* carry out the ministrations. These ministers' fealty is to *the link* alone. As far as they know, tending relays and antennas is what humanity has always done. It is their reason for being. But the real power of *the link* comes from Mega where the technology to identify and direct the energy through interstellar space is based. Greater humanity thrives because *the link* is channeled through our technology. People couldn't just blink their eyes and connect to waves. Don't you see the absurdity of that, Reggie? Think about it."

Reggie was thinking harder now than he ever had, and it still made no sense. It just didn't feel right. What Eridanis said was outrageous. And she said it all with the blankness of wooden table as she moved from artwork to artwork in the room. He wondered what she saw in the art before her. Beauty? He doubted it.

Her back to him, she continued, "We use *the link* for the benefit of all. But there are forces at work causing disruptions to the known order. These disruptions are blamed on the OTH."

If what Eridanis said was true, it meant a handful of people controlled how most of the universe communicated. Ridiculous. Ministers ignorantly servicing *the link* while a small handful of people on Mega pulled the strings? Not possible. Was it?

"Who are these ministers?" Reggie said.

"They serve humanity through the ritual maintenance they perform on a technology they don't fully understand. They know how to keep things running, but that is all. For them, it is the way things have always been. A life of service is passed down from generation to generation. They refer to the energy that comes from the universal contractions as *the breath of life*. The machines they live on, the reactors, are to them *life breathers*, linking humanity to the breath of life." Dr. Eridanis paused and turned around to face Reggie, assessing his comprehension. She approached him, coming to within a half an arm's length. He could see the tiny wrinkles on her eyelids. She stared deep into his eyes with an intensity that roiled with emotion. Which emotion, Reggie wasn't sure. Her brown eyes were opaque but unwavering as they held his stare.

"Recent events have changed everything. There has been a corruption within the sanctum of ministers. And so, the highest level of the Academy has taken the extraordinary action of neutralizing all but a few of *the link* ministers. Most have been brought here to Mega, where they are being scrutinized. A small cadre remains in place to keep contact with the array. The OTH is everyone's main concern.

"Your Earthfolk have been brought here in order to dismiss any connection to the occurrence. The Council does not believe that the corruption within the ministry and the exposure of your Folk to *the link* is a coincidence. I believe it *is*. I believe my brother, and I *will* protect him," Dr. Eridanis said.

"This is all just so . . ." Reggie started to say.

"Impossible," Dr. Eridanis finished his thought.

Reggie began to suspect then that the message he'd received from the Academy just over three rotations ago that had started him off on the path to his botched experiment had more to do with Sig than with what he was planning. It was the only thing that made some kind of sense. Sig must have uncovered a cloaked transmission long ago. Sig wasn't supposed to know about the array, but he did. Sig knew the nature of *the link*. If he concealed this, what else had he concealed from Reggie? Who knows what he's been doing all this time?

"I don't understand how this information helps me help you. Why are you telling me this now?" Reggie asked, trying to piece things together. "You're violating your own secrecy."

"You, along with my brother, conducted an experiment that has given us insight into the OTH. It doesn't appear that your experiment caused a compromise in *the link*'s integrity, and neither did Glimmerwac's experiment orbits ago. But you managed to expose an existential threat. A corruption. I owe it to you to give you the truth," Dr. Eridanis said.

Reggie considered where this was all going. Why was he to be trusted with a secret of this magnitude?

"Again, why are you telling me this?" he said.

Dr. Eridanis moved even closer, almost touching him, but said nothing.

Reggie clenched his teeth and turned his head. He fixed his gaze on a hologram display depicting two stars merging, in multicolor. He thought of Zoe. He could hardly contain his emotions.

Using mystical ministers who worship *the link* to run the order of the universe, though apocryphal, if true was a deception of almost unimaginable proportion. Even if it was being done for the good of all, what about these servants' human potential? What about their right to the truth? And not just the ministers—what about everyone's right? The arrogance of this stunned him. Were they, who called themselves *greater humanity,* even human? It seemed that Folk were more human in the way they acknowledged their passions, struggles, and limitations. There was a purity in the Earthfolk child. And what of love? Was it of no consequence?

As if reading his mind, Dr. Eridanis interrupted his thoughts again. "I share my brother's compassion for Folk, and I believe there is something to what you've said about what Folk children can teach us. I wanted to tell you this before you become permanently corporeal," she said coldly.

The phrase *permanently corporeal* hung in the air. It wasn't as if he didn't know this would happen after what he'd done. But that was before emotion had touched him. That was before Zoe. Being disconnected now seemed a far more grievous tragedy. The same feeling he'd had outside the circus tent those many orbits ago on Earth gripped him. It wasn't fair. His blunder had been worse than he ever could have guessed. Had he not entangled himself with Earthfolk, he might never have come to realize what he felt for Zoe. How could they dance through space, exploring new worlds, exploring each other now? He wanted more than anything to enjoy a life with her in *the link*. She was the one he wanted, the partner his mother had hoped he would find. How could they merge if he was in exile? If *the link* was shut down. It wasn't fair.

"Why not just banish me? Why tell me the truth first?" he pleaded, pained by the knowledge of the grand deception and his impending exclusion from Zoe and *the link*.

"I tell you because it is possible *the link* will never be the same again. Why shouldn't you know? Eons of history are perhaps coming to an end. *The link* is in jeopardy. Sig knows, and now you know. When the Council finds no connection between your Earthfolk and what has happened, the Earthfolk will be returned to their blissfully ignorant lives and you will be disciplined for your insuperable breach. You will have your mind reconfigured to preclude connection to *the link* when—if

—it is restored. You will live as Folk. You may be lucky and not even remember your previous life."

"I won't remember any of it? Not even as a Folk dream?" he said, monotone.

Eridanis looked at him—not unsympathetically, he thought. "You believe in the humanity of Folk? Well, welcome to humanity."

***

ABOUT THE AUTHOR

William Zanotti is a novelist, short story writer, and independent publisher of speculative fiction. He is a former criminal investigator and lives just outside of Washington D.C.

Thanks for reading!

Please consider adding a short review on your platform of choice, and let us know what you thought.

Look for the sequel, *The Link: Farewell to Humanity.*

Visit williamzanotti.com for more information:

ACKNOWLEDGMENTS

I owe many thanks, especially to my author-friends, who suffered through unedited versions of this book. Their willingness to read the entire thing was generous and helpful. I would name them but for fear of associating them with any dilapidations within.

My writing critique groups helped keep the fun in writing. Thanks for being as passionate about reading and writing SFF as I am.

A big thank you to my friend and colleague, J. Fernandez. Solving the world's problems and chatting about our creative works over coffee always recharged my batteries. Friends, editors, professors, acquaintances, baristas, liquor store owners - thank you all. I appreciated every bit of good will that was shown me along the way.

I'd also like to thank my daughter, Kelly, the true writer in the family. Her insight and encouragement were great.

Last but not least, I am most grateful for the patient support of my wife, Kimberly, who shows me everyday how love works.

ALSO BY WILLIAM ZANOTTI

The Link Series:

The Link: Farewell to Humanity

A green planet paradise, the desert of New Mexico, and the decline of human connectivity are the backdrop for this action packed second installment of "The Link" series. The OTH - Other Than Human are spreading. *The link* has been co-opted and Greater Humanity must struggle to survive the apocryphal deception that is *the link*. *Farewell to Humanity* hits the ground running and doesn't stop till there's no ground left.

Made in the USA
Columbia, SC
19 September 2022

67222636R00172